GW00506290

THE SEVENTH RITUAL

THE SEVENTH RITUAL
a race for survival

Clint Adams

Credo *Italia*
San Francisco

Published by Credo *Italia*

Credo *Italia*, 350 Bay Street, Suite 100-124
San Francisco, California 94133 USA

Manufactured in the United Kingdom

Published simultaneously in the United States of America

ISBN 978-0-9768375-6-5

The characters and events in this book are fictitious.
Any similarity to real persons, living or dead, is coincidental
and not intended by the author.

I dedicate this book,
with a lifetime of love and gratitude
to my heroic little pal,
Clinton Dean.

Acknowledgments

Sue Adams, you gave me life, an intelligent one. I will be forever grateful to you for all you've done, for all you mean. When I look back at your life as a single parent, I see your strength and fortitude, and I'm grateful. Thanks for the support you've given me, but more than all else, for the blessing you've provided in order that this story to be told. My love to you always, Mom.

Larry Adams, thanks for giving me brains and your unique set of investigative skills. Just like you, I relish getting to the bottom of things and seeing justice prevail. Our time at Red Rock Canyon is something I will always remember fondly. I love you, Dad.

Shirley Hawes, your name now appears in all five of my books. There's a reason behind this; I want you to know that you'll never be forgotten. Our talks in the East Bay, by the ocean in Half Moon Bay and at the cemetery in San Bruno, helped me tremendously. I will always be grateful to you. My love to you forever.

Samantha, without you I wouldn't be here, no question about it. *Don't Be Afraid of Heaven was* written for one purpose, to say thanks to you the best way I knew how. You've inspired others, teens and adults, to become unafraid of what comes next. *DBAOH* was always the favorite teen novel I wrote. I love you.

Anna Mazzola, without question, your support of me, my writing, and my completion of this book is unparalleled. You are a good soul and anyone who knows you is lucky. Any e-mail you sent arrived at just the perfect time…il destino. E' vero? Grazie sempre; tu sei una amica buona, fedele e premurosa. Alla prossima.

Johan Borg, what can I say? I don't know anyone else I can talk with on the phone for over 2 hours and not get bored. Your loyalty to me, to our friendship, along with your keen understanding of 'me' will forever be appreciated. I'm not that easy to know. You're the greatest; I'm so *incredibly* fortunate to have you as my friend.

Diane Christiansen, our long-lasting friendship is precious. The shared lessons we've been given keep our connection fresh and meaningful. Spending my fiftieth birthday with you was a special treat. Thanks for the great memories we've shared together.

Dr. Vanni Panzera, you are so kind. I loved the time I spent at your house, working on my manuscript, playing with your two dogs and indulging in your fantastic cooking, i tuoi pasti erano molto deliziosi. Our special friendship means a lot to me.

Mads Christensen, I'll *never* forget the great encouragement and support you've given me. I never would have gotten to know DK if it hadn't been for you. Thanks, forever, for being my friend.

Dr. Gernot & Sabine Reisner, Katja, Stefan und Inge. Your whole family is a treasure. Your support, over the years, has been magnificent. Never again will I confuse Australia with Austria.

Holger Bollmann, it all began in Glockenbachviertel. The dark days of life, the beginnings of this book. Thanks for the great, positive spirit you offered. I'm thrilled it's all turned out so well.

John Barker, working with you is such a breeze. The designs you come up with are outstanding and you're so patient with me. I'm so lucky to have met you at the Book Fair in Göteborg.

Susan Wolfe, our chats made me realize how important it is that this book, in particular, be published. I've always looked up to you.

Eva Liljendahl, I learned so much from you. You're a fantastic editor and I only hope my own edits are half as good as yours. Thanks, too, for the flap photo taken in Malmö. Great memories.

Rose Hilliard, you've got class and you know your stuff. You shared some valuable tips with me several years ago and they stuck. You're a rarity in the American publishing business; you gave your time and attention so freely, so generously and that will never be forgotten, thanks a million.

Gen Kelsang Lhamo, Kadam Lucy James, Tim Larcombe and Michele Thorsen, you taught me so much about compassion and much, much more. Kadampa Buddhism and patient acceptance changed the way I view the story that has lived inside me so long. Thanks to all of you for helping me change the way it ends.

Dr. Carla Perez, our writing sessions together that turned into a friendship are invaluable to me. Getting to know you and your family was a prize. I felt as if I fit in every time. Many thanks.

Liz Buist, thanks for having read my previous books. Your efforts to help meant a lot to me. I hope to see you again real soon.

Riccardo & Andrea, grazie per aiutare me trovo il convento perfetto...per scrivere il mio libro. Firenze, e l'atmosfera lì, era una buona esperienza per me, grazie ancora.

Jan-Mirko Krüschet, finishing up this book at your apartment while you were in Hamburg, was a gift. Barrio Gothico kept me on my toes and helped me generate suspense before even placing one finger on my keyboard. Thank you.

Christine Ansell, as a book lover, you get it. The work I did in your apartment got the ball rolling in the right direction. Thanks so much for renting to me. I'll miss those nights in el Raval.

Deborah Granger, what a sweet person you are. You helped me believe in myself and my abilities. Developing my own radio show was fun, I enjoyed every minute of it. Because of you, I hope to return to the airwaves someday.

Josip & Patricia Martinovic, thanks for your eternal belief in what I do and what comes next. I wish the absolute same for you.

Andrea Jaeger, meeting you in Chicago was such a great surprise…you're *so* real; you outshined every other. Thanks for all.

Monica Seles, you will always be my superhero. You inspire me every single day. Seeing your return to Louis Armstrong stadium will forever be the most (positively) emotional moment of my life.

Farrah Fawcett, your life has such great purpose. Thanks for reminding us that we *all* possess the capacity to help others.

Andrea Aringer, our talks in Munich, most of them on the S-Bahn, will stay with me always. Discussing literature, lessons, fear and dreams motivated me more than you will know. Vielen Dank!

Susan Boyle, you've done *wonders* for any and all of us who've ever been dismissed. You rock. Keep going!!!

To all the American publishers, editors and literary agents with whom I've ever shared contact, my thanks. You prompted me to become an Italian citizen and I will always be grateful for that.

To Barry & Tracy Schuler, you both made me stronger, thanks. Your wish for me to proceed with this project entirely on my own was a valuable lesson. I learned much from it, from you and from the collective choices we make.

To Angela Morrison, Leena Flegler, Markus Zusak and the Society of Children's Book Writers & Illustrators, my last day's involvement with teen publishing occurred at your 2006 Munich conference. I am left with pleasant memories and I'm grateful that you propelled me into my present position, thanks to all of you.

THE SEVENTH RITUAL

Introduction

Joan Rivers said, "Yesterday is history, tomorrow is a mystery, today is God's gift, that's why we call it the present." She's also the same person that said, "I blame my mother for my poor sex life. All she told me was 'the man goes on top and the woman underneath.' For three years my husband and I slept in bunk beds."

I no longer blame my mother for anything, but it sure took me a while to accept my present. It's best when you give it to yourself, especially after you realize you've earned it. Way better than a toaster oven, punchbowl, or anything un-returnable.

My mother and I even saw Joan Rivers together the last time I was in San Francisco. Can we talk? Joan made us both laugh. I liked that, sitting there alongside my mom, laughing at Joan's trademark one-liners, "I was dating a transvestite. My mother said, 'Marry him. You'll double your wardrobe'." It really *is* the best medicine. I've been taking a full dose daily for years now; no expiration date on the label, never any negative side effects and the bottle's always refillable. *Rx:* Buy generic and take regularly.

Another favorite quote of mine is, "The truth will set you free, but first it will make you miserable." James Garfield said this. He's no comedian though, just some American President. Maybe if he'd seen Joan's standup routine, he'd be funnier.

There's merit in both perspectives. Don't you think? The truth *is* powerful, but I'd prefer to write fiction so I can laugh a little. This is how I view life; this is why I'm still here. This is my story. My personal wish for you as you read, as you live your life, is that you, too, strive to find lightness in the dark.

-- *Clint Adams, Summer 2009*

THE STARTING LINE

I was so overly eager that even my fingertips got hard. The plastic, painted-over doorbell I'd intentionally passed by so many times on the corner of Bleecker and Seventh was finally staring me in the face. The time had approached to press it. What was she going to look like? What was she going to say? How much was she going to charge me? This was my first time. Perhaps it's only natural to feel a little afraid.

The crimson curtains behind the angelically glass-stained windows had opened and closed without me even being able to see who's in back of them. With no sneak peek at my destiny, the door flung open and there she was. How normal and unadorned-looking, not at all what I was expecting. She still displayed an exotic kind of beauty, yet her expression appeared a little tired and worn. "I rewind. My husband return," was her greeting to me while she carried her cordless phone with her right hand and an unlit, unfiltered Camel in her left.

"What? Excuse me," I said at the same time as I popped a Velamint into my mouth to cover up the oniony gyro I'd just scarfed down.

"No, I talk to the Blockbuster. You come in."

I stepped in and looked everywhere I could for any other living soul, but I somehow knew that she and I were alone.

As I questioned with my hands where I should place the warm winter jacket I had just taken off, the late-twenty-something woman asked, "Upstairs or down?"

"What?"

"Where you want to do this?"

"May I look up—"

Seeming as if she'd worked this room more than a few times before, the woman said, "Sure, sure. Everybody like to get it upstairs."

I could tell that continuing the conversation with the video store was vitally important to her. Forgetting to rewind certainly does come with its price. Walking up the stylish metallic spiral staircase with its period 70's shag-covered lemon yellow steps was like entering a scene from *Shaft*. But as soon as I heard *Don't Wanna Lose You* by Gloria Estefan, I knew our encounter wasn't necessarily going to be as mystical and other-worldly as I'd first imagined. Easy listening had always been like an aphrodisiac to me. The upstairs, composed of three posh black leather couches, red satin pillows, a few chairs and a multi-woofered Bang & Olufsen sound system was more than tantalizing.

As she came nearer to me, wearing baggy gray flannel sweat pants and a shoulder-length, dishwater-blond braided pony tail, I told her, "This is fine. Let's do it here."

"Sure. It doesn't matter to me."

"So, you got the problem with your video worked out?"

"They always do this. Tell me I don't rewind *Die Hard 2*. I hate that. My husband watch it after I rewind, then *he* don't rewind. Is not my fault. Is my husband problem. Why—"

Not having much spare cash on hand, I didn't want to waste time with small talk, so I interrupted her by asking, "How much is this going to cost?"

"What you want?"

"Gosh, I don't really know. What do you have?"

"Psychic reading is twenty. Aura is thirty. Tarot is fifty."

"Well, I think a psychic reading is fine. May we just do that?"

Without further delay I made myself as comfortable as possible in the middle of Lower Manhattan's Greenwich Village. I took a deep breath as my fingers clenched the arms of the red velour-covered seat I was in, while my unclenched butt felt as if it was getting ready for a Loew's bargain matinee to begin.

"What is your God name?"

"My God name? I'm not really relig—"

"No. Just tell me your name."

"Paul Anthony Jacobson."

"Born?"

"October twenty-eighth. Sunday was my thirty-fourth birthday. Oakland, California. But now I live in San Francisco."

"Just date. Don't tell me rest of story."

"Sorry."

Hearing my brief bio. made the woman's eyes shut deliberately. This gave me time to study her up-too-late movie-watching face in depth. But, as soon as I began concentrating on her dangly plastic purple crucifix earrings that looked like they might have been fashioned for extra credit by a home ec. freshman, the phone began ringing. I thought the Blockbuster-rewind problem had already been solved. What's up now? Her eyes remained closed. Someone else answered the phone.

"You are good person. What do you think of when I say the

initial *J?*"

"*J?*"

"Yes, who is this person that make you so sad?"

I was beyond startled. How did she know such a thing? That's Justin. We…well, I decided not to—"

"Don't need to know that either. This man make you very unhappy for the past two weeks."

"Yes, that's why I'm here. How did you—"

"I know these things, I am fifth-generation psychic. You have been thinking about him and that make you unhappy." Then, looking as if she'd heard it broadcast by Tom Brokaw on *The Nightly News* the woman opened her eyes widely and said, "You have always been like this. Extremely sad on inside."

Oops, first mistake, I thought. "Well, I don't know about that. I only want to know if Justin and I are ever going to get back together."

Immediately, without needing time to ponder, she said, "Juspin will come back to you, but it will be your choice. You will decide if you will be friends or more than that." Then, the instantly-absentminded woman appeared to run out of words for a second or two. "Who is this person who is extremely jealous of you? *M?*" she said, with a sour wrinkled-up face.

"Jealous? *M?* I have no idea."

"This person meditates against you daily. Extremely jealous."

How in the world could I even respond to that? How absurd. "Michael?" I wondered out loud.

"No. A woman."

"Mom?"

"Let me concentrate better."

"Well, maybe we should just get back to Justin."

"No, *nothing* will happen with him…until you can get rid of this negative."

"How about acting? I'm thinking of giving it up and maybe doing something else."

"You are good at this. You are creative and you like to help people," she told me while looking even more strained and constipated.

"So, I will be doing something else? I will quit acting?"

"I'm not seeing this. I see no future," she answered with a blank expression.

"Well, maybe you're still thinking about *Die Hard 2*. Perhaps if you concentrated a bit more."

"No, nothing will change. As long as this negative is in your life. Nothing." Then, in an instant, it's like this woman with her dangling crucifixes below her holy earlobes and what looked like leftover muesli from breakfast still stuck in between her braces, gave up. "Nothing. I'm not seeing it." After these words, in her white Keds with candy cane-striped shoelaces, she bolted straight up.

"But, I'm not finished. I have a few more questions."

"Nothing will change. Everything you know is false. You must change. And you must do this *very* quickly."

"Change? Oh, but I *am* changing. I started going to therapy."

"No. Who is *M?* Nothing will change. Nothing good." After a pause, Madame X. said, "I will find who this person is, so you can do something about it. I am very, very busy. But for you, I meditate on this for days, weeks if I need to. You're good person. I do this for you."

"Well, thanks. Because, right now, I have no idea."

"It is much work. But for being nice person, the cost for you only is five hundred dollar."

In a flash, whatever fear, anxiety or apprehension I may

have been feeling had vanished and instead I became completely enraged. Furious. I realized I was being scammed, robbed. I couldn't even reply. I just stared at this woman with my normally optimistic clear brown eyes now only being able to see nothing but negative. "No. I don't have five hundred dollars. I'll figure it out on my own."

"But you *must* do this."

"That'll be my decision. I'm done now. Thank you," I said as I reached into my pocket to give the woman her twenty dollars for my first-time reading.

"You're not understanding what I'm telling you," the woman told me with a fierce sincerity exuding from her bloodshot, baby-blue soothseers.

"I said I don't have five hundred dollars."

"Money for you, in future, is never going to be problem. You can give this to me. I will meditate for as long as I have to, no matter how tired it make me, to help you."

"No. I've got to go."

All the woman could do was watch as I disappeared towards my downward spiral. She disgusted me. I thought, how could my closest friend, Jenna, have recommended this far from reputable crank? Someone who's such a blatant con?

To my incredible disbelief, the woman followed me down the stairs, almost chasing me. Then, calling me by name she said, "Paul Anthony, you've got to. You must to discover the cause of your unhappiness before the end of this year...or you will not live to see the next. I'm not seeing future. 1992 is almost here. Less than two months remain...you must to hurry."

What amazed me more than this latest outlandish prognostication was the look on her face as she uttered my death sentence. Unpredictably, she looked to be genuine, concerned. Even tugging at my arm tightly, jerking me back, preventing me from going down any further. For a moment, while I took my last step before touching ground, my new New Balance running shoes began to lose theirs. The woman's behavior and kind look shocked me. If I had closed my eyes and pretended this woman was not a psychic scam-artist, I maybe would have felt like she was a confidante of mine, someone who's actually trying to help me, someone who really cared.

From one well-seasoned actor to another, I told her with Richard Burton stage presence and my own best diction, "I'll think about it," and I waved my hand goodbye. Of course I was never going to think about it. How absolutely ridiculous.

☠☠☠

Although it would be one of the shortest and easiest of my training, my two-mile run through fall-foliaged Central Park was turning out to be one of the most challenging. Every little uphill incline was like a Swiss Matterhorn climb for me and my legs. It wasn't the physical discomfort I was feeling, it was everything extraneous filtering down from my brain. The training I had done for my past marathons went smoothly on every occasion. I always knew I would finish each one well, based on the by-the-book preparations I had accomplished with little problem beforehand.

Who is this *M*? What garbage. Why did I have to hear all this weirdness just two days before the marathon? And the date. Why before December thirty-first? Absolute nonsense. In addition to my crammed-full head, I was also developing a headache. The timing of everything couldn't have been worse.

If only I could begin focusing on something entirely different, everything would become clear, I thought. Nature's brief oasis amid the manmade mayhem intrigued me, although the humidity lingering outside wasn't doing my straight-acting brown wavy hair any favors.

The hyperactive and most likely horny squirrels running around on the ground as fast as possible then back up the trees again. The other runners, many of whom I could tell would be chasing each other in the marathon now only two days away. So much was out there to occupy my mind. And, like radar, my sensitive ears began picking up every single baby's cry in the park. I had passed by several in strollers, while others were being held lovingly in their mother's arms. Each one of them screaming as if they were all in intolerable pain. I guess teething does that to a person.

Just as my mind reverted back to the peculiar expression on the lady's face when she delivered her proclamation of doom, I was almost knocked down to the pavement by a dread-locked redhead roller-blader. "Sorr—, mahn," was all he was able to offer in a nearly incomprehensible voice. Then, he whisked away from me with no regard for my feelings whatsoever.

It's ridiculous to believe I deserved to have some sort of accident or fatal misfortune coming my way. Perhaps I should just be more careful, I thought. Look both ways. "Better safe, than sorry," my mom had always told me.

☠☠☠

A hot, generically-priced Walgreen's-brand bubble bath had worked every time for me and whatever mood I was in. Everything was in perfect order, all planned out. I could tell my mind would get back to normal once I had finished my most favorite ritual of all.

Just having scrubbed off the hardened Queen Helene's

Mint Julip masque from my freshly-exfoliated face, I grabbed for my custom-ordered and super-sized Keanu Reeves mug filled with Chamomile tea, milk and honey, and I carried it to my bath. The water temperature wasn't too cold nor too hot, it was 'just right,' perfect should Goldilocks pay a surprise visit.

Staying for free in my friend Tracy's apartment in Astoria while she was away in Iowa directing a play was such a money-saver. Although a closet fag hag, Tracy's a natural nurturer to both gays and straights alike. Being two Cal theatre alums, Tracy was the only one sensible enough to remain offstage after graduating. She loved Manhattan, but couldn't afford its prices apparently. Since I'd never known that much about Queens, specifically, the borough of Queens, my stay ended up being a very Italian-American learning experience.

While glancing at my handy-dandy day planner atop Tracy's unkempt desk full of playbills, to see which step comes next, I discovered that I'd dutifully accomplished all that was on my list for the day. Everything checked off.

Putting my newly, lightly-pedicured big toe, with its allover tan, into my makeshift spa as a test, was a success. A well-deserved *A* for effort. Transporting myself into such needed tranquility was going to be heavenly. Total relaxation. Total abandonment. At a time when I needed it most. My closed eyes felt like they were meant to. Alone. Quiet. At peace. Then the phone rang.

Not wanting to drench the bone-dry floor, I did my best to take it slow while still hurrying to get to the phone in time. I wasn't expecting a call from Tracy for another hour or so. Why was she calling me so early?

After picking up the receiver, hoping I wouldn't become electrocuted to death by the 'stepping out of the shower-touching anything electric' myth, I caught my breath and said,

"Hello."

"So, how are your training runs coming along?" my mother Barbara asked, while I knew she was picking at her face needlessly with her right thumb and left forefinger.

"They're OK, Mom."

"Don't forget to eat three bananas right after. If your legs cramp too often, you'll wind up with varicose veins."

"Yeah, I'll make sure to do that."

"I've told everyone I know to watch the race on TV. I'm so proud of you. Did you get the *Oakland A's* tee-shirt I sent you? Canseco on the back? That's how they'll be able to tell it's you."

There's no way in a million years I'd *ever* wear that. Well, only if Jose Canseco's bulges came with it. "Yes, I did. Thanks. I still want to wear something I'm familiar with though. Worn in."

"It's just a thought."

"Mom, I don't think anyone'll be able to see me. There's nearly thirty-five thousand runners." Not really being able to understand her reasoning, I still appreciated my mother's support.

"Well, at least promise to call me after you've finished, hon. I want to know how you did. After all, I'm your biggest fan. I'm always thinking about you."

☠☠☠

Never in a million years would I ever admit to anyone that the TV show that made me laugh the most was *Mama's Family*. It's just too dumb. But, it's one I could watch over and over again if only to hear Mama, Thelma Harper, say, "Well, what the…?" as she smacked her son Vint senseless with a folded-up copy of the *Raytown Bugle*. I loved every easily-predictable second of it.

Just as I became deeply engrossed in the plot's bittersweet climax, Mama with a slight limp, returning home from the Raytown National Bank after having slipped on a roll of pennies, my phone rang.

"Jenna?"

"How'd you know it was me?"

"Lucky guess."

Hearing my petite five-foot-one best friend's voice say, "I just wanted to wish you well, Paul," meant the world to me.

"I'm glad you called. I'm a little nervous. So much has been on my mind."

With her two dogs that flunked out of obedience school barking uncontrollably in the background, Jenna asked enthusiastically, "What about that psychic I recommended? Did you go? Are you and Justin getting back together?"

"Jenna. Are you kidding? That woman was a joke. Why'd you send me there?" I asked while internally scrutinizing the paradox that lives inside her, her great intelligence combined with her faithful belief in this crap.

"Why do you say that?"

"She was nuts. She told me that I needed to get rid of my negativity, to figure out why I was so unhappy, by the end of the year…or I was going to die. Before January first."

"And…"

"You're not surprised? And what? She told me Justin would come back to me, but it's my choice if I want him in my life or not, or something like that."

"And…"

"Jenna. What? It was laughable. OK. And, she told me that someone named *M* was meditating against me daily, someone who's extremely jealous of me."

"You didn't tell her you knew me, did you? You never mentioned my name?"

"No. Why?"

"When I was there she'd told me the same story. Someone constantly thinking negative thoughts about me. She told me the jealous woman was my mother."

MILE ONE

Sounding like an over-the-counter pharmacist doling out drug-interaction warnings, my diagnostic mom said, "I've been so worried about you. I read in an article that diarrhea is a symptom of colon cancer. Make sure you're getting enough beta-carotene in your diet, that's what I do."

"It's just that I have a lot on my mind. I haven't been able to sleep that much here."

"That's because it's so stressful in New York, filled with questionable characters. Always be on guard. You don't know *who* to trust. You'll be back to normal before you know it."

Speaking of characters in question, I got right down to business by asking, "Mom, can you think of anyone that may be jealous of me?"

"Jealous? Well, what in the world…? Why do you ask that?"

"Try not to be judgmental, but I went to see this psychic woman yesterday. She had a lot to tell me. She even knew all about Justin."

Stating in a voice that sounded like it had just inhaled a deep breath of pungent yet antioxidant-crammed boiling broccoli, my mother said caustically, "Justin? I didn't know he was still on your mind. If I were you, I'd forget all about him."

"Forget about him? Mom, I'm thirty-four and I've never had a relationship. I'm getting nowhere as an actor. I'm gaining weight. Always in debt. Everything in my life is miserable. And, it's all getting worse."

"How much debt?"

"No, Mom. Don't get me wrong. I'm grateful to you. Rent. Expenses. Really."

"I'm happy to help out, hon," my mother replied comfortingly. "It shouldn't matter if he's jealous. You'll move on, meet someone else."

"No. *He's* not the jealous one. The lady told me that someone's meditating against me daily, someone extremely jealous of me. A person whose name begins with the initial *M*, a woman."

"I can't imagine such a thing. But, why would you ever go to one of those people in the first place? They're up to no good. I—, your Aunt Shirley says they do the devil's work."

"I just wanted to know if Justin and I were ever going to be together. I was curious, but then she told me all this other stuff. She said I have to figure out who's jealous *and* figure out what made me so unhappy, or else I'm actually going to die. I'm not kidding. She made it all seem so important."

"Die? Oh, my Lord, Paul. You didn't believe a word of it, did you?"

"But why would she come up with something so specific? Seriously, who can you imagine that may be jealous of me?"

"My goodness. Talking about this is making me nervous. There's no one that comes to mind right off the bat. Well, Harry, I'd venture to guess. He doesn't like that I give you so much attention. There's not a single *M* in his name, but it could be him."

"No. A woman."

"Well, she must have gotten that part wrong. It's Harry, for sure. I don't know any other *M's*."

My mother and I went on to try and solve my life's mystery, but going around in circles wasn't doing my head any good. I had so many decisions to make. And, I still had to run in the marathon the very next day. Having the option of turning my brain off, even for a few seconds, was something I wanted more than anything else.

For a little while, in the background with Ricky telling Lucy why she couldn't be in the show, I began thinking about what it was like being a kid. Everything was so simple. Easy. No decisions or choices. No one jealous. No figuring anything out. I was always so happy.

☠☠☠

1959's gonna be over soon. I'm still a little squirt, almost two. I can't talk words out loud yet, but I'm a real smarty pants on my insides, that's for sure. A real chatterbox even. Grownups think that babies don't know what's going on out there. But that's a bunch of malarkey.

☠☠☠

"Marty, you'd better do your training race today. You won't qualify for regionals if you don't do well."

"Stop nagging me, woman. You sound just like the Ol' Lady."

With gobs of Brylcreem in his sandy blond hair, Daddy's listening to his hero Elvis sing *Love Me Tender* on the radio, while his muscles are hanging out of his black leather motorcycle costume. Loudmouth Tillie, our toucan bird, is throwing bits of her half-eaten bananas with its peels still on against the wall. And I'm alone in my room teething, crying, doing your average run of the mill baby stuff. They never know it, but I always listen to every conversation. Mostly none of it I ever understand too good, but as grownups say, "It takes all kinds."

"What are you makin' for dinner tonight?"

"TV dinners. You want chicken pot pie or Salisbury steak?"

"Anything with potatoes in it. Make enough for Bobby. He's coming over."

Maybe Mommy didn't hear Daddy too good, 'cause she didn't have anything to say back for a real long time. Maybe she was busy thinking about supper. When she had a moment, she told Daddy, "Does it have to be tonight?"

"Yes, Ma'am. Just like training. We'll never reach Lucky Number #7 without him."

"Well, I suppose so. He's coming alone?"

"Only Bobby…and his kerosene."

☠☠☠

It's just a normal day at home, waiting. Mommy's in the kitchen cooking up a storm, smashed and warmed-up carrot chunks with tiny pieces of lamb. Yummy. The kitchen in our house is always sunny, bright and clean, completely different from the other rooms. The green-lace curtains were made by Grammy J. She knitted them up real good before her arthritis got to be too bad. Somehow her hands ended up looking like two hooks, the kind that Peter Pan's pirate has, except Grammy J.'s are still human, not shiny like silverware.

The kitchen always smells the lemony-freshest just before and right after everything starts up. Mommy's definitely the best cook ever. Swanson's TV dinners are her specialty. She knows how to cook all kinds of them. Even though they're definitely the most popular thing now, I still have to wait 'til I get to be older to eat any. They didn't invent TV dinners for babies yet, so I'll just have to get patient.

Sunny and bright are the times I try to keep locked up inside, like eating food, any kind of food, makes me want to cheer. Daddy's coming home from his police work soon, but the things he likes to eat are so different from the stuff I'm used to. Once, when he came back from the bathroom, I saw him pull off all the curly black hairs that were left over from Mommy's hair brush, then he put them inside his mouth and chewed on them like they were spaghetti without the sauce. Mixed in was all Mommy's sticky Aqua Net. I'm not so sure that's the healthiest thing to do, but maybe he gets more nutriments in his diet that way.

"You be a good boy tonight. Just pretend. Pretend everything's a dream," is what Mommy tells me like she always does, at least when Daddy and Bobby aren't around.

Mommy doesn't know that she doesn't need to talk to me like a baby. I guess most people think they need to say stuff that way so us babies will understand just right. They should just already know that we pretty much know everything already, whether the other people talk with real words or not. In my opinion, words just kind of take up too much space and get in the way most of the time. Personally, I never cared much for 'em. That's just my two cents. I think Dinah Shore said that once on *The Colgate Hour*. She's my favorite girl singer, by the way.

As I was getting ready to eat my mashed up meal, you know, 'cause of my new teeth and all, I accidentally spilled some of it on the newly cleaned-up floor that still stunk of pneumonia. It was just the smashed green beans though, they never mattered too much to me anyway. Yech! But, instead of cleaning it right up, Mommy walked over to see if the front door was opening. Then, like

Bugs Bunny, she hopped back into the kitchen to get a fresh Brillo pad and some Comet soap. If Daddy saw the beans on our floor that never has waxy yellow buildup, he would have been a little upset. He said once that if I accidentally spill any sort of food on the floor, I still have to eat it anyways. Waste not, want not. I do the best I can to be tidy.

The front door never opened though. It was just Mommy's imagination. She should do what I do most of the time, only listen to your tummy's voice, 'cause it's 100% right every time. That way, you never have to guess at nothing. I *always* know when Daddy's coming home, and I know exactly what he's going to do when he gets there. Nothing new about it. It's Tuesday, and Tuesday's movie night. For sure not like a Kim Novak or Sophia Loren movie though. These are a totally new and unique type. They're different 'cause they come from Bobby specifically, kind of like homemade style.

After cleaning up the dinner dishes that had pieces of green beans and teeny-weeny bacon chunks still left on, Mommy put me in my room with the shades drawn, to be left alone for a bit. But, I had seen this routine millions of times, so I knew exactly what she was doing and what's coming up. Plus, like I already said, the voice inside my tummy tells me everything that's going on. Nothing's ever a surprise for me. I don't really need to see anything with my eyeballs just so I can tell what's happening.

☠☠☠

Bobby came over. I pretended to be sound asleep. It was always my smartest strategy, specially, you know, since I'm still a baby and that's pretty much the best of what my small brain can come up with in a moment's notice.

It was the same old, same old. Instead of just watching the

movie on the projector screen in the living room, eating popcorn and drinking soda pop like at the drive-in, the movies they watch are like the extra charge they all need to get their engines revved up. As soon as the motion picture starts, without even one single cartoon beforehand, Daddy begins touching hisself in private places and then Bobby does the same thing to hisself. Sometimes they all take turns watching each other touching themselves. Maybe that's the polite thing to do, taking turns.

Daddy and Bobby are the ones that come across the most curious. But it's never a surprise to anyone when their peenies turn bigger. That's when Mommy gets involved. She's kind of like the middleman, even though she's a lady.

Most of the time, they never get to see the movie finish neither, they sort of move onto other things. That's not really so smart though. 'Cause that's kind of the whole point, to keep watching so you can find out how it ends. Oh, well. Different strokes.

Somehow I could just tell I was going to get a good night's rest 'cause this time they're all on their own. They don't look like they need me for nothing. Either way it's OK by me, 'cause like Mommy said, "Turn it into a dream," so that's what I do. I just change the channel in my brain and put it on automatic. The rest of my insides don't care. They kind of turned into a wet noodle from a long time ago anyways.

☠☠☠

Strolling through Central Park is one luxury I never seemed to be granted. Walking casually, taking my time. My mind kept reminding me that it's a place I was only allowed to run through. Training, training, training. Forever with a better time, always with less pain at the end. Those were my foremost objectives. Being the best, doing things just right, was constantly at the forefront of my mind. Taking a moment to admire the orange- and yellow-colored fall leaves blow on the ground, being in awe of the striking Fifth Avenue skyline and enjoying the sound of the street traffic becoming fainter as I stepped deeper into the park, were all things I never felt I deserved but stole anyway.

Catching a glimpse of Central Park's manmade natural beauty is something I could have easily done, but instead, I focused on all the people doing the same as me. I gawked at their faces with scrutiny. Examining them, to be most accurate. What had made them all this way? At first glance, they appear so cheerful.

To be close to someone, to have an intimate relationship with a person I can trust, a man, is the one thing I'd always wanted most in life. How come other people have this? A mate. How come I never did?

What I wanted to do next was close my eyes. In order to do this though, I knew I'd have to stop walking, or else I'd ram into some innocent stranger because of my eyes being blinded from their intense curiosity. So, I found the nearest bench to sit on. Locating an empty one though required patience. It was a Saturday, the afternoon before the race, and the park was packed. As a variety of athletically-clad people passed by me, it appeared as if every other person spoke a different language than the one previously heard.

It didn't take long for one of them, actually two, to sit beside me before I could enjoy even one moment of peaceful solitude. They were speaking English, so I didn't have to work very hard at eavesdropping, I mean, accidentally overhearing anything they happened to be telling one another. The couple was discussing the content of something they'd both read, but they had different opinions about its message.

As they unwrapped their pair of alfalfa sprout and soy curd sandwiches on million-grain bread in unison, I heard the woman say, "It's impossible, Breeze. You've got to stop punishing yourself or you'll never be able to heal your aura."

Oh brother, I thought, as I looked over with judgment at the middle-aged couple wearing matching turquoise tie-dyed jogging suits and wire-rimmed glasses. More pseudo-psychologist hippy dippies babbling New Age nonsense, I figured. How did all this ever become so popular?

"Blossom, forgiving is buying into their control over you. They become the conqueror, your master."

"No, Breeze. You're being obstinate. If this is the way you want to continue living your life, that's your concern. Not mine. By the way, Nummie, you have some hard-boiled egg on your chin."

Then, having made the gargantuan mistake of establishing eye contact, and in between nutritious bites, one of them, Nummie, asked, "What do you think? Have you read *The Prince of Tides*?"

"No, I can't say that I have. I'm not really much of a reader."

"You're not? You're afraid of something. What're you hiding?" Rather than reacting to the couple, their questions, and their apparent disregard for my personal space, I just chuckled inside at two people who looked like caricatures from some black and white Woody Allen movie.

"Everyone's got something to hide, you know."

"Oh, not me. I'm an open book. I have no secrets."

"Even the deepest, darkest? No. I don't think so. You're no New Yorker, I can tell. Where are you from?" the man asked me as if he already knew the answer.

"San Francisco."

"Oh well, that explains it," the woman said, sounding like an amateur Mrs. Sigmund Freud.

Were these people for real? "Explains what?"

"You're aloofness. Perhaps you think you're at a higher level of consciousness, perhaps you don't. Everyone from San Francisco gives the impression that they're above it all."

"Hmm. I've never heard that. Um…and, I'm sorry, but I've really got to go. I'm running in the race tomorrow."

"Marathoning. Running away. In a trace-like state. Illusory. Avoiding reality. Denial. Just you and your questions."

Not really knowing how to reply, I could only think to say, "goodbye." Then, after putting enough pertinent words together in my head, I told them, "I hope you reach an agreement on that book you were talking about."

"Oh. I don't. We enjoy disagreeing."

"That's right. We enjoy being disagreeable." Then the two of them both laughed, and after that, they hugged each other with what I could tell was genuine tenderness and affection.

Only in New York City could a conversation with two strangers provide such amusement. On my walk back to catch the *N*- or *W*-line back to Astoria, I found myself snickering from time to time at the recollection of their quirky yet honest, sun-free faces. In my wildest imagination I never could have created such people.

Thinking about them in particular made me want to continue examining the faces of other strangers nearby. Everyone else's looked just as 'out of this world' as the two I had just seen. They made me think hard. But the more I thought about others, the more I was reminded about myself again. If only I had brought a mirror with me on my walk, I would have noticed for sure that mine was the strangest, the most unusual, and the most out of place face of all. Not to sound too pathetic, but a mere veneer that doesn't have the courage to admit that its insides are so perpetually sad, lonely, and vacant of all hope.

To be thirty-four and never have had a relationship must be some sort of world record. Maybe only monks and priests do without love longer than me. But, from what I hear, they get their fair share of what my friend Lowell calls, "goody-goody." For me, the good times have grown tired and old. My frequent, anonymous, and quickie-type sexual antics were satisfying in my twenties, but in my thirties, the gratification of this pastime ritual had begun to wear thin.

Would Justin really re-enter my life? Just as the psychic lady predicted? And if so, when?

MILE TWO

***M**y glands began to salivate as they heard Justin's climax-inducing baritone voice coming from the other end of the phone on marathon morning. Before being able to think clearly, my dream-filled mind flashed back to that lazy, sultry, moisture-filled summer afternoon at his apartment when he asked me to shave off his body hair. The scent of his fresh creamy-smooth skin kept me hard all day long.

Justin's call to me was so unexpected. Is this what the psychic woman meant when she said he'd come back? In a predawn tone I asked, "What time is it there?"

"It's only three, but I had to phone you. You're awake, right?" Justin said, oozing with ~~pre~~ impatience and youthful exuberance.

"Yeah, well, I actually woke up a few minutes ago. Perfect timing."

"I knew you'd be up, dude. I had to talk to you one more time. Man, I miss you so much. Our talks, out time together. It sucks."

"I feel the same. Running together by the yacht harbor. Remember the time you stole a banana right out of that tourist's hand?"

"You said you were hungry. I'd do anything for ya, man."

"I'm glad you called, Justin," I said while melting even more inside from the words coming from deep within his twenty-five year old mouth. As I was picturing his thick brown hair, big brown long-lashed eyes, his tanned skin and worked-out body, my mind began to wander more. Gently touching Justin's 90° right angle-shaped abdominal scar whenever he took his shirt off was something he'd let no one else do. Justin trusted me with something he was sensitive and a bit insecure about. Moments like this brought us closer together.

"So, what's going on?"

There were times when I trusted Justin as well. I wish now I'd taken all those many opportunities he'd made available to touch even more of him. And I wish he'd have called me before I left for New York, it would have all been so different. "What?"

"Paul, what's happening?"

"Other than the race?"

"Oh, yeah. What's up with that?"

"It's in about six hours. Isn't that why you called? To wish me well?"

"Oh, umm. Yeah. Good luck. I mean it."

Unfortunately, truthful reality hit me square in my lost-in-the-clouds brain. It didn't take long for my mind to realize what was really going on. This identical tragic scenario had been playing out to its finish all season long.

With no hesitation coming from him whatsoever, Justin asked, "I've got this huge audition tomorrow." Before he was even able to complete his next thought, my heart sank to the bottom of my being and all my excitement was extinguished. My hope for a reunion waved goodbye. There was no other reason for Justin to call me other than to ask for something, something he needs or wants to get out of me…for his career. The thing he still didn't comprehend was that giving, handing anything out, even one more time again had ended. There's no way in hell. I just couldn't do it anymore. I'd become empty. "You still there?" he asked.

"Yep."

"Good. 'Cause I really need a favor. I need to know what I should say to the casting director. Should I tell him that I also did *The Bold & the Beautiful?* Or should I not even mention it?" I couldn't utter a single word. I was in too much disbelief that that's the sole reason he'd called. "Paul? Paul? I'm not using you, if that's what you're thinking. Oh, wait. My pager."

"Who'd be paging you now?"

"Um, what? Oh, it's one of my…friends."

"Why are you calling me about this?"

"Because, Paul, you're the best with advice. You're the only one who can help me. You've done this all before. You 'da man."

"Yes. I suppose I am."

"Well…"

Remaining disgusted, part of me didn't feel strong enough though to just hang up or provide no response whatsoever. All I could say was, "Do whatever you want. You know what you're doing. You don't need my help anymore. And, if that's the only reason you have to call me, then, I'd prefer if you wouldn't."

"Come on, Paul. We're buddies. You and me. I love ya, man. You're being too sensitive again."

"You know what? I really need to get ready."

"For what? You have an audition, too?"

☠☠☠

Taking the phone off the hook was something I should have done hours before. Better late, than never. Only minutes remained until I'd head over to the Starting Area at Fort Wadsworth on Staten Island on a bus packed full of other half-asleep runners. As I closed and locked the only window in my friend's Astoria walkup, a sudden nor-east breeze forced its way in. It was like a brisk slap on the ass in a cruisy locker room. The uninvited gust was sobering; it reminded me why I was in New York in the first place.

Walking out the door of the apartment with an empty mind though, I knew for sure, wasn't ever going to happen. Just like arriving cross-country, I'd be bringing all my baggage with me. My sturdy Nautilus-ed shoulders were prepared for the added weight, along with any tagalong burdens that may be joining in. There was no getting around it, I had a strong task ahead of me.

Still dark outside, it was an odd sight to see, so many nerds huddling together in the dim streets of New York City with these strangely-numbered, fluorescently-colored bibs identifying them as 'official.' Runners, not nerds. On the bus passing from borough to borough, en route to the Verrazano-Narrows Bridge, no one said too much. As usual though, there were many chatty Italian runners. Always talking. Loudly, almost disturbingly, breaking the silence. Then, one very thin, tall and somewhat pasty-looking man hovering above me, speaking superb English said, "Ahoy, mate."

After taking a second to glance at his securely pinned-on race bib with every one of his stats listed for everyone to see, I said, "I know where Rio Vista is. It's in the delta, right?"

"Yes. Very hot in the summertime."

"I heard it's popular with boaters. You have one?"

"No. Not anymore. I sold it. I'm done with that. That whole scene."

"Only running now, huh?"

"Yep, that's it for me. Just this marathon left, then that's it."

"No more? None?"

"No more nothin'."

I don't know what exactly he'd just said in his enigmatic reply that made me think so much, and as a result, my mouth couldn't come up with anything to say back. But I had to smile after I noticed he was doing the same. He was so happy, constantly smiling. He appeared pleased that whatever it is he's decided, is the best way to go. Thinking again about his obvious contentedness made me want to respond, maybe even validating his contagious good mood. "I don't know why. But I'm excited for you. I don't even know…, but I feel glad for whatever you do—, whatever comes next for you."

"Cool answer. What's your name?"

"Paul."

"My name's Per. Nice to meet you. Good luck today," the giant, blond-haired Viking-looking man said while opening up my zip-locked throwaway jacket. Studying my race I.D. long and hard, Per continued by saying, "5626. I'll be looking for your number in the list of finishers. You're a winner, a survivor. It's obvious."

That certainly was a peculiar thing to tell me. I never did ask what he meant. My mouth closed again for a second, and I just looked out through the windows of the bus to discover that the dark horizon beyond had turned to light. And almost not even noticing it below us, amongst the army of sirens and official ceremonial hoopla that surrounds the marathon, the New York Harbor underneath the bridge appeared to be so calm, even with the teams of fireboats shooting water high up into the heavens.

When we all exited the bus near the staging area, I said "goodbye" to the man that seemed so at peace. Among the other thirty-thousand-plus runners impatiently waiting hours prior to the Start, I thought it unlikely that I'd see him for the rest of the day. But, as it turned out, I kept running into Per several times at the spacious grounds there, the urinal, the water table, and other locations at Fort Wadsworth. One time when he didn't happen to see me, I observed him sitting alone on a wrought iron bench under the shade of a maple tree that still had a few leaves remaining. It looked as if he might have been praying, maybe meditating. This stranger was a mystery to me, and I never knew why I cared.

Being surrounded by so many people and absorbing the adrenaline rush that was exuding out of them left little opportunity for me to reflect on my own self. There wasn't any room for that. Next, the time finally came, after waiting nearly two hours for each and every one of us to be herded over to the starting lines. I was in the Blue Start, containing the elite male marathoners. I had no idea why I was placed there, peculiarly positioned only a few feet away from the Number #1 marathoner in the world, pencil-thin Juma Ikangaa of Tanzania. It felt strange, all of us sweating together prior to having accomplished even a single stride, already smelling like we just stepped off the mat in an over-crowded P.E. wrestling class before we even had the chance to snap each other's jockstrap. More than anything else, I was hoping for another surprise cool breeze to join us for the entire length of the race. Maybe there'll be a Right Guard dispensary adjacent to one of the many water and E.R.G. stations along the course, I thought, while reeking of pre-must. Dream on.

☠☠☠

A jubilant and dutiful Mayor Dinkins fired his starter pistol into the sky. The amplification of the gun going off startled me a little, just as it probably did for everyone else. Finally, the time had arrived for all of us to make our strategic move together.

It took several minutes before we were able to complete even one trot, with the mass of every runner compressed together. But, before long, we were off. For most of us there, this is the event we'd been preparing for all year, perhaps our entire lives. Marathon running is special and scrupulous, appealing mostly to those who relish alone time, time for clearheaded-ness, time to ponder. Especially because there's so much of it during the ample hours of training required.

We weren't on Staten Island that long at all. Most of my first mile was spent looking down below at my feet, making sure not to trip or step on anyone else's. Definitely not the most roomy or relaxed way to begin.

From the two previous New York City marathons I'd run, I had already known that much time on the course was going to be spent in Brooklyn. Nearly thirteen miles from what I recalled. Another thing I remembered is that that's where the crowd of spectators begins, immediately at the Brooklyn base of the Verrazano-Narrows Bridge, just as we exited. Two million people standing on the streets to cheer for people they may or may not know running 26.2 miles, concluding at the swanky and over-priced Tavern on the Green restaurant in Central Park.

It was all so completely exciting, to say the least. But, having done this race already, combined with the five marathons outside New York I'd completed, I felt like this one was turning out to be more final. My thoughts sometimes returned to that tranquil man I'd been speaking with on the bus and kept seeing over and over at Fort Wadsworth. I felt like maybe my desire to continue beyond this particular marathon, to ever do this again, was evaporating.

Fourth Avenue in Brooklyn was coming up. It went on and on, an eternal straight line that lasts forever. No twists, no turns. Always the same. 'Til the very end at the Williamsburgh Bank Building. This always seemed like the most boring part of the race, from what I could remember. Like watching a *Laverne & Shirley* rerun for the two hundredth time, knowing full well that Laverne's going to voh-vodee-oh-doh in the backroom of the Pizza Bowl, while Shirley stays at home petting Boo-Boo Kitty. With little activity going on in my imagination, this opportunity made me think again about all my years, about the many ways in which all courses led to the same boring, uninteresting and unfulfilling path I'd been following…life. All the thirty-four years I'd been around equaled the extremely predictable, unending and never-changing Fourth Avenue in Brooklyn.

The cheering and screaming spectators weren't able to drown out all the other noise coming from my head. My legs were doing their job, but the energy that was being spent from my clogged-full brain was already beginning to rob me of what I needed to perform at my peak, positive mental energy. There was no way to turn it all off. I knew already, with less than three miles completed, that this particular marathon was going to turn out radically different from any I'd done before.

For only brief moments, my mind reverted back to Justin. Although the situation was so clear to anyone who knew me, I only, inside my head, considered myself a sorry sap for having fallen in love with someone who was such a blatant and unabashed user and manipulator. The strangest thing of all was that I somehow felt for certain, in some strange way, Justin loved me back. But how can a person feel love for someone they only use? Thinking about Justin, feeling the sadness that comes with all that emotion, occupied my head for the next several miles. In my eyes, every man and boy around me running resembled him.

While still traveling the eternal straight line, I'd find myself looking across the plastic partitions on Fourth Avenue to see the women runners on the other side, the ones who were part of the Orange and Green Starts. This made me reflect on Jenna and the love and loyalty I felt for my overly-competent best friend, many times regarding her as some sort of sister I never had. Her call to me, wishing me well for the race is the one that meant the most.

She always wanted what was best for me. Jenna and I seemed to be so much in 'sync about many things in life. I wondered what she, along with those two dogs of hers, was doing.

A little bit beyond the Eight-Mile marker, the point where all the multi-colored starts containing all the men and women merged together to become one, I saw a hand-held sign carried by one of the spectators that stood out miles from the rest. It said, 'I'm with you in spirit. Now and forever. Love, J.' Seeing this banner not only made me reflect, it chilled me to the bone. *J.* This initial symbolized so much to me. Justin, Jenna. Two *J's.* Two people that loved me, but in such completely different ways.

My warm thoughts of Jenna filled me with gratitude for the great friendship we shared. I knew she was staying busy at work in Los Angeles. Her new high-powered executive job at an upstart production company in the San Fernando Valley meant so much to her. The passion and dedication Jenna felt for the work she did made me happy for her. In my imagination I pictured her greeting me just beyond the finish line.

☠☠☠

No one was there to hug me when I was done.

For someone that not only liked things being done correctly but demanded it, my finishing time of 04:17:56 was without question the worst finish of any race I'd ever run. Nearly one full hour slower than the fastest race I had run only six years earlier. My self-imposed emotional exhaustion took its toll on my body. I had nothing left, and I could tell that what was to come next, my necessary recovery time, most probably needed to be doubled what it had been in the past.

I could barely walk after crossing the finish. I felt like such an absolute loser, a total failure. Running a marathon in over four hours is something I swore I would never allow myself to do. How could this have happened? Many of the other runners looked ecstatic that they had finished with similar times. They must have been beginners, happy to be finishing any marathon at all. "Paul, you're never satisfied. You're *way* too hard on yourself," Jenna had always told me. It's a shame, I wouldn't know how to live any other way. I'd never been so humiliated. I wanted to die.

☠☠☠

The added insult to my marathon catastrophe was not being able to get a ride back to Queens. Taxis were impossible to find, and the few I was able to flag down refused to take me back to Astoria. "No, not there. Sorry," the drivers told me. It was Sunday afternoon and the subways heading out of Manhattan operated on a limited schedule. Normally, always trying to see only the brighter side of things, it was difficult for me to see anything but despair on this gloomy and dreary day.

☠☠☠

Upon entering my temporary quarters in Astoria, I was barely able to peel off my stinky, perspiration-laden, heavily-salined running clothes. Once I did, after glancing down at my body in the bathroom mirror, all that stared back was a bloody mess. My pain intensified as I realized that I hadn't lubricated my inner thighs enough to prevent chafing. The same was true for my nipples. The scotch tape I'd initially put on had come off, allowing the sweaty salt to rub continuously between them and my saturated singlet for over four hours straight.

My joints were stiff and my muscles were frozen tight. In my subconscious, I had then planted the seed that vowed, "Never in a million years will I ever do this again." What a relief, I thought. To not have to be in pain anymore. An everlasting blessing. I just wanted to go home.

☠☠☠

Closing my eyes tightly felt so comforting. I could still hear the taxicabs honking and people chatting two floors below outside the building, but at least I didn't have to look at them. At a time when I least wanted to hear the phone ring, it did.

"I didn't see you. Were you wearing the shirt I bought? Everyone was watching, Paul," my mom said while blowing her nose.

"They only show the top finishers."

"No they don't. They interviewed people from all over the world. Oh, Lord. Some of the oddballs. More like a—"

"Mom, don't you want to know how I did?"

"Well, of course I do, Paul. I'm sure you did your best. No shame in that. That's all that matters. You're a survivor."

MILE THREE

"I've got the clap."

"No. Not again."

"Yeppers. Tonight, it's just you and Marty I'm afraid. I'm the odd man out."

"Marty, that means Pauly probably has it too. Poor darling. And you know I can't take him to the doctor too often. He always wants to know every last detail," Mommy said, while her wobbly hands jumped all over the place.

"Give him some of my pills. It'll knock it right out of him like an out-of-the-park homer. You got any beer?" Bobby said as he stooped over to find the missing plastic tooth that fell out of his shirt pocket.

"Bobby, alcohol? That'll make it all the worse, won't it? You remember what the doctor said."

"Stop being an old bitty. Get it. Now!" Daddy yelled out loud enough to make Tillie quiver on her perch.

Like I'd said from before, sometimes I don't know about too much stuff. But, I learned from Ed Sullivan's show what clapping is. It's what the people in front do just before and right after Burl Ives sings his folks' songs real good. I never really knew why I got the clap, but it sure hurts real bad when it happens. I'm pretty sure the clap's not something that most kids have like the measles or chicken pops. Maybe just kids like me.

Seeing Mommy get the bottle of ice-cold Burgie that's going to make Bobby's weener sting was like watching one of those shiny slow-motion robots on *The Twilight Zone*. You know, the kind that does whatever it's told, just 'cause that's the way it's made in the factory.

I wonder if Tillie the toucan ever got the clap like Bobby and me. It's a lot worse than the common cold, in case you didn't know. And, by the way, you can't get it from just clapping. That's silly.

☠☠☠

From my bedroom I can hear everything. Daddy's becoming cranky like usual. And this time it's not 'cause he ended up with a bad haircut. No, he's mostly mad at Bobby who wasn't even there to hear his yelling. Bobby'd gone out for some cigs and he hadn't come back yet. I guess it's making them all go off track for the special final ending they've been planning all along. They keep calling it Number #7, Number #7. I don't know why that number's more special than the rest, but I'm sure I'll find out sooner or later.

"Nope. Damnation! The full moon's *tonight*. Now we'll have to wait another blessed month to have this chance again. Damn it to hell."

"Marty, calm down. You'll wake Pauly."

Then, as I was waiting to hear the next word Daddy thought to say, I heard a dinner dish smash up against something, probably

Tillie's cage or next to the burning fire. It sounded like it burst into a million bits. The loud noise made Tillie screech real big, even with the white, nighttime sheet pulled up over her cage for when she goes beddy-bye.

I knew for sure that whatever Mommy picked out to stay next, she'd tell it in her shaky, scared Betty Boop, baby doll voice. "I'll clean it up, Master."

Watching Mommy pick up the broken plate pieces I'm sure made Daddy really happy. It usually always did. As a matter of fact, that's the only time's he's ever happy at all, right after getting so mad at Mommy or anybody else. It's funny, I'm just the opposite, and I'm just a kid. Maybe I'll learn the other way around when I get to be a grownup.

"You forgot that one, over there in the corner…Not there! Near the fireplace."

"I'll get it, Master. I live to serve you."

Again, although I couldn't see her, I imagined Mommy just like those robots again. She's not from outer space though. She's a real live human person, just like the rest of us. Another thing that always happens right after is that the water starts up again in the kitchen. Even if there's nothing to clean up, Mommy turns on the water faucet full blast in the empty sink. It's only make believe, the way she does it. Like she's playacting. Mommy wanted to be an actress ever since she turned into a lady, specially 'cause she's so pretty and glamorous. Tons of people say she looks like Gina Lollobrigida, but without the fake-Italian voice that goes with it.

Daddy, from the get go, wanted to be a policeman, so his dream came true a few years back. He doesn't need to go ape to feel good about that. Wrestling is another thing he likes a whole bunch. Wresting against other mens. That's how he met Bobby in the first place. They became real good friends right after they wrestled each other the first time. I heard them tell that story over and over again.

'Cause Daddy likes him so much, that's how Bobby got his job as Daddy's partner on the South Oakland Police Force. That was definitely a good deed on Daddy's part, for sure. I don't really know what they do exactly when they drive around together while they're working, but Bobby says they're mostly just "cruising the streets, huntin' down jigaboos."

Mostly all of Oakland is changing from what I can tell. Where we live at the very end of Hillmount Drive more and more colored people are moving in. I could never tell why Daddy and Bobby need to hunt them down anyways. My most favorite neighbors of all lives down our street, Mr. Reverend Pointer and his wife, pretty Mrs. Reverend. Everybody just calls him Elton. I'm not sure what they call her. At first he looks kind of gruff, but whenever Elton catches me playing in the front yard, he always stops his car to wave real big and say something nice like, "Glory be. Praise you, little one." He's got tons of daughters, and they all sing real good out loud in their very own church. When I grow up, I want to go see them and clap bigger than anyone else so everyone'll know I was there.

☠☠☠

Whether in the mood or not, I still went ahead with Jenna's recommendation to go to a play she had seen on Broadway only one month earlier. Since I was able to purchase my ticket for half-price at the discount booth in Times Square, there's no way I could end up not going.

Still sore, my feet full of blisters and a bit tired from running the race only a few days before, I wanted to collect one moment to be entertained, enjoy myself whilst hobbling around, and not have to think about anything too serious.

Everything was going my way. I was able to catch a train heading into Manhattan immediately. No waiting at all. And I even got a window seat with no one next to me. This never happens on the subway. The headache I'd had for more than a day or two was beginning to vanish and I was able to walk around the city with more of a joyful and carefree attitude.

Eating my spicy, peanutty Thai dinner was heavenly. My cute, chatty and not to be hyper-critical but most likely small-girthed waiter, Tenchi, was Japanese. With dyed blond, spiky, gel-enhanced hair, and his five-foot-two inch frame, Tenchi made me think a lot when he said, "Everything's a lie. You'll see," as he discussed my nighttime Broadway drama to come.

"That's what you got from seeing the play?"

"This is what I learned about life."

"How easily we're fooled?"

"No. Not everyone. Only the purest, the most good. These are the ones that are the most easily deceived. Then *you* must decide, Paul. Where does your conscience lead you?"

After I'd reached my flirting quota for the day, Tenchi, a philosophy major at NYU as I discovered, and I, went on to talk about many more things before I left to see *Six Degrees of Separation.* He still remained a little vague about what I was about to experience. Tenchi mostly wanted me to know that it's a play that'll make me think…as long as I'm receptive.

"Pay attention. Close attention."

"OK. I sure will."

"Everywhere you go, everything you do. Pay close attention, it all means something, it may even be vital to you." I never would have guessed in a million years that ordering a spicy duck dinner with mushroom rice on the side was going to unfold into a night of such significance. "Symbols," Tenchi said, somehow now appearing taller to me. "They're everywhere."

☠☠☠

It's just a play, I thought. And, I was led to believe that it all had to do with some notion that somewhere, somehow, every one of us is linked together by knowing six other people, six acquaintances. Six degrees. Six degrees of separation. Maybe I was wrong. The strangest thing about the evening was that the main character is a man named Paul. Is this what Tenchi the waiter had meant? Did this fictitious person in some abstract way symbolize me? My life?

Perhaps. Paul is endearing to the people he meets, he's popular. The affluent middle-aged family living on the Upper West-Side that takes him under their wing has compassion for him, giving the impression of being inspired about his goals and dreams. They genuinely appear to care for Paul, especially the female protagonist, Ouisa. She and her husband appear to have every material thing life has to offer but feel removed from the 'real' world. They also seem to be impressed that twenty-something Paul is the supposed son of actor Sidney Poitier.

As the play progresses, the socialite couple discovers though, that they have been completely deceived by everything Paul has done, everything he has told them. None of it ends up being the truth. Everything they had come to love and admire about him is false. How could they have been so gullible?

The strangest thing however is that 'there's got to be more to life than this Ouisa,' continues to feel a connection to Paul and is intrigued by his cloaked compulsion to lie and take advantage of others. At this particular point in the play all I could do, personally, was to conversely think more and more about Justin, about being deceived. How could I have felt love, and continue to feel love, for someone who finds so much pleasure in hurting me?

What a weak person I must be to attract and still care for someone who is such a brazen opportunist. Is Justin the one who made me feel so poorly about myself? Or was it only my doing? I hated this feeling of not knowing exactly who to blame. Sitting in the audience, absorbing the messages I was receiving, was making me so uncomfortable. Mainly because the questions I'd been having about my life, about the way I view myself, seemed to be growing in relevance. Again, almost out of nowhere, I stopped thinking about my mealtime sage as my prospective messenger, but I instead recalled the psychic woman in the Village.

She had told me the exact same thing. "Everything you have ever known is false. All you've known is a lie."

☠☠☠

The solitude of the rest of the night and early morning left me more time to reflect on the questions surrounding my life. Why did mine appear so radically different and out of place from most others? My right to happiness had always lived in some foreign, undiscovered hemisphere. Why? The many failures of my nonexistent acting career were beginning to add up as well, now too much for me to handle. Something about me knew for sure that these days were about to end soon.

☠☠☠

My Manhattan reunion with Stefan was something I was really looking forward to. An old friend in his mid-to-late twenties from way back, all the way back to my tennis-playing days when we used to team up together for the Golden Gateway Tennis Club doubles tournaments. Stefan was forever optimistic, never said a bad word about anyone, and usually felt some sort of personal guilt anytime anything critical ever came from my mouth.

Everything about Stefan was impressive to me. He was almost like the kid brother I always wanted to have. Stefan graduated from Boalt Hall, Cal-Berkeley law school with ease, then moved away to have a new life outside the Bay Area shortly after his father's apparent suicide. Just as I was, there's no question Stefan's father would be proud of his son and the way he's turned out.

Stefan was living comfortably in Manhattan, the Upper East-Side somewhere in the 70's with his girlfriend, and I couldn't wait to see them both that evening. What I wanted to do most was treat them both to a play that night, something special. Standing in the half-off line once again in Times Square was something I didn't mind doing, even though it never moved along. Then the rain started coming down. Luckily, the street vendors had plenty of umbrellas to sell to the unsuspecting tourists that didn't want to get wet, but at the same time, weren't happy about shelling out the inflated price of fifteen dollars for something so flimsy and dispensable.

Standing for hours in the pounding rain was taking its toll on my patience. Was this really worthwhile? I was beginning to wonder. The bulletin board up at the front was filling up with all the names of the plays for which they'd run out of tickets. Once in a while, they'd also make an announcement over their loudspeaker, but with the pelting drops, disgruntled prospective theatre-goers and the traffic noise that filled my ears, I never heard what was still available and what was not.

Stefan repeated to me over and over a few nights earlier, "anything *but* a musical." Not that, never. He always acted like such a flexible, go-with-the-flow guy, so much more than me. But, he and I were on the exact same page regarding musicals that offer nothing but fluff and lack substance. I was so hoping he and his girlfriend would be pleased with whatever I was able to come up with.

☠☠☠

"It's so great to see you, Paul. But why did you get tickets for a musical?"

"This isn't a musical," I said absolutely, after being seated in Row 22, Orchestra Center at the St. James Theatre on Broadway.

Stefan looked away from me, stared into his girlfriend's face, not really knowing what to say next. "Yes, it is. Didn't you know that? That's OK. No problem."

"Stefan, this *isn't* a musical. What makes you think that? It's a mystery of some kind. *The Secret Garden.* Maybe a murder mystery." Then, after tearing through the pages of the free playbill, I got it. It *was* a musical. I was wrong, but how could I have made such a mistake? What a fool.

"It's OK. I've actually wanted to see this. But, Stef never wants to go. I'm glad you picked this one," Rebecca, Stefan's newest and embarrassingly polite ringlet-headed girlfriend said without looking me in the eye.

Rather than going back and forth in my mind, I just had to admit to myself that mistakes happen…to everyone. What an evening of agony we three were about to experience, I thought.

After not taking in anything even remotely memorable in the first act, at intermission I had to ask, "Are you guys all right? You're surviving?"

"It's interesting," the ever-diplomatic girlfriend said to us both with a lack of sincerity showing on her face. Boring was what this thing was. Awful. A waste of time, nothing at all worth paying attention to.

In the darkness of the theatre after its much too brief

intermission, I whispered to Stefan softly, "You wanna get drunk after this?"

"You're drinking these days?"

"I'm making a joke," I said while attempting to create at least one entertaining moment during our evening out.

☠☠☠

We ate and drank a lot after the musical at some local deli, then bar. Only a Perrier with a twist of citrus for me. We needed to. It was *that* bad. Maybe it was just something for kids to enjoy. It was some sort of fable or fairytale, something like that. I knew for certain I'd end up forgetting its transparent plot the very next day anyway.

☠☠☠

On my way to the subway to get back home to Astoria that night, somewhere near Broadway and 42nd Street, something unexpected happened. I ran into Tenchi, the talkative waiter from the Thai restaurant I'd eaten at the night before. "How are you enjoying your trip, Paul?" he asked with an attractive tall, blond girl attached to his right arm.

"Fine, I guess. Definitely a mixed bag."

"Oh…but it's not."

"Right. I remember," I answered back with a grin.

"No. I'm not kidding. Like I told you before, pay attention. Do you think you've learned anything, anything in particular, from your experiences here?"

While us still smiling and the girl not, I reluctantly admitted to Tenchi, "Maybe, yes. Like I'm a big boob. Someone who makes mistakes. I'm someone who's *not* so perfect."

Without saying a word, Tenchi just looked at me, rolling his eyes in every circular direction imaginable. If Tenchi were a kid, he would have said, "Duh."

Instead, being a wise beyond his years adult not juvenile, he told me, "You're not finished by any measure. What a long way to go ahead of you. You'd better get on with it. Time's running out."

That comment just made me stare at him with a smidgen of fright oozing out of my clogged unmasked pores. What did he mean exactly? "Tenchi, do you—"

"Who knows? It depends how badly you want to find the truth. Maybe if you have enough desire to learn, you might uncover a lifetime of answers."

MILE FOUR

*"T*hat mutt that's wandering up and back, it belong to anyone?" Bobby asked while licking his chops.

"As far as I know, that negro family that recently moved in, over on Tompkins. I think they own it," Mommy said as she popped a pimple on her face that wasn't even there.

"You sure 'bout that? Looks like a stray."

"Like you, butch."

"Marty, shut up. Ain't talkin' to you."

"Not that dog, Bobby. Maybe you should look somewhere else. Too many questions from the neighbors if another one turns up missing," Mommy said next when she moved her pointer finger up to her mouth. "We don't need that."

"I'm on the *force*. I can damn do whatever I please. Nobody can tell me nothin'."

That's sort of the attitude Daddy and Bobby have about tons of stuff. Like they can do anything they want and never get scolded for it. Not like me at all. I can't wait to be a grownup so I can be just like them and get away with murder. Mommy and me are the only ones that get punished for whatever it is Daddy thinks we do wrong. He sure can be picayune sometimes. Maybe it's just the flu bug that's going around that makes him act so crabby.

"Find a different one. Or, go down to the pound like last week. You know what? I'm more in the mood for doing a cat this time."

☠☠☠

"Yes, Master. Anything for you, my Lord and Master."

It was one of those evenings. Daddy was in the living room with his Bell & Howell movie projector running and that automatically makes the air inside our house as thick as pea soup. Again, the girlie movie he's showing wasn't a Walt Disney one. Those are my favorites, and since I'm such a little kid, those ones are the most easiest for me to figure out.

It's good that *Old Yeller* never visited our house when they do their secret barbecues in the backyard, 'cause Bobby probably would have cooked him up real good. Mommy never tells Daddy that Bobby's crazy or nothing, she just says that he "marches to the beat of a different drum." Whatever that means.

Like every evening right after mealtime the water kept running full blast in the sink, but nothing was inside it to be washed. All the plates and glasses and bowls and stuff were already shiny clean. Auntie Shirley says it makes her nutsy cuckoo to have a sink like that. Auntie Shirley's Mommy's kid sister. She's skinny and she's crazy for sports. They're like two peas in a pond. Auntie Shirley always treats me extra nice, like I was her own kid. I can tell for sure she doesn't like Daddy too much. I don't know why. Daddy doesn't seem to like Auntie Shirley too much neither, just 'cause from out her living room windows you can see the whole bay. From ours you just see the street, the Chevys parked on it, and the empty trash cans. At least Auntie Shirley pretends to act nice to

Daddy the way everyone else does, just so he won't be rotten to them.

"Barbie!"

"Yes, Master."

"Why aren't you in here?"

"The dinner dishes, Master. They're piled sky high. Got to keep the kitchen in order before Bobby get here."

But there were no dinner dishes. I could see that for myself, from the chair I was sitting on inside our dining room. Mommy was fibbing. The dinner dishes were washed up a long time ago.

Then, the strangest thing happened, Mommy started putting the spanking clean dishes back into the sink and then she began to get them all soaking wet again, to make them look like they were just getting ready to be cleaned. Why'd she do that, I wonder? For Pete's sake.

In between the splashes, Mommy'd hold the dishrag over her mouth so her crying wouldn't be out loud. "Hush now, Mommy. Don't fret," I said from my tummy. Poor frightened thing.

Like I keep saying, it's just a typical night at our house on Hillmount Street.

☠☠☠

Watching *Queen for a Day* is always one of the mostest favorite things I like doing at my babysitter's house, Mrs. Pusey. She's a big lady 'cause she eats bacon fat from her Miracle Whip jar on the stove all day. Mrs. Pusey lives down the street over on Partridge, and since I'm not even two and not old enough to talk to other people, she keeps asking me questions as slow as a cartoon turtle and in the most annoying way. "Now, how'd this happen? How, little one?" I wish I could have answered. Although I had plenty of 'em, she probably could have figured it all out for herself, if she'd only have listened to her inside voice like I do all the time. It gets me out of so many jams.

Sometimes mine tells me the strangest things though. More than just stuff like when Bobby's coming over, when Tillie's going to spit out bananas, or even when Daddy's going to yell. The voice that lives inside my tummy tells me all the time, "Everything's *not* so hunky dory. You're being fooled." Fooled is just another word for fib, in case you didn't know. I haven't figured out yet what the fib part of it is, but maybe someday.

"Oh, I love my little darling so much. Yes I do," Mommy said to me.

I love Mommy a whole bunch too. She's the best Mommy ever. Even when she does all those things to me that Daddy and Bobby tells her to. That's the times when she acts like a *Twilight Zone* robot again.

☠☠☠

"No. Not Tillie. You just can't," Mommy said.

"I'm not going to say it again," Daddy repeated.

"The trouble with you two, you're too stuck on that damn bird."

"Tillie's like family. We got her when we were first married."

"Horse pucky."

"Find something else for tonight. Pick something out of the Frigidaire. It's loaded with sacrifices."

"No, dopey. It's gotta be fresh. Blood still drippin'. Somethin' that's freshly stopped breathin'."

If I was a grownup, I probably would have understood why they do the things they do. But, just like all kids, I've gotta wait 'til later, and for now just mind my P's & Q's. Don't stand out like a sore thumb, that's the trick.

Mommy didn't do a very good job of hiding what's going on inside her stomach, 'cause right after Bobby started talking about the animals he likes to hurt, Mommy ran straight into the bathroom. Right after she does that, she always comes out smelling real freshly-scented, like a Christmas cinnamon stick snatched from a mug of apple cider.

Just when Mommy's her shyest right after her face gets blushed, that's when Bobby comes at her like he's sweet on her. After that, they make whoopee. Daddy likes it too. He watches the two of the when they playact together. Sometimes, to a stranger person, they might guess that it's Bobby and Mommy are the ones that're married. They only pretend in front of Daddy though. It makes him glad to see. And, just like when he watches his special movies about the people who forgot to put their clothes on, on the projector screen, he reaches for hisself down there. Daddy grabs onto his private parts a whole bunch. Not when he has sores on it though. He needs to just let it be then, and give it a rest during those tough times.

I never feel myself there. For me, it hurts too much 'cause of all my scabs and scratches. So, whenever I want to do something fun, I just play with my green Play-Doh instead. I don't really know what exactly I'm putting together, you know, being a kid and all. Someday, I'll probably build something that's for real.

From the kitchen I could hear a loud screech. It wasn't Mommy, Daddy or Bobby. I'm not really sure what made the sound, but all I heard next was Bobby yell out, "Got it! Hot damn. Let's get started."

☠☠☠

Four seventeen. Four seventeen. That's all I could think about. How could this have happened? The feeling I was experiencing was like what I imagine a murderer must feel immediately after killing someone. Shock. Not being able to take back what they'd just done. Did that really happen? In my case, yes. Not kill anyone, of course. But finishing the marathon in four hours and seventeen minutes, a total humiliation, something I should be ashamed of. How could I even tell anyone I knew back home? I never lied, I'd just have to go completely out of my way to avoid talking about it altogether. That's the strategy.

Soon I'd have to make plans to return to San Francisco, back to reality and all that goes with it. Little was left for me to do in New York. Nearly a week after the marathon, my leg muscles nearly back to normal, I decided to go for a long walk all the way down to Battery Park City from Columbus Circle.

Walking had always been good for me. It cleared my head and forced me to put one foot in front of the other, to get outside, and hopefully see things differently. Going from neighborhood to neighborhood in a southerly direction took me closer and closer to the Village. Bleecker Street was coming up soon on my path, it was unavoidable. I knew that seeing the place where the psychic had been would make me think again. Inside my head I wondered if she was remembering to rewind just as she'd promised. Certainly not my problem, that's for sure.

But seeing her place once more made me reflect. Just like she had warned me, the clock's ticking, with seven-or-so weeks now remaining in the year. I wonder how she thought I would go. Car accident, a burglary-gone-bad, disease, murder, suicide, a random attack. Who knows? Instead of being a coward hiding from her view, I stopped walking and glanced over at the building in which I had my reading. I stared straight up at the second-floor window I had looked out of. How many other people have been scammed by this gypsy woman upstairs, I thought?

The wildest thing though, part of me began believing more and more that I wasn't being taken advantage of, not completely. I started growing more curious. Maybe if I asked once more she would tell me she was wrong and come up with a more agreeable and pleasing scenario. I stepped up close to the seven-story, dark gray-painted building with a broken window on the sixth I hadn't noticed before, stood right in front of it, the entrance, and just waited. I even peered through the downstairs window with the red satin curtains on the ground floor, but was unable to see or hear anyone or anything. It was deadly calm.

Part of me wanted to and the other part didn't. It wasn't a matter of mustering up enough courage. Or not. I wasn't that afraid. I really wanted to forget all about it, but deep down I knew I never could. The feeling was growing bigger and bigger, in importance as well as urgency. So I rang the bell. That's when I became nervous and scared. There she'd be...whatever her name was, telling me off for not getting on with it all. But she never answered. Being persistent, I rang the bell a second time, and still no response. I was so relieved inside. I'm sure she was wrong all along anyway. Or, her dialogue was lifted from some stale master script she's been using for years and years.

☠☠☠

"You'll never believe what I found out," Jenna said sounding as cool as a cucumber, not at all star-struck after just having finished a conference call with Tony Danza.

"Tell me."

"I don't know what made me think about it. Actually, well, you've been on my mind, too."

"Think about what?"

"That psychic woman in the Village. When I had been there. What she told me about my mother."

"Yeah. The details that were so similar for both of us."

"Right, Paul. My brother, Nathan. I told him what she said. At first, he didn't want to hear any of it, and then he began laughing. But, he stopped when I told him everything."

"What was it that made him stop?"

"Nathan told me something he was afraid to tell me earlier. He said that when we were younger, he was in Mom and Dad's bedroom and he opened and read her diary."

"OK."

"In it, he said all Mom talked about was how jealous she was of me. She spoke about me like she was obsessed. In the diary, Mom wrote that the only times she was able to feel happiness in her life was whenever I happened to be feeling miserable."

"Jenna, wow. Did you ever know any of this? Before?"

"Definitely not. It creeps me out. On the other hand, maybe Nathan was exaggerating. He does that sometimes, you know."

"Yeah, I do."

"Frightening, isn't it?"

"For sure. But I don't get it. Why? Why would she feel this way?"

"Paul. Who knows? I just keep thinking that this is maybe something she was going through when I was younger. Not now. No way. We're so close. My mom and I love each other so much."

"I know you do. This is how I feel about what that woman had said to me."

"So, you don't think your mother's the one who's extremely jealous of you? The person that meditates against you every day?"

"No, Jenna. It's hard for me to believe that, any of it. Plus, it wasn't the FedEx commercial I ended up getting, it was UPS."

"So, none of it's true."

"I guess not. I don't know. Although it's garbage, I still thought about that stuff all day today. Honestly, I think about it all the time now, every day. I can't get any of what she'd said out of my head. As soon as I get home, I'm gonna get you back for sending me to her. Just kidding."

"Paul. I'm so sorry for referring her to you. Well...as long as you feel there's no truth to it. What she did tell you was pretty serious though, you know."

"I get it. Before the end of the year or else I'm toast. I know."

"That's not funny, Paul. I'm concerned about you."

For best friends, the feeling's always mutual. As I hung up, my memory took me back to the night when Jenna talked so openly about her private sex life after she'd slurped down two mango margaritas. She opened up about her secret afternoons in the local dog walk where she's had quickies behind the bushes with strangers. Just as Jenna had concern for me, I had the same for her. What astonished and bothered me most of all was her confession that she's never had an orgasm in her entire life. How peculiar. How sad and tragic, I thought. If I never had the ability to climax, my body would have shut down and died long ago.

☠☠☠

Leaving New York behind would be an easy accomplishment. No problem. I had several things to look forward to upon my return to California, and getting together with Jenna was one of them. All I kept thinking about was how wonderful it was going to be to see her again. I couldn't wait. I knew she'd be coming up from L.A. for a visit, so we'd have plenty of experiences to share, lots to talk about.

Extra patience was a requirement on my return flight however. I never learned that much about aerodynamics, but one day I hoped to understand why it takes nearly two extra hours going from New York to San Francisco than it does the other way around. Someday, I thought.

Sleeping became Priority Number #1 for me, but so much stayed on my mind. I found myself developing a fierce determination to "get on with it all," whatever *that* was. I always loved returning home to San Francisco from any trip I'd been on. My tidy urban apartment would be right there waiting for me, and I was eager to sleep in my own waterbed again, and do nothing more than doze off for an eternity.

All I wanted to do before getting there was nod off into oblivion while reclining in my economy class seat, especially with this middle-aged pervert still staring at me from his center aisle seat. Night flights can be so bizarre sometimes. Just ignoring him was the best strategy, I thought. But, to be honest, it never offended me. After all, having just come from New York City, and living in San Francisco, encountering sexually-aggressive types wasn't really so unusual…but on a plane full of people. He was beginning to get on my nerves.

Making any kind of eye contact I found to be a huge error. Every time I'd glance over to see if he was still looking, he'd just be more obvious and eager while apparently beating himself off with his right hand underneath the paper-thin blanket.

"Just let yourself fall asleep," I kept repeating inside my head. But I couldn't.

It started making me so upset. Upset to the point that I became obsessed with the anger I was creating. I felt so violated. Why did this bald-headed stranger wearing a telltale wedding ring and a mouthful of cold sores single me out? Without glancing over anymore, I still found my mind focused on the whole notion of him, some stranger so ferociously stroking his dick, up and down, around and around, while he was watching me…on a plane full of people headed westbound.

I don't know if it was the plane full of half-asleep/half-awake passengers, but somehow I couldn't find the courage to confront this guy. Perhaps there was something about me that attracts these kinds of psychos, an energy I give off that tells people it's OK to be crude with me. I don't know. My anger penetrated deep inside me, still as swollen and throbbing as ever.

The only thing I knew how to do was fake it. It was somehow the only answer I was able to come up with at the time. I pretended to be asleep when I wasn't even close. I pretended I wasn't even there. I pretended that this wasn't even happening, and that I wasn't on a plane full of travelers. And, I just knew if I ever told any one of them what was going on, they'd never in a million years believe me or offer to help. Maybe this is what I deserved.

MILE FIVE

"So...how'd things go?"

Wearily, I told muscle-bound on the outside soft on the inside Andy, the carrot-topped day doorman, "It was OK. I'm just glad to be home," while his silver flask quickly disappeared from my sight.

"Well, it's nice to have you back, Mr. Jacobson."

Andy's a likeable guy, but I hate it when he calls me that. I'd known him for nearly ten years, and being so formal and proper just doesn't feel right. It never did. It's like Andy is always playing the part of a doorman, instead of treating me as a friend. Actors.

Taking the elevator up to the twenty-first floor was the very last leg of my journey home. Apartment #2102 was coming up soon, and I couldn't wait to step inside. It was going to be heaven. After opening the door though, it somehow didn't feel so sacred anymore, something was out of place. It all looked the same, but something was wrong inside. The toilet was dripping, but it's always done that. Not so unusual. The noticeable difference was that I kept hearing some sort of continuous and constantly unmistakable clicking sound in the nearby distance. When I stepped into my bedroom, there was a sea of white pages scattered on the floor. Crinkly paper.

Over a dozen of them.

Stepping further into my bedroom, I quickly discovered that they had come out of the fax machine I had on top of my file cabinet. I hadn't been expecting anything. And so many of them. There must have been fifteen to twenty pages. After picking one up, I could see that they were sides, part of a script. For the soap opera, *As the World Turns.* My taquito-sized San Francisco commercial agent, "30-30 Barry," who proudly brags to any gay man that'll listen, 'thirty blowjobs-in-thirty days,' knew when I left and when I'd be returning. This must be for an audition coming up soon, I thought.

While thumbing through the pages of the sides, what stood out more than anything was the cover letter. It was addressed to Justin. The audition was for him, not me.

I had no idea why, but my mind immediately reverted back to the chrome-domed pervert on the plane. Being violated in the most inappropriate way possible. Although the two experiences were nothing similar, I somehow felt dirty.

Before being able to think any longer about what was appropriate and what wasn't, my anger was just about to surface. But, prior to erupting, the phone rang in my bedroom and it startled me. "Mijo, you're back. How many'd you do in the Big Apple? You kept track?"

"What?"

"Did all the pages come through? There should be twenty-two altogether."

"Twenty-two pages of what?"

"Candi had some problem faxing them. You got 'em alright?"

"What's going on? Why are you sending these to *me*?"

"That *protégée* of yours, Justin, said to. He's always over there.

Doesn't he live with you now? You lucky fuck. What's his body like?"

"Barry, I have nothing to do with him. What are you talking about?" I wasn't able to understand any of what was going on, what was being said, but I did take a moment to glance around my bedroom. In a room I always kept so perfectly organized, with all things in their proper place, everything was completely out of order. "I've got to go now, Barry."

"But, you did get all the pages? The casting director's really interested. The part may even go recurring."

I don't remember what I'd said after that. But what I was beginning to notice was that my bed wasn't crisply-made and wrinkle-free the way it's supposed to be. Someone had been in my bedroom. Pulling back its brown satin comforter told all. There were cum stains on my copper-colored satin sheets, stains that weren't there before I left. Justin had been in my apartment while I was gone, and he had sex with someone in my bed.

☠☠☠

"Do we really need to get Pauly involved tonight? Or can we do it without him?" my mommy asked politely.

"Of course," said Daddy. Without waiting long and looking like he was about to do the Pledge of Allegiance, Daddy went on to say, "Pauly's the one who's going to save us." The three of them were in such an all-fired hurry. I didn't know why. Maybe they had to burn one of the neighbor's front lawns like they do once in a while in the late night. "Time's running out."

"And, we ain't gettin' any younger," Bobby told him back.

I'll just pretend I'm asleep. That worked once before. That's the best way, I figured. I'll just pretend I'm sound asleep, then not one of them will touch me, none of them will have to lift a finger.

Plus, I wasn't really in the mood. Grammy J. had taken me to Children's Fairyland at Lake Merritt all morning and my dogs were barkin', even though I still didn't know how to walk too good.

I've done this a whole bunch of times, so I was getting really good at playacting. Maybe I'll be an actor someday when I turn into a grownup. I can be on some of those television shows Mommy likes to look at dreamy-eyed during the daytime, like *Edge of Night, Love of Life* or *As the World Turns.* Those ones are really high-tone.

My idea didn't work too good, 'cause they came in after me anyways. The person I didn't like picking me up the most was Bobby. He's just way too rough, like the way Marshal Dillon is when he throws his saddle onto his horse's back. I think being a policeman makes Bobby probably feel more official than he really is. Especially on the nights when him and Daddy put on their dark blue police costumes just before they do their business.

I didn't have any clothes on, just my diaper.

☠☠☠

In a rather desperate moment, I did it. I called the psychic, Debbie, the woman who'd issued my death sentence. "The baby…not yours. I'm certain of this."

"Excuse me?"

"Your girlfriend has not been fateful. She sleep with anyone whenever you turn your back."

"What?"

"Oh, which one— Nothing will change. As long as you have anything to do with this person, *M.*"

"Well, what about Justin?"

"Nothing. I keep telling you this."

"I need to know more."

"Paying this money to find out who this person is will be nothing for you. In your future money will never be issue."

"Who will be my first relationship?"

"No, you don't understand. Nothing will change. You will have no future if you don't find out."

☠☠☠

My need for answers, or some sort of clue at the bare minimum, was all I could think about. Not necessarily because the New Year would be approaching in a little over six weeks, but because I began to become so curious. The psychic's prediction, or forecast, or whatever it's called, never gave me cause for concern. But, what filled up in me was an insatiable hunger for some sort of answer or maybe a variety of them. The therapist I'd been going to was fine, but his methods seemed rather usual, routine. Nothing really stood out about them. We talked about guys, my mundane auditions for the week: Toyota; Burger King; Alitalia; HP; JC Penney; the *New York Times*, my part-time work teaching comedy traffic school and of course, sex, all the typical stuff. It came in handy that Matthew was also gay.

"Do you like sailing?" I asked him.

"Sailing? I've been once or twice. I recall having liked it."

"So, you'd say you're into it?"

"I'm not really sure. Why do you ask?"

My gut just had to laugh, while my conscience remained a little embarrassed.

My mouth couldn't really answer flat out, he'd think I was nuts. Prefacing is what I needed to do. That's not so hard. "And, you like reading, don't you?"

"Paul, this is about you. Not me."

"Yeah, I know. I'm just curious."

He had a sort of disgruntled look on his face, like the questions I was asking were sending him into overtime. "Final answer. Yes, I like reading."

"I've just been thinking lately about all those things the psychic told me. That woman in New York."

"You discussed my interest in sailing?"

"Well, no. Like I said, I'm just curious. When I'd asked her about the first relationship I was going to have in my life, she told me it's someone who has books all around them, a scholarly-type, someone who loves sailing. *M.* Matthew."

"So, you're fishing."

"It's just kind of interesting. That's all."

Matthew, my therapist, could only stare back at me, maybe because he's paid to. I liked him as a person, yet I knew almost nothing about his personal life, if he has a boyfriend, if he believes anything that a psychic would say. It was just weird that so many things happened to match. It wasn't so strange telling him any of this after all. Only fun and entertaining.

Seeing my therapist as a prospective mate was a crazy idea though. What was I thinking? And, how did this psychic woman come up with these specific notions?

☠☠☠

Meeting Mom at the Denny's restaurant in Walnut Creek was a good idea. She really wanted to help me out. In between the Cobb salad and normal conversation, I was beginning to put together a few of the pieces inside my head. "So, you think it's Harry," I said to Mom decisively.

In a subdued voice, my mother replied, "Well, yes. He could very well be jealous of you."

"And you think he would meditate against me daily?"

"I'm not so sure I know what that means, but you never know. He does spend a lot of time in his woodshed."

"But why?"

"Maybe because you're younger."

"Well then, I need to have a talk with him. This needs to stop."

"Oh, Paul. I don't know why you're taking what this girl said seriously. For heaven's sake. I'd forget all about her if I were you."

"No, it's not her. Something in my life's not right. Nothing is going well. Nothing ever has. I've got to find out why."

My mom gave the impression of being concerned, but the look on her face was one that presumed all my worries would pass naturally over time. She probably figured that I'd soon forget about any of this and just keep living the way I always had been. She was wrong though. "What's been going on with that...acting of yours?"

"Acting of mine? You mean my *work*?"

"Yes. How's that coming along?"

"On Tuesday, I'm doing a Mars bar commercial. It's just for France though, not here. No residuals."

Mom didn't answer. She just munched on her celery instead.

So did I, until I remembered something and said, "Didn't you always want to be an actress?"

"Oh my, well I was the star of *Oklahoma!* put on by the Pleasant Hill Players. That was so exciting. Many people had told me that I should have gone in that direction."

"Why didn't you?"

"I had to take care of you, of course."

"So you would have been an actress if you hadn't had me."

"Oh, no. It's not that, hon. If not you, I would have had a different one, some other child. I'd never have the time. It's probably for the best that it worked out the way it did."

"But, that's what you wanted to do?"

"Maybe. Maybe not." I knew there was more going on than

what I had been asking and Mom had answered. Perhaps there'd be another opportunity when I'd be able to ask more questions like this, I figured. Mom never liked me discussing any of my acting gigs. And, whenever I'd begin mentioning anything about them, she'd immediately change the subject. I never knew exactly why she did that. "What's happening with that Jameson?"

"Justin."

"Oh, yes."

"Nothing. I don't know."

"Well, what? You don't still think about him, do you?"

"No. Not at all."

As Mom was preparing to respond, she had a shy smirk on her lips at the same time she said, "Oh, it's a shame that never worked out."

☠☠☠

"I've been thinking about Charlie so much."

"Tell me again what the woman told you about him."

"She said we'd only be friends. More than that if I get rid of my negative block."

"What is that exactly?"

"She said it's like a dark cloud hanging over my head all the time. Nothing will ever go well 'til it's gone. My friend Julianne told me her psychic told her the same thing or something very similar."

"So, it's a bunch of crap then. Right?"

"I don't know. It's the specifics that get me. They sure know a lot of the small details. But, no more for me. I'm done with them."

"But, Jenna. You wanna know the truth? I don't regret having gone to that woman. She may have been weird, but I'm still so eager to get to the bottom of…life."

"As long as you don't pay her the five thousand she wanted.

That's insane."

"Five *thousand?* You mean five hundred."

"No, when she called me, she asked if you were going to send the five thousand."

"She called you? How'd she get your number?"

"It doesn't matter, Paul. Are you going to send it?"

"Send it? I don't have five thousand dollars!"

"She told me to tell you to send cash, after you've mediated on the hundred dollar bills under your mattress overnight."

"Yeah, I remember her telling me to do that. But, I did it with the five hundred. Making two stacks in the shape of a cross inside a starched white handkerchief, and then putting it under my mattress, along with my ten greatest wishes written down."

"This sounds so crazy. I wonder if anyone ever falls for this."

"I know. It's nuts. Who would ever do such a thing?"

Me. I almost did it. I couldn't admit it to Jenna, but I had actually addressed the envelope and was ready to send the package full of cash via Express Mail to New York. Something made me not follow through though. A person would have to be so desperate to do that, I thought. All of this was still new to me.

☠☠☠

Closing the windows in my bedroom on a Sunday was something I never usually did, I never needed to. The financial district was like a ghost town on weekends. Only occasional murmurs coming from the ground, twenty-one floors below, so I was able to fall asleep immediately on a quiet afternoon.

My brain slowed down enough for me to finally doze off after not being able to all night. I needed it so badly. My mind began traveling in a million different directions, and somehow while sleeping, I began sweating profusely. It wasn't at all hot. And, while in the middle of the strangest dream that had nothing to do with Tom Cruise lying on a beach towel, one that had no relevance to me or my life whatsoever, I heard two loud bangs coming from the outside. A few times in the past, the noises coming from the park below would wake me up. They were mostly made by homeless people that sleep there in the late night and early morning, but this time the park was vacant.

Whatever it was, was so loud, so unnerving, that it not only woke me up, but made me leap right out of my bed while my dick stayed as completely hard as a gay jackrabbit's in heat. I was terrified.

MILE SIX

"**M**y headaches keep getting worse. Sometimes I can't even get out of bed."

"Try not taking naps during the day. That'll help you sleep better at night," Matthew, my soft-spoken, dark and distinguished-looking sounding board said while stroking his slick salt and pepper beard up and down.

"I can't sleep then either. I'm always tired."

"You've been thinking of Justin again?"

"No. Well, yeah I have. But, I've been thinking about everything else, too. It's like something's going on out there for me to solve. And, I don't even know where to begin."

"Maybe the answers will come to you…if you let them."

"Matthew, no New Age crap…please. You make it sound so easy. That is true though. It's like I never *let* anything happen. I always feel that I have to make everything happen. Nothing *just* happens. I'm a control freak. Never one spontaneous moment, remember?"

"Perhaps that's something for you to explore."

"Do you believe there are clues around us that we should pay particular attention to?"

"I'm not sure. Do you?" Although Matthew's responses may have appeared pat, I knew he was insightful and always managed to say just the right thing, even if it's only a word or two.

"I never did before. I never had to."

"Well, if that's something you want to do, you feel you need to do, make that change now."

☠☠☠

Getting to spend any time with my perky Auntie Ina, who wears a smile on her face every single day but sometimes forgets to comb her hair, was always the best. She's got tons of patience 'cause the Maker made her born with a daughter that's retarded. I think for sure the Maker only does that for special people who can handle something big like that. Although she'd never hurt a fly, Bonnie's a handful for sure. Anybody'd say so. A regular-type mommy wouldn't get too far. They'd probably just give up, and that's something you can never do if you're a grownup parent. You just can't. 'Cause retarded people, just like babies, need extra attention from their mommies and daddies. And with retarded people specially, they'll need it for life. With kids that aren't babies anymore, they eventually get to be grownups and be by themselves later, then it's the wife's turn to take care of you.

Auntie Ina rolled me outside in the fancy shiny silver stroller with bright red tassels she bought with her Blue Chip stamps. Eleven books. Going down the block from where she lives to the park was like her showoff time. I felt proud of myself when I was with her. Auntie Ina and my uncle live in the most old-fashioned part of Oakland. They live in a part where it's just people like them, the same-looking kind you know, with just white-colored skin.

Like I'd noticed from before though, Oakland sure has its share of worrywarts. That's all they think and talk about, how many colored people are moving into their neighborhoods. How come? Auntie Ina's not like that. Whenever she takes me to the playground, it's always Albertina she likes me playing with most. Albertina's a year older than me and she's got brown-colored skin. But, she's exactly the same as me. We never did talk about it, 'cause I can't talk yet. But, I know for sure that her parents do some of the same stuff that mine do to me. It's just harder for you to see all the scratches 'cause her skin stays dark all the time.

"You've lost a few pounds, haven't you?"

"I've been drinking my strawberry Sego in the mornings and vanilla Metracal every night. Variety, you know. Thank you for noticing."

"Where's pretty little Albertina today?" Auntie Ina asked the grandma who was sitting all by her lonesome on the swing set.

"Oh, she's not doing so well. Heaven's sakes. Last night, she took a spill. Oliver, her daddy, drove her into the hospital, and she came back with seven stitches on top of her head."

"Oh my goodness."

The grandma only got it half right. Albertina didn't take a spill. I'm not really sure what that means, but when the daddy hit her, he smacked her too hard. It must have hurt Albertina real bad. I hope they don't kill her or nothing. I like playing with my playmate Albertina a lot. And, since I don't have any brothers or sisters, I like having other kid friends to be with sometimes. My older sister Maria didn't hang around too long. She left before I came around, so we never got to play together. I forget how to explain too good, but she went away while she was snug as a bug in a rug. Crib death, it's called.

I'm still trying to decide if I was the lucky one. Not having to share my toys with nobody, I mean. I'll know someday. That's my motto. Captain Kangaroo says everyone's got to have a motto. They're real important. Mr. Greenjeans always says his bright and early every morning, but now I forgot what it is. He's funny to look at sometimes 'cause he's as thin as a railing.

"Well, it looks like it's only you and me today, Punkin Pie," rosy-cheeked Auntie Ina told me. She calls me that sometimes since my birthday's close to Halloween, not 'cause I look like a pumpkin.

I just stared up at her, and with my eyes, answered, "That's perfect. Definitely OK by me."

She understood exactly what I'd said. She and I talk the same lingo. It's the same language she talks with Bonnie, who's in her special summer school right now. It's just for kids, I mean, grown-up kids that go there. I'm not so sure how old Bonnie is, so I guess she's kind of in between being a kid and a grownup. And, the thing is, she's going to stay that way forever. She's never going to change. For sure, that's the best way to be though. When you never get to be a grownup, the rest of the people expect a whole lot less from you. Your life's a whole lot easier that way, I think. You do the best you can, and that's just fine.

The lazy, hazy days I spend in Sunnyhills Park always make me the happiest. It's the place where all the kids go to get away. In the sandbox or on the grass, we always get to do everything just the way we want, as long as we don't get into fist fights with the other mean kids. That's a no-no. Sometimes those jokers do get on my nerves though. They can be, you know, competitive, just like Daddy and Bobby are when they play Roman gladiators.

Inside the park Auntie Ina always lets me pet every one of the kitties that comes up to me. Even if I don't give them any groceries. The ones that don't know me too good claw me a little at first because they don't know any better, just like a baby would. I have my favorite ones, too. All the time I ask them their names, and they always give back this answer, "We don't do that, we don't have names." That's pretty smart, if you ask me. Personally, I'd get confused if everyone all had the same name, Kitty. It's like if someone calls me, "Boy" or "Baby," when there's really a whole lot more to me than that.

The place I like to take my kitty friends is inside the red brick playhouse that's built like a barn. Auntie Ida doesn't think I'm a weirdo 'cause I do that, she thinks it's adorable. Somehow, without her knowing the factual realities, Auntie Ida understands that the kitties love me and I love them back, and that's the most important thing. The kitties never hurt me, they never make me do things I don't want. They always love me no matter what.

Later on every afternoon, Auntie Ina takes me to Bonnie's school so we can pick her up together. It's a place where everyone's happy, 'cause that's all they know. For outside people, it's like the retarded people are the ones that have less, but what they don't realize is that they're the ones that were born with something extra. They don't know ache like the rest of us. When someone hurts them, it's like they only stubbed their big toe, and the ouch goes away. It's not like when someone does something real bad to them, making them have to hurt real bad, and the ache stays inside them for always.

☠☠☠

I'm glad they made me stay in my room. I didn't want to have to be out there.

And, not just 'cause they weren't going to do anything to me for a change, it's because of what they're doing to Fluffy. Fluffy's the orange and while-haired kitty that scratches at our backdoor screen sometimes when no one else gives her food to eat or water to drink. Whenever I'm crawling on the floor, I push the backdoor open, and I always make sure to give her tiny pieces of my tuna fish sandwich. Not the relish part though. That gives her the runs.

"I'll do it. You two, stand back and watch."

"But, are you sure? Do you have to…cut its head off?" Mommy asked.

"It's the only way. It's what pleases Satan most."

"Let him do it, Barbie. He gets a kick out of it," Daddy said.

"Oh, I've got to tend to Pauly. I've never heard him cry like this before. I'll be right back. Maybe he hurt himself again."

"No, let him be. You'll miss all the fun."

"Hurry on, Barb. Then bring him back so he can watch too."

When Mommy walked into my room, all I thought to do was spit up vomit. I figured that might make her stay inside my bedroom instead of having to go back out there and take turns in what's going to happen next. Poor old Fluffy.

In between the vomiting and Mommy trying to fix me, I heard the most scary scream of my life. At first, I wondered if that's how I sound after they do stuff to me.

When Bobby screams like that, I know something real bad happened. But, I also know that Fluffy went up to the sky. She's so lucky.

I stopped crying. And Mommy went back into the kitchen. Since Fluffy got to be away from them for good, my heart didn't need to be sad anymore. I just kept listening.

"Skin it real good now. Get over here, Mart," Bobby said.

"I'll just watch from over here. Remember, I'm the Master tonight. Next time, it's your turn."

"Okey dokey. Barbie, where's your skillet? That big one."

"It's in the pantry. What do you need it for?"

"Got to get the innards nice and spicy. Like Almighty Satan, our glorious leader, I like my eats with a little heat."

"Would you like some Tabasco to go with that, sir?" Daddy

asked like a wisenheimer.

"You fooler. This is serious business, Master. What's next?" Mommy said as she handed Bobby her penny-bottomed frying pan.

Then, Daddy began reading from their special holy book with its specific instructions written in. It's for sure not like a bible or a phonebook, more like the opposite. Well, maybe it is. Maybe it is kind of like a bible, but for this Satan guy, not the Jesus kind. Inside my head, it didn't matter at all what they were doing to Fluffy and her insides. I knew the very next day I'd crawl into the backyard, pretend to play, but really dig a special grave hole for Fluffy, and I'd just bury whatever leftover pieces I could find. Like I said, she's lives inside the sky now. That's all that matters.

"Subsequent to removing all the animal fur with your bare hands, and after gutting the corpse, place the carcass on a platter, preferably made of sterling silver. This will later be used for the offering to Our Beloved Savior, Our Most Blessed and Sacred Master."

"Praise be to You, Most Holy Satan," all three said at once.

Then, the lights began to flicker in our whole house. I don't know what made that happen exactly, 'cause I don't really understand electricity too good yet. Maybe all of Oakland was doing the same thing that night, and Fluffies all over the city were flying into the sky at the same time. I hope it had room for all those cats up there, and let's pray its sandboxes are fresh.

Thinking about the peaceful sky again made me relax instead of needing to cry anymore. I fell asleep, knowing that the Man upstairs heard my special wishes for my special friend Fluffy.

When I woke up the next day, I was as patient as could be. I was a real good boy. I looked over the kitchen from top to bottom, but I found nothing. Every time Mommy cleaned up after, there was never anything left. It's like the whole thing could have just happened in your magination, because there was no evidence leftover, like the kind they have to find on *Perry Mason*.

That's OK. I did something even better. Like I said, I was patient. I waited until after lunch. Mommy didn't know, but I hid the biggest part of my tuna fish sandwich inside my clean diaper. She'd never find out, I thought.

Later, when she put me on the ground to crawl anywhere I wanted, I got the backdoor to open, and I went into the yard on an extra bright and sunshiny day. It was real nice, because I got to be all alone. Just me and my tuna fish sandwich. When Mommy was on the phone talking to her friend Millie, I dug a little bitty hole in the dirt with my very own two hands. I pushed four clumps off to the sides. But before making the next step, I had to do one real important thing. Instead of beginning with 'Dear Most Holy Satan,' I began saying,

☠☠☠

'Dear Maker, Billy Graham from his television show calls you that. Is that Your nickname, by the way?

He said that if people talk to You, stuff gets better. Really? I don't seem to understand any of this too good. You know what I mean? After all, I'm just a baby, and I'm not the smartest person on earth by a long shot. Pretty soon Mommy's going to get off the phone, so I gotta hurry. But, I want to tell You for sure, 'Please take care of Fluffy.' Sometimes she never had too much to eat, and sometimes she ran out of fresh water from our drainage ditch. But, Maker, even though we were mostly strangers, I loved Fluffy a whole bunch.

I want her to know this. Can You please tell her. I know You're like me and You don't need to speak any of the languages that people talk. You just do it without knowing the words. By the way, kitties do it the same, in case You didn't know that already. And, like the kitties in the park told me, they don't have names neither. They're all unanimous. You know, without being called nothing, just like the bad guys on Dragnet.

Anyway, Fluffy's not a bad guy. She's the one that went up above last night. Just so You can keep track. Please love her and take care of her. And, more than anything else in this whole wide world, please tell Fluffy that she'll never be forgotten by me. And, one more thing, please tell her that someday I'm going to make up for this. Someday, I'm going to make this whole thing right. I'm going to turn it all around. They may be my mommy and daddy, but someday. Just You wait and see.

So, for now, bye, Fluffy. I love you a bunch. The same goes for You too, Maker. I'm sure I'd like You if I knew You better. Amen, Pauly."

☠☠☠

With only love coming out of me, I put the teeny chunks of tuna fish and pieces of breads into the hole in the ground and then covered it up real good.

☠☠☠

"He was real nice to me. Especially after I drove to the wrong town. Oh, brother. I can't believe I did that."

"Harry's a tough nut to crack. Difficult to read sometimes. I bet it's him."

"No, Mom. I'm positive it's not. I knew that, somehow only minutes after being there with him. He said a lot interesting things though."

"Like what? He usually talks about firewood whenever we get together."

"Nothing like that. Personal things."

Mom had a worried look on her face. Like I was somehow unearthing a family secret or something. My mother cherished those. To her they're undiscovered gold bullion. "Well, I'm happy he's opening up a little. He never says anything very meaningful to me. I wonder why he confided in you. I hope it's not because you paid for his breakfast."

"No. Breakfast? No. I felt that he really liked talking with me. I enjoyed talking to him."

"That's nice. What did he have to say that was so personal?"

"Well, one thing he mentioned was about you. About the way you view me, my life."

"I told you, I do my best with you being..."

"That's not what I mean. Harry said that you see me as being a child, seventeen. He says you always will."

"Oh, did he? That's not true though. It's a free world, he's entitled to his opinion."

What I hadn't repeated was that Harry insinuated, rather frankly, that my mother needed medical attention, help mentally, therapy of some sort. I had never looked at my mom this way before.

MILE SEVEN

*S*o, it's *not* Harry. He can now be officially crossed off the 'jealous' list. All signs point to Mom. But how could that be? Why would she be envious of anything I've got? There's no conceivable reason why anyone would want to trade places with me. My life totally sucks.

The fact that I was still alone, never having had a relationship at age thirty-four, had become my biggest and most obvious failure. I hated not being able to spend my life with someone. There's got to be some reason, I thought. Something big. It's just not normal. Most of my friends have had several meaningful long-term commitments, even marriages, by this time. What made me so different from them?

At my loneliest and most desperate moments, my mind always strayed back to Justin. Sometimes I'd force myself to recall what my friend Sally always used to tell me, "Would you still feel the same about him if you put an 'ugly' bag over his face?" She's absolutely right. There were some good times when Justin and I got together, but his looks are what took up the most storage in my memory banks. I hated and loved that about him. Everything was so easy for Justin, all good things coming his way, presumably because he's so beautiful to look at.

But there was more. When we first met I felt something inside, like we've known each other from someplace before. There was a familiar sensation to our first-time meeting at the mostly all-gay and locker-room friendly Central Y in the Tenderloin. As if on purpose, it was explicitly-in-your-face Justin that came right up to me on the Stairmaster. It wasn't the other way around. Right there at the gym, with a hole in his shorts, in the most strategically eye-catching place, giving me enough visibility to know if he was circumcised or not. Sexy Justin, squatting right there in front of me, doing sit ups on the ground facing me with his dick and presumably shaved balls targeted straight at me.

I wish sex wasn't on my mind so much. Everything about Justin was so enticing. If he hadn't been so overt, maybe I would have taken my time noticing him.

The afternoons we spent together for lunch nearly every day at the economical Hunan Empire on Union, our ritualistic Chinese restaurant-meeting place in the Marina, was something I missed a lot. I wondered if he did as well. Trying to forget about Justin was so hard. Over and over again, I'd get so close to putting together a relationship and then it all comes to a screeching halt. Always the same. The identical pattern. I wished so very badly to know why.

Answers about Justin were all I was looking for, nothing extra. Maybe if I ask about him just once more she'll be more direct, and not try to sway me in another direction. In one of my weakest and most confused moments ever, I called the psychic woman in New York one more time.

"All will be the same. Unchanged. He will not come back to you, nothing good will happen, as long as this middle-aged woman is meditating against you."

"So, then it *is* my mother. You're positive it's her? Debbie? Hello. Are you there?"

☠☠☠

"I just don't have five thousand dollars. What's she thinking?"

"Paul. Are you sure? I feel so bad about this whole thing. You know I'd give it to you if I had it."

Quietly reiterating inside my head my private nickname for Jenna, Miss Moneybags, I was positive she had plenty, but still I insisted, "Jenna, no. I'd never borrow it from you anyway. You've got your own life to deal with. Am I nuts?"

"No, Paul. You're not. I'm so torn. I have no idea what that money would do. It's your choice."

"I wish there were some sort of Better Business Bureau for psychics or something like that, an expert to ask which're reputable, which aren't."

"Maybe Ralph Nader."

"Well, I know it's my mother. That's for sure. And, I've told her in the nicest way possible to knock it off."

"That'll work. After I had the talk with *my* mother, it seemed to do the trick. And, all those hang-up phone calls I'd been getting stopped. It was a misunderstanding, that's all."

"I don't know if it's that easy for me. I'm not really sure if my mother's so agreeable to that. There's no way she'd ever admit to being jealous of me."

"Well, even if she is, a little bit, what harm could it do? I take that back. Meditating against you daily…that *is* pretty severe, but it still sounds somewhat farfetched. I'm sure that woman was just trying to scare you. Finagling money out of people is how she makes her living."

"Yep. Off of suckers like me," I said from my gut, rather than my perpetually wavering mind.

☠☠☠

The clock kept ticking. Just like that psychic lady told me, "before the year ends," this is my mission…or else. There's no way I would ever let this psychic woman's opinion outweigh what I really felt I had to get done in life, but where did she come up with an idea so outlandish in the first place? How outrageous. Somehow, somewhere, there's got to be some shred of truth to her story, I thought.

One thing I knew for certain is that I still felt love for Justin. Maybe time was what needed to pass in order for him to appreciate me the way he should. Or, again, was I being completely naïve?

Just as I was thinking about Justin and our imaginary reunion, my phone rang.

Sounding out of breath from a few too many Marlboros, the voice calling me said, "Hello. Pauly? This is Christina. From New York."

"Hi, Christina. What—"

"I haven't heard from you. I've been so worried. I've lost sleep thinking about you. You are OK?" The woman said, almost hysterically.

"Well, yeah. I guess so. I'm fine. I thought your name was Debbie."

"I never heard from you. And, I've been asking your friend…there in California. She tells me she knows nothing." That's how this crackpot got my number.

"About sending you the money."

"No, about you. I ask her all the time how you are, how you're getting by. You are doing all right?"

"Debbie, Christina, please don't bother her. But, yeah. I'm doing fine, I guess."

"It doesn't sound so. This is the truth you are telling me?"

"I figured out that it's my mother who's jealous of me. If that's what you mean."

"And how do you know this?"

"I asked lots of questions. The process of elimination."

At a time when I wanted our discussion to be interrupted most by Blockbuster or Captain Video, it just never happened.

"But, it's not finished."

"Yeah, it is. We talked about it. She didn't really admit to it. But, my mother wanted to be an actress. I think that's what it's all about."

"No, nothing better. Things will only get worse. Much, much worse."

"But, Justin will come back to me. Right?"

"No. Nothing good. You will have no future. Nothing at all. And you must remove this soon."

"Remove what?"

"This negative block. Your dark cloud."

That's all I needed to hear in order for me to terminate our conversation. It took this long, weeks instead of days, for me to realize that the only dark cloud I had in my life was this crazy woman and the things she was telling me. They were both bogus. How can I ever forgive myself for being so stupid to believe in this nonsense, even temporarily? I'll just have to try, I kept repeating to myself.

A huge weight had lifted from my shoulders. It's like this constant, nagging pressure I had had ever since I was in midst of drama central, New York City, had disappeared. Vanished into thin air. Happy to know that I was going to see the next year after all, I began thinking about the things I'd like to do. Figuring out what to do about my career, or lack thereof, was at the top of the list.

☠☠☠

With the clearest head I've had in quite a long time, I chose to try something I hadn't attempted since I'd come back to San Francisco. I decided to go for my first run. I wasn't very prepared for a long one, just something quick. Even though most of the shorter courses near my apartment were filled with traffic, I at least wanted to get out and attempt to keep going.

My legs were rested and ready to do their business, and heading up the Embarcadero with its odd-numbered piers was just like old times for me. Without the expectation and anxiety of having to perform well in a 26.2 mile marathon, I was on my way. I felt free, completely liberated from my past.

During the mornings, that's when there was the least amount of tourists milling around. I loved that a lot. For some reason though, there were so many more pedi-cabs than normal, cyclist-drivers whisking city visitors to and fro. Their destinations every day were always identical, Pier 39, Fisherman's Wharf, and maybe Aquatic Park after that. From a tourist's perspective, these locales *are* the very heart of San Francisco.

Although the calendar was now entering late-November, it resembled, much belatedly, earthquake weather outside. Rather warm, with the air being as heavy as could be. As I continued running, I began feeling it all. Like the pressure I had known previously was returning, just from the atmosphere alone. The air was pulling me down. And then it all began weighing heavy on my mind, the thick and humid air.

As long as I could make it past Fisherman's Wharf to Hyde Street, I was going to be fine. Beyond that point, I'd have a clear path. Very few tourists after it, with only one small hill to scale, Fort Mason. An easily doable one for sure.

Making it up and over the Fort Mason hill and entering into the Marina district was a breeze. It felt like old times. Like I was training all over again, but without all the stress that accompanies it. For me, my run was becoming easier, yet when looking around, I found only tension. All the other runners, roller-bladers and bikers appeared rushed. A storm was blowing in from the Pacific, and I'd assumed they wanted to beat it. I didn't care. I kept going.

This was my chance to begin erasing the huge failure I'd created in New York City. Well, maybe some of it at least. I was starting to think that since I had made it all the way to the Marina, the Yacht Club and beyond really wasn't that much farther to go. So I did. Running through Crissy Field, adjacent to the San Francisco Bay, was refreshing and rugged on its gravel-laden trail. As I was moving along, I was feeling as if I was genuinely accomplishing something worthwhile. I felt so strong and durable. I felt like I could do anything.

At lightning speed I was running in a very deliberate westerly direction, away from the protected, enclosed and safe bay towards the wide open Pacific Ocean and the fury that's generated there whenever a storm's coming in. Something about me felt like I was defying nature and all the limitations that go with it. I didn't care at all what came next, I was ready.

Almost at the end of San Francisco's now-defunct military post, The Presidio, and with Crissy Field almost a memory behind me, I kept prodding along. Yet what was directly in front of me was my main hurdle. Not the gloomy weather but Fort Point, the crashing waves blanketing, intruding upon, every sole runner's path. And, more than anything, the huge uphill climb connecting me to the Golden Gate Bridge at the top. After twelve years living in San Francisco, this bridge continued to amaze me. Although it's not one of the Seven Wonders, I can see why it remains to be the most photographed man-made object in the world. It symbolized everything to me. Freedom.

Up, up, up. "Don't *ever* stop," was my motto. Never. Even when only feeling pain, don't stop. Never. Not for any reason. This is why I'd lost so many my running partners. They couldn't tolerate this 'only seeing the world in black or white' mentality.

Within a matter of minutes I would be on the east-side pedestrian pathway of the Golden Gate Bridge. Only a handful of tourists were headed there. Perhaps the bad weather had scared them off. It was a blessing. Not having to outmaneuver anyone or anything to get to where I wanted to go. I had no idea what motivated me to want to go the distance. All during my training this was always my longest run. Nine miles to the end of the bridge from my financial district apartment and nine miles back. Eighteen miles was my max. I still had no idea if I had enough stamina to run all the way back or walk. But…no stopping, no walking. Never. That's for losers, I'd always thought.

From up above the bay, headed north to the Marin County-side of the bridge, Sausalito, I looked out to the vista that appeared unparalleled, unlike any other I had ever seen in my entire life. It was the most perfect sight, like being in the vicinity of what comes next.

Midway across the bridge, I looked in back of me to the view of all San Francisco. The best city in the world, in my opinion. But, something had changed. As I turned my head to the right, I began missing it. It's like I imagined I was never going to see it or be in San Francisco again. Why was I thinking this? Each step I took, running forward, running away, was like I was abandoning it, leaving something behind. But, as I started looking ahead, I began feeling the same as my eyes observed the northerly direction as well. I began to miss Sausalito, Marin County, Angel Island, and Alcatraz. And I didn't know why.

Inside my head, I began considering how easy it would be. Wouldn't it all be easy if…? Imagining anything like this had never happened before. Not so spontaneously at least. Not so natural-feeling. Hundreds of people have jumped off the bridge. What difference would it make if I were to join them?

There I was, smack in the middle of the Golden Gate Bridge, dozens and dozens of cars whizzing by in both directions, all of them not noticing what's going on alongside either pedestrian walkway. I stopped. I stopped running, something I had never done before. Right there, mid-span between the two gigantic towers. My feet just stopped like they were meant to. It was all so easy. So natural, I thought.

Now what? What would they do next? I took two steps to the railing and just gazed out to the view I felt I would soon be missing. Then, I looked down to the undiluted and potent salt water below me. It was so big, the sprawling San Francisco Bay meeting the almighty Pacific Ocean. Vast and deep. Endless. I felt as if I knew exactly what the people had felt when it was their time to become a part of something so never-ending and infinite.

I took another step, the only one left. I didn't allow myself to think about any of it too much. If I did, I would have begun to recognize my own fear. It was the right thing to do, I thought for sure. Sooo easy. Sooo final. But not.

My foot only dangled on the railing for no more than a second. At the same exact moment my foot was at peace, two of the dozens of cars, going in opposite directions on the bridge at high speeds, during non-commute hours happened to crash into each other. The sound of the collision both startled me and awakened me. I couldn't make out the particulars when I turned my head to see. It all happened so fast.

The two colliding cars propelled me into the real world. Somehow though, one split-second before I heard the crash my mind flashed back to Oakland, the city where I was born and lived in as a little kid. That's all that stayed inside my head. Oakland and the crash. Glaringly impressed there like a granite tombstone. Why?

After exorcising the image of Oakland from my head, the truth set in. An accident just occurred. People were hurt and I had to do whatever I could to help.

I spent the next several minutes tending to others who desperately needed my assistance. The thought of what I was about to do on the pedestrian walkway of the bridge disintegrated forever, almost like it never existed in the first place.

MILE EIGHT

"It's lucky no one else hit you."

"I guess you could say that."

"Well, of course. You knew exactly what to do. It must have been terrifying."

"At least there were witnesses. Many. The parking lot was packed. Macy's was having a huge sale."

There was a reason Jenna was my closest friend. Instinctively somehow, we always knew the best way to comfort each other, even in the aftermath of a minor fender-bender. When the time came for *me* to confide, I couldn't. Plus, it was Jenna's turn. Discussing anything about my own life seemed too self-indulgent. I had told her that I had gone on a run, and that it took me to the middle of the Golden Gate Bridge. I never told Jenna that I had stopped. Never did I attempt to mention what I contemplated doing after that.

Walking along Stinson Beach while Jenna took a timeout from La-La land was always one of my favorite things to do with her. Even though I wasn't much of a dog person, cats have always been my favorite pets, she always brought her two cherished hounds along. Whenever I thought about them, I always imagined them as being her children or something else formally adopted. They were so loving to Jenna and all three adored each other. Wilma and Pepsi gave the impression that they liked me as well, but I'm sure they were able to detect somehow my preference for their counter species.

Being as bullheaded as Jenna sometimes, I said, "No, we have to keep going. Never stop. We can't."

"But, I want to rest here for a while. I'm still a bit shaken up."

Looking as if Jenna's feet were coming to a standstill, I promptly said, "Oh, no. We've got to keep going. Then it doesn't count. You can't stop, ever."

"Paul. You're too much."

"Seriously. It's not a good way to exercise. You have to keep your metabolism, or whatever it is, up and active. You've got to continue for over twenty minutes consecutively…or else you have to begin all over again."

"Paul, you really should take the time to stop and smell the flowers. Chill out once in a while."

"What flowers? We're on the beach. Plus, I can't smell anything anymore since I had to smoke for that Japanese shampoo commercial. My nose stopped working the very next day."

"You know what I mean."

"No, stopping's for losers."

Defiantly, while picking up her pace, Jenna said, "I stop all the time. So, I'm a loser?"

"No…of course not, Jenna. But…it would be better if you kept going. Stopping just isn't right.."

"Paul, how did you get to be like this? Everything with you has to be all or nothing. You either have to do it all the way, the hardest way, or you…dismiss everything, all your effort."

"I don't know. Maybe I was born like this."

"Well, to me, it just feels that you're much too hard on yourself."

Rather than listening anymore, I pretty much ignored Jenna's commentary for the rest of our nature walk together. Not being intentionally rude, I just wanted to keep going. It's "good for you," I said before not speaking, persuading Jenna to take her mind off her scratched rear end. Sometimes I can be as manipulative as Justin. As we approached the three-quarter mark from the beginning of the beach to the very end, Jenna said, "No, Paul. Really, it's too tiring. I want to stop for a while."

"Loser."

"What?"

"Oh, nothing. Oops, did I say that out loud?"

☠☠☠

"Marty, it happens to everyone. Not to worry."

"What did you call me? Did you say Marty?"

"I beg your forgiveness. Of course I meant to say, Master."

"Put your peter back in its holster. Give it a rest, pally," Bobby said as his was standing at attention.

"Shall I deliver the ingredients unto you, my Master?"

"Yes, you may."

Daddy's really harsh on hisself sometimes. That means he's never happy with too much stuff that's going on, he always wants to get it all more right, and even more than that for the next time. He must have learned that from Pop, 'cause he's the same way. That's why he snaps back at Grammy J. sometimes, even though whatever it is is never really her fault. It's just that she's right there to listen to the yelling whenever it's time for him to do it.

"Bring me that cheese grater. I want it now."

Like I said before, although I never seem to understand most stuff too good, I think for sure they're going to make something for dinner that most ordinary people don't eat. I still haven't figured out if most other mommies and daddies are as much fans of Satan as mine. I don't think so, 'cause Ozzie and Harriet aren't really interested in stuff other than just being a friendly good neighbor.

It was time for Ritual Number #2, and they were all so thrilled about it. Remember, there's seven altogether, and for every single one of them except Number #7 when it takes its 7th-inning stretch, there needs to be a full moon up in the sky. A full moon is where it's totally round and not just a sliver of one. Like pie.

Daddy couldn't do his part full-way, so he sent Bobby in as the pinch hitter. Like the way Willie Mays and Willie McCovey does in their ballgames sometimes. But, Mommy, Daddy and Bobby weren't playing baseball. And every time, Daddy's the coach. There's never an umpire, 'cause whatever it is they do is always right on the mark. No errors, no fouls. No scoreboards neither. Mommy, Daddy and Bobby always hit homeruns.

The bright white moon still had a ways to go before it got to be like a hula hoop. At first, like always, I thought I got to sleep in for this one, but I was wrong. I had to be right in there with them. I'd just have to catch up on my sleep some other time. Probably when the moon starts looking like one of those crescent rolls from the Pillsbury Dough Boy again.

As soon as Mommy grabbed me to take me into the main room, I began remembering Fluffy. I wish I could see her again. I thought of her being away. Maybe if they were going to do to me what they did to Fluffy, then I'd get to go way ahead of schedule…and I wouldn't have to hang around for whatever's left. That would be such a breeze. Just getting to stay a kid.

At the very same time that Mommy, Daddy and Bobby were

gearing up for their wingding, I could hear piano music and singing coming from down the street. The windows in our house were all opened 'cause it was like earthquake weather, and it's way too hot for them to stay closed. The music made me wonder so much about stuff. The singing music was from the church where Reverend Pointer and his girls were. I think it never mattered too much to them if they had a round moon or not. They always sing for the Maker. Songs like *Swing Down Chariot* and *Amazing Grace.* And, I'm pretty sure the Maker listens full-time, no matter whatever's going on up in the sky at night.

The singing coming from the Pointer's church was getting louder and louder. It's all I could hear for a while. Then, Tillie even joined in, and she's not the best singer in the world, believe you me. It's not like listening to Doris Day when she does *Secret Love* at all. "Shut up," Daddy yelled out.

"Should I close the windows, Master?"

"No, it's a test. That's all it is."

"Like at the Academy."

"No, you moron. We must concentrate better. We've got to go under. Right now."

A trance is what Daddy was talking about. At first I never knew too good what that was, but it's like when you let your brain turn numb. Sort of like a dummy. Just not a real stupid one. Whenever they did their trances, they still stayed normal…they just talked really different, with new voices even. Daddy was the biggest faker of them all. He made hisself talk real slow and burly-like. Kind of like Clint Walker, where the big voice he's got comes directly out of his chests.

"Our Most Holy Satan. Let these serpents lead us down the path to Thee," Daddy said, while sounding sorta spooky and not nearly as friendly as Casper.

Then, something happened that I had never seen before.

Bobby walked over to near the fireplace and let five slippery brown snakes out of a cage. And, at the same time, Mommy opened Tillie's. They just let her fly around all over the room. Not into the kitchen though, maybe 'cause Mommy had left a Betty Crocker cake out on the counter and it was still cooling. It wouldn't be proper. You couldn't eat it if it had bird plop on it.

Tillie just kept flying. Flapping her wings every which way. Screaming louder than ever. Getting over-excited about the snakes that were wandering all over our floor. Then, Mommy and Bobby started doing their stuff. The same sort of things they do in the movies Daddy brings home. Then, Bobby grabbed me, and started doing the same things with my bee-hind. I just made my mind think more about Fluffy, the kitty. What's it like to go away?

Right then at that very moment, over Tillie's loud screeching, I heard the word 'heaven' from the church singers as clear as a bell. And, at the exact same time, I remembered pretty Fluffy again. I wondered if when I go away, the Maker or whoever's in charge then could change me into a kitty cat for the next time, so I could visit the insides of that church. Just to see with my own two eyes all the stuff that happens there. I don't think they'd care if a kitty came in to see. Kitties don't have any skin, they only have hair all over. And, since I don't have the right kind of skin to get inside their church right now, maybe I could get in 'cause I'll just have hair.

Plus, I think all kitties are the same. There's not some that are better than others, they're all equal. They're not like people, where you've got to be born with either brown-colored or white-colored skin in order for you to know what neighborhood you're supposed to live in. This is all I thought about while they kept touching me like they do. The ouch was normal for me to feel. I knew for sure I'd have bruises or scabs the very next day. But, for sure, I didn't want to have the clap again. It stings my peepee too bad.

The whole snake squirmish didn't work out too good neither.

Those little rascals were just as scared as Tillie and me. They just hid underneath the couch most of the time. It sounded real crunchy later on though when Bobby started feeding them the freshly-stabbed mice he pulled from his gunny sack. Even louder than when Daddy stomps on the cockroaches that live in our pantry with his police boots.

"I am the warrior," Bobby said.

"Conquer me. Oh, conquer me," Mommy yelled out.

From some of the gladiator movies I'd seen on our Motorola, I could tell what the acting speeches were all about. I didn't need the *TV Guide* for that part, even if I could read it. Babies can't read too good. Remember?

When they finished up with my part, Mommy put me back into my crib and kissed me goodbye. Then she switched on my very own sweet baby Jesus nightlight. The air outside stayed hot, and there was still singing coming from the church. Their songs always put me fast asleep. Just before going under myself, my brain couldn't help but join in and sing along right with them. Just like kitties, brains don't have skin neither. So, inside my head, I sang in my best singing voice. A song the Maker upstairs would hear for sure.

☠☠☠

Maintaining order and tidiness had always been a priority for me. Leaving my apartment in such a mess after having returned from New York nearly three weeks before was highly unusual. Why? I just didn't care. I was too tired, and demanding order was not really a priority for me anymore. Being social inside my apartment wasn't either. It was a space only for me. But, like always, so many different hoots and hollers were coming in from the opened window in my bedroom.

Indian Summer was long gone, and with it, scorching temperatures no longer existed. Fall was in full force, and some sort of precipitation would be the norm for some time to come. What amazed me, while glancing at my bedroom floor, were all the things I had collected from my trip, souvenirs that I normally never would have bothered bringing back with me in my checked-in flesh-colored Samsonites. I had playbills from the plays, lots of marathon items, including my foil blanket they give out to the runners to keep them warm once they've crossed the finish. Lots of junk lying around that would just have to wait until I'd no longer be able to tolerate the clutter.

My sleep at night continued to be nonexistent. Not because of more sounds and noises coming from the street twenty-one floors below. I didn't know why exactly. Once again, I just couldn't shut off my brain.

As soon as I felt myself begin to doze off, the phone in my bedroom began ringing. It was close to midnight. "Hello, darlin'," the Vodka Gimlet voice blurted out.

Twenty-eight year old Lowell and I had met behind a secluded bush above Baker Beach in 1987, a not so unusual first-time meeting place for a good variety of horny gay San Franciscans. He eventually wanted more than the ten to fifteen minutes I had to offer, but we stayed friends anyway, after our one-time only interlude. Oops, I nearly forgot, there *was* another time after that.

I wasn't in the mood to listen to superfluous distractions. But, I decided to be cordial with my always over-the-top friend, Lowell. "It's almost twelve o'clock."

"I know. Who're you in bed with? Half the fleet as usual?"

"No one. Please."

"Can I borrow that martini glass again?"

"When? You don't need it now, do you?"

"Yes. I'm going out…and I need to be fab-ulous."

Lowell was talking about my aquarium-sized martini glass he uses from time to time whenever he dresses up as a young Endora from *Bewitched.* He looks just like her when he gets made-up, with the red wig and all the flailing arm and hand gestures that go with it. Even turquoise mascara with sapphire eyeliner. The perfect complement. "I'm in bed now."

"I'll be right over. You should come with. Paul, you really are a yawn these days. Get with the program, tiger."

"No. Well, if you come right over. I can't wait up all night."

"Thanks, sweetness. You're the best."

"And, I want you to keep the glass. I never use it."

"Really? Endora lives on…"

"Yes, I guess she does."

Lowell was always so spunky. Or maybe erotically-energized, to be most accurate. I never know. And, he's always had much better luck at relationships than me. I wonder why. Maybe he's just more flexible.

Lowell did come over, wearing one of Endora's finest emerald green cocktail gowns. More than anything, I'd hoped none of my neighbors had seen him. My apartment building's very straight or straight-appearing. Maybe I really was the conforming prude Lowell always made me out to be. Dressing up or acting anything like Endora is something I could never do in a million years. It's just tooo much. Too much to shave.

"What...a…dump," Bette, I mean, Lowell, said after taking a quick glimpse inside my apartment.

"I know. I haven't had a chance to clean up after New York."

"Girlfriend, that was nearly a month ago. Don't worry about chipping those nails. Drag out the Mop N' Glo and get crackin'."

As Lowell stepped in to look at my bedroom I heard her, I mean, him gasp from fright. "Who've you got buried under all this?"

"I just haven't felt like doing laundry. Gimme a break."

"I guess you haven't been *entertaining* lately." Although I never did drugs or drank, Lowell labeled me a trashy Grade-*A* slut long ago, often referring to my bedroom as the 'arena.'

"No. I'm not in the mood."

"Honey, when you say you're 'not in the mood,' something's W.R.O.N.G."

"Lowell, I've just had a lot on my mind."

"Well, dearie. You look like hell. There's not enough Maybelline Erase in the world to cover up the bags you've got living under those tired eyeballs."

"I'll make you a promise. As soon as you leave, I'll go right to sleep, wake up fresh tomorrow morning, and I won't even need a touchup later on. How's that?"

"Good girl. I say, Get with…" When Lowell snapped his fingers up in the air above his head, my mind immediately went back to the Greenwich Village psychic the first time she told me I'd be finished. I had no idea why I was subtly being reminded of her so often. "or else…"

MILE NINE

Resting my head on my soft pillow felt predestined, a perfectly natural fit. What I wanted to happen next though was a notion very distant from reality. For so many months all I imagined was Justin and his well-chiseled torso lying beside me in my bed, something that had never happened before. How wonderful that would be, I felt. No sex, but being close, next to each other, occasionally holding him. As the end of the year drew closer, I knew that all my cozy thoughts and visions about Justin were indeed no more than full-fledged fantasies. The harsh realities of life on that breezy November night began to take hold of me, with little room left inside my head to entertain ideas of what might be.

☠☠☠

"It's so meaningless to me now," I told Sally, a stage-trained, early thirty-something acting buddy of mine.

"You'll get over it. I've been there too, my friend. I think about quitting all the time. Maybe you just need to get laid."

"Oh, please. That's not it at all. I keep feeling like it's never going to happen." I was referring to the falsehood all actors live by, the idea that they're, we're, going to "make it someday." What a joke. Jenna, like Tracy, was so smart to leave and move on. They're too smart for most things that don't make any sense. Trying to make a living from a career that offers no respect and no more than ten thousand a year was most definitely the thing that made the least sense of all.

On the outdoor set of a commercial for BP Oil, in the dark and still gusty early morning, only one idea occupied my head as I remained the most depressed I'd ever been.

"Shut your windows, before the doors open. Is that how they say it?" Whatever words come out of Sally's mouth always arrive unadorned and pure, much like her incredibly striking yet make up-free face. This advice didn't come out quite as polished as the 'ugly bag on the pretty face' line she delivered earlier, but I decided to take it nonetheless.

"I know what you mean," I told my streetwise friend back. But, somehow I realized that there was so much more to what I was hearing than just quitting acting. I was meant to hear these simple words. They were about my entire life.

☠☠☠

Still being the perpetual problem-solver, my mother said, "The reason you're not sleeping is because of all that yelling that comes through your windows at night. They really should do something about those homeless people that live down below. Doesn't your complex have security anymore?"

"There will always be homeless people in San Francisco. *They're* not the problem."

"Oh, I know what. Buy a fan. An air purifier. Close your

windows."

"A fan? In winter? Nope, I'll figure it out. It's still going on."

"What?"

"The mystery. My horrible life. That's all I can think of. Something happened to me, something was done to me. I know this for sure. Without a doubt."

There was silence on the other end, and I had no idea why.

"Well...why do you say that? Do you need money?"

"No...thank you. My life is just *too* strange. I'm going to end up doing extra work forever. Or be a professional traffic school teacher or even a census taker. It's not normal. Nothing about my life is like anyone else's. Everything's a huge mess. I've always been so sad."

"You're a worrier, that's all. Look on the bright side of things. That's what I do."

"Something happened to me. Something happened to make me this way."

Again, silence. "You haven't been watching *Creature Features* on Channel 2. Have you? I bet that's what's causing this. Those kinds of movies keep me up every night."

"No, I haven't. Something happened. When I was little...in Oakland."

Then, the longest silence ever. And even more after that. "It's all those bills you have. Those debts are what's on your mind."

"Oh, I doubt that. When have I not had debt?"

"Well, you see, that's the whole thing. Bills."

"I know. But, I haven't gotten that many new commercials lately. I can't pay anything off."

"You know what? I'd really like to help. It'll make me happy. Soon I'll be able to borrow on my retirement. How much would it take for you to get out of debt? Or at least pay off your really big bills?"

"Oh, no. That's OK. They're my concern, not yours."

"But, Paul, I want to. I'll be able to take out about twenty thousand. Would that help?"

"No, seriously."

"I won't take no for an answer. It'll take the pressure off. A clean slate. You'll feel like a new person."

Something about me knew that this was probably not the issue at all. But, it *would* help tremendously. I felt that it was maybe OK to agree. Why not? "Well, if you really would like to help, that would be great. I'd really appreciate it."

Something in my mother's voice sounded relieved as I agreed to her plan. "Then that's settled. It should take a few weeks to come through, but after that…smooth sailing."

My mother made it all sound so easy.

☠☠☠

On warm evenings, sometimes everything turns silent. Quiet enough to sit on my balcony without having to hear the muted chattering of the financial district executives coming from the ground level. Alone, with none of them staring at me eye-level to eye-level from our respective twenty-first floors. Or at least that's what I'd imagined they did. Maybe they really *were* working. Maybe I was being paranoid. The structure immediately next to me, the smoked-glass Alcoa building, was close enough to lip read the conversations of its occupants, if I'd ever wanted to. I needed more privacy. So, that's why I waited until the after work evening hours to enjoy my outdoor urban solitude.

I appreciated the openness of it all. No hiding behind the curtains in the dark this time. Many nights I'd be offered the occasional racy after hours peep show, something I felt guilty about watching, but I enjoyed nonetheless. Straight and sometimes gay sex amongst my late-night high-rise corporate neighbors. What a spectacle. Always worth getting up for.

It was about nine o'clock and the slight wind I felt on my cheeks was stimulating. The nearly century-old Ferry Building and its clock tower all lit up on my left, the TransAmerica Pyramid on my right, and Nob Hill beyond that in the near distance further down Washington Street. This is the same balcony, with its three-times replaced royal blue outdoor carpeting, I have been spending nights on for nearly twelve years, and I never got tired of it. The view straight down below intrigued me as well. Twenty-one floors above what used to be the exit from the once vital Embarcadero freeway, a freeway that had been sitting empty and abandoned, closed down, after the '89 World Series quake had damaged it so permanently.

Never tranquil enough to hear the detailed conversations of others that high up, the background noise of the entire city always drowned out specific words, sentences, and my favorite, dangling participles. But, on that night, I could clearly hear faint sobbing. Someone was crying quietly, and at first I couldn't figure out where it was coming from. It wasn't loud enough so many could hear. It remained hushed at times, almost secretive. Like it was meant for only my ears to hear. I tried not to listen to any of it. But, I was somehow able to make out nearly everything.

While still trying to figure out where it was coming from, I heard someone's telephone. It was a special, classically-toned, Mozart-sounding ring I remembered having heard once before. I recognized it. It was coming from Miss Francine's apartment, a woman I knew somewhat well, who happened to live one floor above me. Forever and always *Miss* Francine, every time with a 'Miss' preceding her first name, and *never* a last spoken. I don't know why. She worked in the complex's adequate health club, a nice enough sixty-ish, French-twisted woman who appeared to like me, and I liked her. Miss Francine was different, very different. Unique and quirky in every way. Whenever she gossiped about anyone, and always with lipstick smudges on her teeth, she'd only spell out their names. "The other night, I saw S.u.s.a.n. leave the building with J.a.m.e.s." And, I hate to admit it, but amongst many of my younger apartment complex-mates there, I guess myself included being in my early-thirties, it seemed OK to sometimes make fun of this eccentric woman, merely *because* of her eccentricity.

When not working at the health club handing out precisely-folded starched towels or using the electric 50's-retro flab-stimulating exercise belt during her lunch breaks, she'd play harp music at a variety of functions in and around the City. Always wearing on those formal occasions what looked to be a period, lemon yellow evening gown, Miss Francine displayed her exposed, un-toned upper arms with pride. Gossip to Miss Francine was only fact-stating, like reading about it on the front page of the *San Francisco Chronicle.* Unlike me, she never said an unkind word about anyone, but still my neighbors and I occasionally mimicked her behind her back. It was her crying voice that answered the phone, Miss Francine from the health club. Why?

"But, you don't understand. I did the best I could," I heard above the faint hushed humming coming from the far-off Bay Bridge traffic.

Who was Miss Francine speaking with? And did she realize that I was able to listen to everything?

"That was so long ago. I didn't know how to handle your father's temper." Then, more crying.

I had never known anything about Miss Francine's personal life. Perhaps no one did. She was a sociable enough person, always cordial and talkative, always asking about the wellbeing of others, but never divulging anything about herself.

"That's all I could do. I had no idea it would affect you this way."

I thought I remembered her having grown children somewhere, a son, or maybe even more than that. It must have been him she was speaking with. An attorney living in Seattle, if the gossip I'd heard from others was credible. I couldn't believe I was able to hear the conversation so unobstructedly. Then, I began feeling guilty that I'd learned any of this back-story that was coming to me via my balcony and an open window.

"Hello? Hello? Nicolas?" Then the controlled bawling began all over again. It seemed to never end. It probably did though. Eventually it was my time to leave the open air, walk back into my apartment, and stop eavesdropping. I didn't know what to think. Without being invited I had found out, I mean, accidentally discovered so much more about this different-but-interesting woman from my apartment complex health club. A woman who would maybe never have volunteered the information I'd overheard to anyone.

The next morning, while waiting for the down elevator, en route to buy low-fat milk for my morning Special K, its doors eventually opened for me to find Miss Francine already inside. "Well...hello, Paul."

While still being the actor, I put on my best mask snugly, the one that shows absolutely nothing from inside. I didn't look nervous. I probably didn't look concerned. And, most likely, I didn't appear that intelligent either. I just looked...and said, "Hi, Miss Francine. How are you?"

"Oh. Wonderful. It's the most glorious day. Isn't it?"

Small talk. The easy way out. Once in a while we'd gossip about some of the other health club members and neighbors. But, I'd always done it in a way that I hoped she'd never assume it was actual rumor mongering. Miss Francine was my inside source for so many juicy tidbits, so I took full advantage. "I heard it's supposed to be seventy today."

"Relith."

"What?" Sometimes Miss Francine mumbled whenever her upper plate happens to slip.

"Really? Oh, how lovely."

Before reaching the first floor, I felt something inside me, something that needed to come out. Anything that wasn't trivia. Also, nothing that would make Miss Francine uncomfortable. I thought carefully. Maybe I wore my fake blank mask with a little too much Krazy Glue underneath because nothing intelligent nor meaningful came to mind.

Instead, I gently touched her shoulder. At first she flinched. Never had I done that before. I also didn't remove my hand immediately. It's all I knew to do. My hand on her shoulder said all the right things, "It's OK. Everything's going to be all right. It'll all be fine."

I knew she knew that I knew. At first, rather than feeling comforted, Miss Francine looked at me kind of squeamishly. Then she acknowledged the positive gesture, and she returned to being a bit shocked as we both exited the elevator. The moment she saw me walk towards the front doors to leave our building, Miss Francine headed the opposite way to the garage. It was definitely not my intention to make her uneasy, but I did. I was sincerely sorry for that.

Running into her at our holiday-hours Safeway downstairs two minutes later was something we both should have expected, but we still offered a simultaneous fake-surprise reaction to one another. When our paths crossed one more time in front of the pitted prunes, I didn't initiate another awkward conversation, because I knew for sure it wouldn't be welcomed. That's cool with me. But my smile to her was the best I could offer. It said what my hands had forgotten, "You're not alone. You never will be." That's what I wanted to relay most. Sometimes conversations are supposed to be overheard in order for the truth to come out, sometimes people are meant to listen in. Maybe that's the way it's supposed to be. I don't believe in God, so maybe these are just lucky coincidences. I'm glad I got to say all the things I wanted to Miss Francine. Maybe the best form of communication happens without actual words being spoken. Perhaps, at certain times, they're unnecessary. I hope I'd have more to say whenever I had the opportunity to speak with Miss Francine again.

☠☠☠

"Mom, why do you have to go out on another date tonight?"

"Oh, hon. I'll be back before you know it."

"But, it's my birthday."

"Pauly, we already celebrated. You had a good time. Didn't you?"

"Yeah. It would have been better if the batteries worked."

"Tomorrow, tomorrow. I'll get the right size first thing in the morning. They'll be here before you know it."

My new red Johnny Speed racecar with remote control was so boss. The most bitchin' thing I'd ever seen. The best present to get when a boy turns nine. But, with no batteries to work it, what's the point? Duh. How could Mom have forgotten that part? Maybe she was thinking about her date too much.

"Are you going to marry this one? Is he going to be my new dad?" I asked.

"Pauly, you never know. We'll just have to keep our fingers crossed."

Although Mom and Dad got their divorce when I was six, I still don't have any memories of Dad from before then. I wonder how come. As usual, he didn't call or send a present. But, that's OK. He usually gives it to me some other time. It's just that sometimes, I wish I could have gotten to see him or gotten my stuff on that day. After all, birthdays are supposed to be special. Not just some run of a mill, crummy day.

In just a few minutes, one of the Robertson kids was going to come over to baby-sit me. It was always a mystery which one shows up. I always liked Joanie the best, mainly 'cause she lets me smoke her Lucky Strikes. Joanie's so cool. And after Mom goes away, Joanie usually lets her friends inside, and they always have tons of fun together. Sometimes she calls up her boyfriend, Wayne. He's a tough kind of surfer, but acts the best he can around me, treating me like a perfect gentleman. Every time he sees me he tells the same old joke, "What's the stinkiest show on TV?"

"Gomer's pile." I always answer back. Duh. That one's been around the block more times than the Good Humor man.

Sometimes after Joanie puts me to bed, she turns on *That Girl* in my bedroom, and then she closes the door. It even comes in living color now. I'm always supposed to stay in my room and watch it. But sometimes I sneak out. Sometimes I act real, real quiet and tiptoe into the living room to see what they're doing. Wayne likes Joanie a lot. They're really friendly together a lot of the times. Like the way married people are with each other.

Sometimes I don't understand too good what they're doing, but I like to watch anyway. I like it when they get undressed. They never know I'm there. It's top secret. In case you didn't know, what they do is a private thing, and it's not meant for small frys like me to see. I still like it. I like it when Joanie makes squealy sounds when Wayne comes at her. I like to watch it and hear it.

When it's time for them to finish, I rush back into my room. Sometimes I go back to watching *That Girl* or *Bewitched*, sometimes I don't. Sometimes I do other things, private things I don't want anyone else to see.

Right at seven forty-five on the dot the next morning, my Phillips clock radio woke me up just like it always does. The Real Don Steele on KHJ-Los Angeles was playing my favorite song, *Let's Hang On!* by The Four Seasons. I could smell the ocean in the air. It was going to be a super cool day.

While I was in our kitchen when I was supposed to be making my peanut butter and jelly sandwich for school, I did something I hadn't done in a while. In one of the top drawers next to the refrigerator, there's always stacks of pictures inside. Once in a while, when I'd get bored, I'd look through them. Just after I rinsed off my hands to get the raspberry jelly off, and when Mom was doing her make-up in the bathroom, I looked at the photographs again. There were always old pictures of Dad there, when we were still a family. Mom liked looking at those over and over again.

It was cool seeing myself as a baby. And I really liked the pictures of that bird we used to have, the one with the long, yellow pointy mouth. But, out of nowhere, I saw some new photo, one I had never seen before. It was of Dad, in some kind of costume, like from the Army or something. It was neat, but sorta weird. He was wearing two horns on the top of his head. He wasn't smiling, and he had a real stern look on his face. It was the strangest thing.

Horns, an Army costume, and that really serious face. It must have been Halloween.

MILE TEN

"*Y*es sir-ee, bub. Right there in the heart of Malaria. They buy 'em as fast as you can ship 'em."

"Malaria's not a place, you nincompoop."

"What do *you* know? You don't know nothin'," Bobby yelled back to Daddy. "One of these days…p-p-pow…right in the k-k-kisser." Bobby gets real mad and shaky once in a while when his expression turns into a volcano, and most of the times his temper comes at you by surprise, like a sneak attack. You never can see it beforehand. It's just like what Walter Cronkite's always saying, whenever he's talking about Cuba on the television set. Lots of people are cranky these days. Way more than just Bobby.

From the new playpen Mommy put in her bedroom, the room Bobby calls "the arena of the vessel virgins," I could hear and see everything. Most of the time I didn't need to. But, since I had to be right there, I really didn't have much choice. I just kind of wanted to be absent like from nursery school. But really from home. The part I did like to see is when Bobby has one of his spells and acts up. So does Tillie. She gets real hot under the collar sometimes.

Once in a while even, the bananas she flings from her mouth misses the wall completely and lands right next to me on top of my powder blue baby's blanket in my crib. Mommy keeps reminding me not to eat it though. You know, 'cause it's been in Tillie's mouth first and all. It's probably not polite.

"Would either of you care for some rhubarb pie?" Mommy asked them all. "It's fresh from the oven."

"And there you go. Changing the subject. Are you with me on this one? Or not?"

"Bobby. We're not going to ship body parts off overseas."

"We'll make millions. You got no get up and go. No courage. Just like that lion on TV."

I knew exactly which lion Bobby was talking about. The Cowardly Lion from *The Wizard of Oz*. Duh. That's the one he's talking about, even though Daddy looks nothing like him. The coloring's all wrong.

"Too chancy."

"Nobody's talking to you…*woman*."

"Of course. My mistake. Please forgive me, Master," Mommy said right before darting back into the kitchen to whip up another fresh one.

"We can hide 'em in those pies she makes. It can be some kinda export bakery business. They eat them meat pies over there in England all the time. Ain't nothin' new about it."

"Where'd you hear about this in the first place?"

"Down at headquarters. Where else?"

"They talked about this there?"

"That's *all* they talk about. Malaria, Malaria, Malaria."

"It's Mala*ysia*."

"Well, thank you very kindly, Miss Manners. Malaria. Malaysia. Same difference."

Bobby and Daddy went at it for a while longer. While I minded my P's and Q's, I just kind of laughed on my insides. Bobby's funny to look at when he gets riled up. Like Daffy Duck when black steam sprays out of his ears.

Some of the shouting was extra hard to avoid listening to, but I still tried my best. For the second time in a row, Bobby called Daddy, "Miss Manners," and Daddy's face became flaming red like a fire engine. Well, that could have easily been fixed if Bobby had gotten the names right in the first place. He should have said, "Mister Manners," because, duh, Daddy's a man, and 'cause his last name's Jacobson. A simple mistake I guess, but crazy Bobby should have learnt from the past time he got it wrong.

After things calmed down a little bit, Daddy and Bobby still argued, and nobody ended up with a fat lip after all. "You only landed that promotion because you happened to be in the right place at the right time."

"I got it 'cause I earnt it."

"And how'd you do that? When your evaluations come back they're *always* lower than mine."

"Nobody pays attention to those anyway."

"Why don't we begin, boys." Mommy said.

Although I was still crying, nobody in our house paid too much attention to me. Maybe I just wasn't being loud enough. So, I turned up the volume a notch. It worked out perfect, because Daddy and Bobby ignored whatever it was Mommy had said, so then she ran right over. For about two seconds, Bobby forgot to be mad at Daddy and what he was saying, 'cause he always likes watching me drink the milk from Mommy's chests.

"Come on. My turn, my turn."

"Oh, you."

When Bobby finished eyeballing Mommy's headlights and he talked to Daddy again, he said, "You're just jealous. You're pea green. That's what you are."

Daddy couldn't speak right away. Maybe he had a slight touch of amnesia at first. 'Cause he didn't know which words to tell, Daddy just picked up one of the huge smooth black rocks near our fireplace and heaved it right at Bobby's big fat yapper. It didn't hit him though. Instead it landed smack in the middle of Mommy's huge beauty mirror on the wall. "Oh, my Lord in heaven," she yelled out.

Before you knew it, one of the cracked pieces of glass, I mean, mirror, fell off onto Bobby's hand and blood started to spurt out of his skin. His bleeding happened so fast. Mommy almost fainted. But instead of getting Band-Aids to put on, Bobby yelled out the strangest thing, "Go get my camera, get it. Number #7 strikes again."

"Bobby, you're talking crazy. Calm down."

"Seven years bad luck if we don't do somethin' 'bout it. Hurry!"

With all the fighting over with, Bobby's cut-up and bleeding left hand had given him and my folks a chance to celebrate. They said that the blood coming from his hand was a sign, a sign directly from Mr. Satan down below in Hades, and the sign said that He needs to have a blood donation right quick. This Satan character sure sounds like an odd duck, if you're asking my opinion.

Daddy took tons of pictures close up from Bobby's new Brownie Hawkeye camera that's really black. Its extra bright flashing light made Bobby's cut-up face look real glossy from the fresh blood he'd smeared all over it like Coppertone. Their scrapbook was getting bigger and bigger by the day. Mommy showed it to me once. All the photographs in it were funny. I didn't understand them too good, but the one that's my favorite is the picture of Daddy when he's wearing his horns. He doesn't look like Bugs Bunny neither when he does it, 'cause those are ears not horns. Duh. And, when Daddy does it, he's not doing it just to be like a cartoon in the funny papers. His face turns a whole lot more gruesome, sorta like the Big Bad Wolf. It's like those two men that are the same one, Dr. Jekyll and Mr. Hive.

Daddy and Bobby changed their whole moods around when the picture-taking time was over. Bobby's hand stopped bleeding. And the face I'll always remember most was Daddy's when Bobby said he was jealous of him. Maybe there's a part of that that's the truth. My tummy's voice says so. The truth is always easy to see. But, it only comes to you when your head stops working. The more you think, the less you can tell the difference from the truth and what's made-up. "Just stop thinking," that's my motto. "Stop thinking" and "never remember." Start out fresh every time, or else you'll be carted off to the loony bin, for sure.

☠☠☠

Thanksgiving Day feeding time had arrived. The weather had definitely become winter-like in its unpredictable aggressive approach. More rain, more wind, more storms coming in from the northwest. A relentless driving force was making its presence known. And the clock never stopped ticking.

Although she appeared noticeably fatigued from the effects of her chemotherapy, my aunt, Shirley, somehow managed to gather enough energy to create another feast for us to remember for years to come. Not nouvelle, but traditional excellence offered in the most generous portions. Attempting to describe it in detail still wouldn't do it justice. Beyond being a brilliant cook, Shirley was a master storyteller, an absolute pro, the best at putting words together. She could hold your attention for what seemed to be forever, and she never failed to deliver the most amusing endings. They weren't punch lines because her stories were always spontaneous, never scripted, never rehearsed.

Glancing over at Shirley once in a while, without being too obvious, realizing that she might not be around much longer, made me think back to the years she had taken care of me. We used to watch *The Dating Game* and *The Newlywed Game* side by side on her purple paisley-patterned couch during our mid-60's afternoons together. Most of that time I was supposed to be taking naps or doing my homework, but I didn't care. It was fun, and so was Shirley.

In twenty years, her house in the East Bay town of San Ramon hadn't changed much at all. She and my uncle redecorated a few times, but to me it always felt familiar, just like home. I liked that a lot. Whenever Thanksgiving dinner came around, Shirley was the best at making everyone feel, individually, like they were special, unique, that they mattered the most. She never played favorites, but the attention she gave me was always distinctive, and it never went unappreciated. "Paul, how about more turkey?" she'd ask many times over.

With Shirley and me, it was never about turkey though. It's not like I had ever felt an uncommon bond between the both of us, but Shirley always gave the impression of being more concerned about me. Not in a worrisome way like my mother. Shirley always hoped that someday my luck would change, that I'd start doing better in life, eventually being happy. She's the only one who seemed to see me as a success, rather than a poor misfortunate.

Shirley probably weighed less than one hundred pounds by this time and was wearing a new brown wig, but she always appeared vibrant and wiry. Kind of like a young Granny Clampett from *The Beverly Hillbillies*, another 60's favorite of ours.

One time at dinner in some restaurant in Alamo, I had just come from an audition in the East Bay. Shirley had asked to look over my acting resume. It wasn't really the right time or place, but that didn't matter. Acting resumes need to be perpetually updated and revised, always adding the most minor of parts, to make any actor appear the least pitiful and pathetic as possible. So, I showed it to her, and after I'd proofread it at least a thousand times, Shirley still found one error, *Sistter Act.* At first I was upset inside that she had discovered the mistake, particularly after I had just paid to have so many printed. Then, as usual, I was grateful. More than anyone else, Shirley always wanted me to get things right. Having the best possible chance at everything.

While still at the dinner table at Shirley and Uncle Lester's house, one of the tales Shirley had been telling turned into something unexpected, not necessarily amusing. It was a story that took place during her adolescence, a memory that my mother, her sister, also shared. The main character in the story was their mother, Maria Gemma, my maternal grandmother, a woman I'd never met because she had died four years before I was born.

The emotion being felt inside came from a story about the last Thanksgiving they were all able to share together. At first, there were just sniffles. Then, Shirley had to excuse herself from the room because she began crying so hard. Just a few minutes after that, my mother did the exact same. It had all turned so sad. But, most unexpectedly after my mother's departure, *I* did the same thing. I had to immediately retreat into seclusion by running inside the bathroom, and I became emotional. It made absolutely no sense at all. Feeling sentimental about someone I'd never known. Or was I emotional because I could see that Shirley and my mother were? I had no idea.

When I returned from the bathroom, all my Uncle Lester had to say to me was, "Why did *you* go?"

But, I had no answer. Although I had never met her, I had heard many, many stories about my grandmother. And, the most coincidental piece of information was that we were born on the same day, October twenty-eighth. What a strange and bizarre fluke,

I'd always thought.

Having had this strange experience of running away crying over someone I had never known, was mystifying to me. Shirley had always been extremely intelligent, but conveying emotion never appeared to come easy to her. When we were alone in the kitchen together, after she had returned from her bedroom, all I had to ask was, "Are you OK?"

She didn't really know how to respond. But, it was my hand on her shoulder that seemed to make her feel more calm and soothed.

I went on to say, "Everything's going to be fine, Shirloots."

Again, no response. Or at least a much delayed one. "What?"

"I mean, Shirley."

"That's what Mama used to call me."

☠☠☠

"Oh, come on. You've got to be here. It wouldn't be the same without you," Jenna said stubbornly.

I wasn't in the mood, but maybe Jenna was right. Any time spent with her was well worth it, especially with so many things happening in our lives. A loving holiday distraction. She, along with those dogs, had always been there for me. This is something I'll remember forever, I thought.

It wasn't a Thanksgiving dinner or party, and it was too early for Christmas, but it was something in between. Whatever it was, Jenna felt like celebrating at her beautiful home in the Malibu hills. It had been a long while since I'd been in Los Angeles for a weekend, with my last visit having already been exorcized from my memory.

After having landed at LAX, Jenna was right on time as usual, seventeen minutes after four, greeting me just outside United baggage claim. But, it was the weirdest sight. A she walked closer to me, I didn't notice Jenna so much, but instead, what she was wearing. It was utterly eerie. From head to toe, her wardrobe matched mine identically. Hers being a more feminine version, and mine masculine, I'm assuming. Red turtleneck sweaters, khaki pants, white tennis shoes, and a low-key burgundy belt.

After exchanging the obvious, Jenna said, "Oh my God. This means something, you know."

"Yeah, it means we shouldn't be using the same personal shopper at Macy's."

"No, you fool. It means there's something one of us needs to know."

"About clothes?"

"OK. I can tell it's going to be one of those weekends."

"No, Jenna. I get it, I think. I know what you mean," I said, while detecting the out of character bags under her eyes.

"Paul, something serious."

"I know. Really meaningful. I think I've been having this same feeling for a while now. It's like we're living out the very same story."

"Pepsi and Wilma are waiting in the car. Let's talk as we walk. Do you have everything?"

"Oh, they're in the car? Now?"

"Absolutely. Ever since my neighbor told me someone had been opening up the gate in my backyard, I never let them out of my sight. They've run away three times now."

"But, who'd do that? They do it deliberately?"

"My neighbor said she saw some middle-aged blond woman coming from behind my house…on two occasions."

As I closed the passenger-side door to Jenna's car that aspired to smell as sanitary as an SPCA kennel, I yelled out, "Let's hit it."

"Paul. Are you trying to learn more about what the psychic talked about?"

"Jenna, are you kidding? Not this again. Hell, no. What a waste."

Jenna just shook her head sideways. "No, you shouldn't."

"And why do you say that this time?"

"I had a dream last night. It scared me to death."

"About me?"

"No. Stephen King, fool."

"OK, OK, OK. Go on."

"You were in your apartment. I'm not sure where I was in the dream. But, you were right there, and you weren't doing very well."

"Wait. Not doing well in what way?"

"Emotionally."

"Go on."

"I don't really know if I should."

"It's just a dream. Go ahead."

"Right. Just a dream. Well, anyway. You were about to step inside your apartment, and from the bedroom came a burglar or someone horrible. Oh, it was awful."

"Yes?"

"Oh, Paul. He had a gun…you were caught off guard. He came from nowhere and…"

MILE ELEVEN

"*M*aybe that's the dark cloud that's going to kill us both," I said while irreverently pointing upward.

"Toxic rain? With me it was a *black* cloud. And *no* silver lining," Jenna said as she meticulously blotted, not rubbed, SPF 35 onto her freckled, fair-skinned face with a Q-tip.

"You missed a spot," I said while poking the tip of her nose. "Bullshit."

"Hooey. That's all. More than that, the money."

"I'm with you on that one."

"It's insane. But, she knew all about Charlie, our breakup. She told me several other things that were the truth. To you, too."

"No. Don't stop."

"I won't, don't worry."

"With the walking, I mean. You stopped."

"Oh my God. Here you go."

Jenna and I were doing what was the most familiar to the both of us. Quality time for each. Walking down Malibu beach, having one of our most important talks while doing our best to sustain maximum heart rates. They were never typical, always deeply felt, and every time divulging something we'd never known about each other before. Perhaps something we were supposed to discover.

"OK. You can stop if you want to."

"That's a first. And...we don't have to walk all the way to the end?"

"No, I guess not. Not if you don't want to."

Looking like she was in shock, Jenna stayed on track by saying, "You know what? Paul, there's something I've got to say."

"Yes."

"My Charlie played an important role in all this. If you think about it. As did Justin for you."

"Why did you bring up his name?"

"Without him you'd never have taken a look inside, at your life."

"Are you kidding?"

"Sure. You started therapy the same time I did. You and I sought that woman out for the same reasons. Because we loved them."

"*Love.*"

"OK, love. And, again, it didn't work out."

"Thanks a lot for reminding me."

"No, there's a reason, Paul. There's got to be. For you and me both. You've got everything going for you. There's something there that made things this way."

"And, you're sure it's not a curse, dark cloud, black cloud or negative block?"

Jenna didn't respond, nor laugh. Next, her face froze stoically, just before her left foot crunched down on a sand dollar that had recently been devalued. Maybe she was thinking about that weird dream again. She tends to give so much credibility to them, much more than I could ever give mine.

We continued to walk. Jenna continued to appear lost in thought. It's easy to tell when she's doing that, she always looks straight down at her shoes or bare feet. "I love you, Paul," she told me.

Letting it sink in, how from-the-heart this conversation was becoming, I responded, "I love you too, Jenna."

"For me, please take one more look at yourself. Not about what the woman said. Imagine that her warn—, the advice, came from me…and look one more time."

☠☠☠

Dear Justin,

So many things have gone through my mind over the past two months, and I find that I really need to share these, my thoughts, with you.

I sincerely hope you're doing well in life. I'm sure you are. I hope you get everything you audition for…and much more.

To me, you were always a lot more than an acting friend. I'm sure you knew that. Every time I told you I loved you, I meant it. I said it from my heart. But, all along, I never knew exactly how you felt about me. I know it's something we've discussed before, and I know you don't want to hear it again…but, was it your intention to use me all along? From the very beginning?

I know you never saw things that way, but it became so obvious to me. You kept saying, "It's just friends helping each other out. That's what friends do." Yes, friends do help each other out. But, when that becomes the sole purpose/focus of the friendship, me helping you with your acting career, then I am left with nothing for myself. I was used. Whether you want to hear it or not, you used me.

So many times I was happy to help out. I was excited about seeing you progress. But, like I said, I gave and gave, to the point where I became completely empty. As a result, and all else considered, I'm pretty sure I'm going to quit acting for good. It makes little sense for me to continue in a career that has given me back next to no rewards for the energy and effort I have put out.

I actually believe it's time for many, many changes in my life. So many things have never worked out for me, and I guess it's time to figure out why. There's got to be a reason. Perhaps there's a cause for everything that I'm not even aware of yet. But, I've got to find out.

I'm thirty-four now, and our time spent together equals the closest to a relationship I've ever come, Justin. I really loved you. But, it's like you never recognized or appreciated how special I am. I'll never know why. To me it's obvious. Just kidding.

It was sad, being in New York, remembering that we were supposed to take that trip together. I missed you. I did all the things I told you we were going to. I ran the marathon, but it was a disaster, the worst finishing time I've ever had. I kept feeling all along that this is something I'll never do again. I still feel this way.

As I'm writing this, I'm wondering if you care anything about these words I'm putting together. Or is it just a nuisance for you to be reading? Did you ever care anything about me at all? I have the feeling that I may never know.

I realize that we're both invited to the STARS Christmas Party coming up. I'm sure you're going. We may even run into each other there. I don't know about you, but if we happen to see each other, it may be nice to talk once more. Don't you think?

There's a play I saw in New York that made me think about you. It's called Six Degrees of Separation. *The title implies that each person on earth is separated by anyone else by only six people. Interesting, isn't it? But, there was more to it than that. The main character in the play wonders about many things in life. The most important one being that separation from different kinds of people isn't healthy. Well, at least that's what I got from it.*

The central female character, an affluent 40's-50's-ish woman, also had something else going on with her. She befriended a boy in his early-twenties, someone she and her husband actually cared about, cared enough to want to help him. They believed he was the son of Sidney Poitier, that he was a friend of their kids in college. But, in actuality, everything the boy had told them was a lie. It all was untrue. The boy completely used them; this was his intention from the very start. His motive for doing this was never really clear. To get money out of them, I guess.

But the strange thing was, even after the truth came out, the woman still wanted to assist the boy, give him a hand any way she could. The husband, after feeling completely deceived, wanted nothing to do with him. But the woman recognized that the boy needed help. Because of her continued concern, even after having been completely used, the boy wanted to know her even more. Perhaps he had never met anyone before who wanted to help him become independent from needing to use people.

I hope you don't take this the wrong way. I know a lot about you, and about your life, Justin. Even after being used, I would still want to help you. I know that you're a recovering alcoholic, and I have heard that alcoholic people often times use other people. Perhaps this is none of my business. After all, I don't know much about it, but if you would like me to find help for you, please let me know. In the meantime though, I need to continue helping myself. There are many answers I need to uncover.

There's a psychic woman I talked to in New York who knew all about you, about what was going on. Isn't that freaky? She said, well, she said lots of things.

I guess I'm kind of going on and on at this point. Anyway, Justin, I've got to say that you are someone I truly loved. And, despite all that happened, I wish you the absolute best in life. Love, Paul

☠☠☠

At the same moment I put Justin's letter into the mail drop on the first floor, I found the mailman behind my see-thru box calling out my name, "Paul Jacobson? Is that you?"

I stepped behind the normally securely closed door to find the goatee-faced, out of uniform mailman impatiently waving a package directly in front of my face. "Sign here," was all he had to say to me.

Finally it had arrived, I thought. The all-important day planner I had left in Tracy's apartment. "It's from San Ramon. Right here," he said while pointing to the triple X's next to the single dotted line.

My mother. It was a large, oversized, hurrily-wrapped but tightly-sealed envelope. Not a square or rectangular box. I began opening it on the elevator ride back up to my apartment. As I rummaged through the insides, its contents made no sense. The envelope was full of photographs. Pictures of my mother. Why? I didn't get it. Was she going to die? Were these pictures sent as a way for me to remember her? I had no idea.

On my small but size-appropriate pressed-wood dining table I'd purchased from Montgomery Ward, I laid all the photos on top. I was in a few, but the majority were of my mother. In one, she was dressed up in a cowgirl costume, standing on the middle of a stage somewhere. Mixed in were a variety of greeting cards and letters I had written to her. Why did she still have these? What did they mean? And why was she returning them to me?

The pictures and old greeting cards I had given her were like a chronologically-incorrect history book of my childhood, my mother's life through the years, not mine. A quick phone call would be the solution, I thought.

"I received this package to—"

"Oh, didn't I mention that? I should have told you to be on the lookout for it."

"But, why?"

"Well, you said that that psychologist you're going to wanted to know all about your childhood. I thought these would be helpful."

"That's true, thanks. But all these pictures are of you."

"Oh, are they? I thought I'd slip in a few of me as well. Keep them if you like."

"And these letters and cards. They're all written to you."

"They're nice mementos. For you to have. Don't you think?"

"Sure. Yeah, thanks."

"Now, you're positive this one's reputable? I've always heard it's psychiatrists that have the most problems."

"No, he's a nice guy."

"Is he like you?"

"Gay? Yes. Just like me."

"I'm just dying to know, do you ever discuss me in there?"

"Sometimes, I guess. We talk about lots of stuff. Mostly about Justin. Why I'd still have feelings for someone like that."

"Oh my, Paul. He's bad news. I knew it the minute you first told me about him. I'm sure you'll find...some other boy," my mom said, setting off my internal fire alarm.

Something about me wanted to end our conversation as soon as possible. My head was beginning to hurt from talking with my mother. She never seemed to care or understand that I really did feel love for someone, and that it never worked out for me. Why ?

"Mom, did you and Dad ever fight before you two got a divorce?"

"Well, that's certainly coming out of left field."

"I'm only asking because it must have affected me in some way, when I was a kid."

"Oh, never around you. You were a child. You were too young to remember such a thing. Arguing of any kind."

"Matthew says that even if you're too young to remember, to have a memory of anything, it'll still leave an imprint on some level."

"Now, wait. I'm confused. Matthew? Is that that new boy?"

"Matthew! My therapist. And, please stop saying *boy*."

"Oh, I'm sorry. I didn't mean to upset you."

"That's OK."

"I gave you everything you ever wanted. You had the perfect childhood. I sacrificed so much for you, Paul."

"I know. And, I appreciate it, Mom."

"Being a single parent, working three jobs. Even trying to find you a new father. I did my best."

"I remember. You had many boyfriends. Lots of dates."

The silence on the other end most likely meant that I'd blurted out something offensive to my mother. I didn't mean for it to be. It was merely the truth or my interpretation of it. Either way, no direct response was offered at first. But after a minute or so, my mother said the strangest thing.

"I betcha it was one of them. Shelton. Or was it Sidney?"

"What do you mean 'one of them'?"

"Did they ever touch you?"

"No. Of course not."

"Maybe you just don't remember. That's what that Matthew's trying to get at. Yep, it's one of them, I'll bet."

"Touch me? What do you mean?"

"Well, that's all they talk about on *Oprah Winfrey* these days. Everyone remembers being molested. Then, they need to tell the whole world about it."

"I never would have thought about that."

"You probably forgot. That's why. That's what they say people do."

"No, there's no way. Something like that never happened to me. Besides, I would have remembered that. No, never."

"That could be what that gypsy, that teller, meant, when you were in New York. And, well, being touched by a grown man that way may make a person…you know, the way you are."

"What? Why are you talking about any of this? I'm gay because I was born gay."

"Paul, please don't get upset. I'm only trying to help."

MILE TWELVE

"Excuse me, boys. I've got to go put my face on."

From my room I can see everything that's going on. Mommy's pretending to be a photo fashion model for Daddy and Bobby. She's fixing up her hair real nice with curls and bows. On her face she put red on her cheeks and lips and light blue cream on top of her eyes. She laid out her best fancy-pants black dress with gold spangles and got out her link stole. But then, with her highest high heels on, that make her as tall as the Jolly Green Giant somehow Mommy must have forgot to put her clothes on, when both of them, well, Bobby mostly, started taking photographs of her that way.

"Marty, you get into this one," Bobby begged Daddy.

"No, just Barb."

"Come on. For me. Pretty please."

Daddy shook his head so it said "OK," then the strangest thing happened. Just like when they all three playact with each other, Daddy took off all his shirts, pants and even underpants for the whole world to see. Just so Bobby could take the pictures that way.

I'd never seen that before. 'Cause in all the magazines I'd ever seen, you can only be in them if you're wearing all your clothes, or your swimming trunks at rock bottom. Maybe this was the latest style, I thought.

"OK. Now, what?"

"Do your stuff, Daddy-O."

"Yes, Master. Give me something to work off of. My director told me that once while we were preparing a scene."

"Well, I'll do my best. What if I put my hand up here?" Daddy said as he grabbed Mommy's left-side boobie.

"Yes, perfectamundo."

Mommy and Daddy both pretended to be like the people in *Photoplay*, but neither one of them really looked that much like Marilyn Monroe and Rock Hudson. Well, I guess that's 'cause they're movie stars and all. That's a totally different story.

"OK. My turn, my turn," Bobby yelled out.

Next, something even zanier happened. Or else, it was just some kind of joke. Daddy pushed Mommy up to the front so she's the picture-taker. And, then Bobby started taking off his shirts and trousers so he could be in the photographs just with Daddy. They were both in their birthday suits, but they didn't even notice. Daddy looked happy that it would just be the two of them, maybe 'cause they're such best buddies and all.

Bobby even started poking his finger at Daddy, even down there. Then, Bobby said, "Gotcha!"

"Good one," Daddy said as he chuckled at Bobby's joke.

The two of them just stood there like best friends. Then, Mommy, since she was the odd man out, snapped a few photos. After that, Daddy took some more pictures of Mommy and Bobby together, and they playacted like the three of them were whole lots more than friends.

I wondered which magazine is going to have these kinds of

pictures next to its store coupons. What made it the most interesting is when Daddy let Tillie out of her cage so she could get into some. Tillie never had clothes on, because duh, she's a bird and she doesn't ever wear any.

"Not too tight, Bobby," Mommy said.

"No, the tighter the better. Now, put your hands around her neck, Bob. Squeeze as hard as you can."

☠☠☠

"You wear this nice bonnet now. It'll protect you from the sun. Stop crying, dear. Please stop crying," my mommy told me before she began to panic.

It's a perfect day for a picnic outside, so that's what Mommy decided to do with me. We're joining up with Grammy J. at Children's Fairyland over at Lake Merritt. Grammy J. likes going there a lot. She'd probably bring along her transistor radio with fresh batteries in it and her flesh-colored earplug, because she knew the Giants were playing a double-header. By the way, those same giant baseball players came all the way across the world from New York 'cause they like San Francisco a whole lot better. Grammy J. never misses one of their games, specially a double one.

"You be nice now. Don't cry too much in front of Grandma. She's elderly and it'll upset her."

That wasn't really the truth, but I played along like it was. You see, Mommy's a worrier. She probably figures that if I make too much of a stink, Grammy J.'ll start up with all her questions again. Like, duh, "Why do I cry so much?" For me, the answer's a no-brainer. 'Cause I'm a baby, that's why. Plus, like I'd said from before, most of the times, I pretend I'm invisible when they rough house, but it's impossible to ignore by the same tokens. Even though I'm just a tiny little kid, I think there's probably better ways to be. A person who looks a heck of a lot like the Maker told me that one time when He was in my room at night. He's tricky that way.

He visits me lots. But, I think 'cause of the language barrier, I still don't understand Him too good. Maybe someday He'll learn English. Most of the times He's just there. I don't really know why. But, it's like, with Him being there, I kind of feel OK. Someday when I'm older I'll understand more, if I get old enough to be a grownup, I mean. I realized I wasn't even two years old yet, but I can still count to twenty-one with all my fingers, toes and my tongue. Inside my head I always felt that that's when things will probably finish up from. 21. Twenty-one. Two-plus-one. Twenty-one. That's the magic number that's stuck in my head like a statue.

While waiting for Grammy J. to show up, Mommy kept looking into the teeny Max Factor beauty mirror that she took from inside her black patent leather handbag. She wanted to look extra special, I guess. She kept putting more glamorous make-up colors on, but then she'd wipe it off right away. Just at the same time she felt she got it just right, there was Grammy J standing in front of us. She was happy to see us for sure, but a stranger would never be able to tell, 'cause Grammy J. never smiles out loud too much. Daddy calls her "Ol' lady." Not to her face though. That's bad manners.

"Well, they lost another one. To the Dodgers. Thank heaven the second's about to start," she said in her bumpy voice while adjusting the stay-in combs attached to her blue hair.

"Oh, no. Not again," Mommy said back.

"And, how are you, little precious?"

From the mouth inside my stomach, I told Grammy J., "Same as usual. Can't complain." I decided to fib, rather than go into the whole story.

"Oh, did I tell you? Jocelyn and Ned are expecting again." Jocelyn is my aunt, my daddy's baby sister, but I never call her Aunt Jocelyn 'cause I still don't know her too good.

"No, really? Well, isn't that wonderful."

"And, Ned just became a partner in his law firm. At his young age. Can you imagine such a thing?"

"He certainly is a hard worker."

"Disciplined. There's a word for ya. Something that Marty never had," Grammy J. said while shaking her head. Not from Parkerson's disease, she just doesn't agree too much with Daddy's work.

"Marty's doing well though. You'd be proud. He may be promoted to captain someday. If all goes well."

"Oh. Motorcycles, the Police Department. Glorified hooligans are what they are. Nothing more than trouble."

"Well, he's doing his best. That's all that matters."

"And, that partner of his, Robert. The look he has in his eyes. Scares me to death whenever I see him." Then, I don't know why. But, as soon as Grammy J. said that, she looked straight over in my direction. Like she knew more than anyone ever told her. Maybe the Maker upstairs spilled the beans. Grammy J.'s from Scotland, so maybe He told her in Scottish.

"See all the ducks over there, dear? Ducks…in the water," Mommy told me.

Yeah, I get it. Ducks…in the water. If you've seen one, you've seen 'em all. I may look dumb on the outside, but there's more going on under my noggin than most people give me credits for.

As I noticed the very same dead turtle with a crack in his shell I'd seen in the pond from a week before, Grammy J. said, "Pauly looks well. I don't see one single bruise on him today."

Poor little thing. I guess someone forgot to bury him in their backyard.

"You're right. He's walking so much better now. Hardly ever falls over anymore."

☠☠☠

"Oh my goodness, Marty. What happened?" Mommy said to Daddy, rushing up to him right after he stormed inside our home.

"No, don't touch it."

Daddy's face was all bloody, like he got into one of those shootouts you see on *Gunsmoke.*

"Let me get some liniment." Mommy ran into our bathroom's medicine cabinet to get some ointment to put on top of the bloody parts pouring out of Daddy's puffed-out face.

As she dabbed the clear medicine onto his right eyelid with a cotton ball, Daddy grabbed Mommy by the back of her hair and said, "If it hurts…," then he showed Mommy's eyeballs his fist up close. Daddy's such an exaggerator sometimes.

"Never. No, never, Master."

When all the bleeding and bandaging stopped, Daddy's face looked even worse than mine does during the mornings after. It's strange to see that it happened to Daddy this time 'round.

Daddy calmed down and Mommy stopped shaking from when Daddy was teasing about giving her a knuckle sandwich. "We shot a couple niggers tonight."

"You did? Dear Lord, what on earth happened?"

"Nothing new about *that.* It's Bobby that gets me steamed. He just doesn't know how to play by the rules. You must maintain order at all times."

"He's getting himself too far ahead? In the game? Is that what's upsetting you?"

"No, nothing to do with that. The force. Down at headquarters."

"Yes, the force, where you both work."

"Bobby was picked over me as night shift supervisor."

"But, he's under you…so to speak."

"I know, I know. They don't care."

"And, you've served more time than he has. I'm sure it's only an oversight."

"It wasn't them. It was Bobby. He got it by shining boots again. Our sergeant. He likes having his boots shined by Bobby."

"Oh, I see."

Personally, I don't know what the fuss is all about. The day I get old enough to wear boots, I'd want them to be spic and spam. After all, looks count.

"Our sarge is a member of the club too. That's what they have in common."

"I had no idea he was in the Klan."

"Never say that. It's always Club, not Kl—, the other word."

"I beg your forgiveness, Master. Club."

"Well, anyway. You gotta play by the rules. That's the way it works in life. You gotta do things in their right order, to the *T*. The way they're intended. You don't get anywhere in life with chaos."

"No, sir…Master."

"It's like if you go to bake one of those pies of yours, and you start cooking it before you put all the ingredients in. No, follow the recipe, play by the rules. Bobby doesn't do that. Too much in a hurry. He skips steps."

"So, that means I shouldn't bake his favorite, strawberry rhubarb pie? For after supper tonight?"

"He's not coming over tonight. Or any other night."

"But without Bobby, doesn't that mean we'll never get to Number #7? The Sacred Seventh? He took an oath that he'd follow through 'til the end."

"I know. We'll just have to find another person. Start from

scratch, that's all."

"Oh, my. Well, you know what's best, Master."

"Yes. Of course I do. We must do all that's humanly possible to please Our Almighty Satan, so we're not damned eternally."

"Maybe Lester can join in. Shirley's always saying how enthusiastic he is about trying out new things."

☠☠☠

"I know I was sexually abused," I told my mother while ordering off the late-night menu, a double, rare cheeseburger with fries and side-salad at some East Bay Denny's that all look alike.

"Oh, I knew nothing about this. How horrible. And you still don't know who did it?"

"No. Not a clue. It's something that happened, but I don't remember any of it."

"And, that man you're going to see…has he been of any help?"

"We've never talked about any of this. This is my own theory. Well, not a theory. It's just something I know, something I feel certain about. Something happened."

"Well, I want to know who did this. Let me know the minute you find out."

"Oh, definitely. Maybe one of my babysitter's."

"You know what? Come to think of it, I bet it was one of those Robertson boys. That oldest one, the one who surfed."

"Bobby?" Mom looked completely startled as soon as I was able to identify him by name, someone from so long ago. She didn't even know how to respond after that. "Do you feel the same, Mom?"

"Oh. Oh, yes. Bobby was his name. I bet it's him, for sure."

"It's just that he was my first babysitter after we'd moved to L.A., and I was so young. Maybe that's why I don't remember very well."

"Those surfers certainly are an odd bunch. Maybe all that salt water affects their brains. Don't you think?" my mom said while trying to lighten the mood.

I just looked over and had to laugh a little inside. Even though I was searching for whoever it was, somehow I felt it wasn't some wave-curler, not to mention totally hot, tanned, well-toned and always bare-chested Bobby Robertson. That's something I would have remembered, for sure. He was definitely a more quiet type of guy, but my memories of him were that he treated me well, never mean.

"I think I need to drive back to the City soon. I feel a little drained."

My mother shook her head, looking as if she had just the right answer to everything. "I love you, hon. Don't forget to take those B complex vitamins I bought you. Have you been?"

"Yes, I have. Thanks."

"And don't ever buy generic. They tell you they're the same, but they're not." After a pause and a long hard look, my mother went on to say, "Please, please tell me if you're taking drugs. Are you?"

Hearing that remark again sparked something inside me, something sharp and painful within the pit of my stomach. It left me speechless, I couldn't say a word at first. Then, this bottled-up anger I'd never recognized before just had to come out. "Of course not."

"Oh, thank heavens."

"What an absurd question. I've never done anything like that."

"Paul, lower your voice, please."

"Drugs. Are you serious? Something happened…when I was younger. I'm sure of it."

"I believe you, Paul. I'm only concerned about your health."

"But, drugs. That's crazy. Something happened. Something was done to me and you knew all about it."

My mother wasn't shocked, but her face turned as red as mine. "Paul, how could you say that? I'd never let anyone hurt you. Never."

MILE THIRTEEN

*A*fter tossing her misguided blond hair like a green salad, my perpetually-partying running buddy Lizzie blurted out, "Paul, you look like shit."

My eyes gave back what Lizzie calls my 'Scorpio' look and my mouth told the rest, "Can we just get going?"

Meeting Lizzie in the lobby of her building immediately next door to mine on Battery Court was a long-standing ritual for both of us. Always in the lobby, and never in her apartment. I figured that's where she'd kept her stash of hot guys left over from the night hours before. Lizzie swore she was no tramp though. "They're just fun and games," she insisted after every one of her infamous nights out.

Before I had time to paste on my smile, Lizzie said, "Eek. Don't look now, but guess who's headed our way?"

As soon as I turned around to see who Lizzie was talking about, I heard, "Well, hello. Where are you both running off to today? Napa?"

"Oh. Hi, Miss Francine. How nice to see you," Lizzie said in the most fake-polite way.

"Hi, Miss Francine. How are you?" I asked with a bit more sincerity and a more believable smile.

"Well, hello, Paul. How sporty you two are today."

That's because we're both going running. Duh. "We're not off to Napa though."

"I was teasing, Paul. You don't look like you have enough energy to run *that* far. And, Elizabeth, I realize you probably couldn't."

Still not knowing Miss Francine necessarily all *that* well, I was a bit offended by her insensitive remarks.

Unphased Lizzie chimed in by saying, "Paul, you do look a little strung out, you know. Every time I see you, in fact. Doesn't he?"

"Hey!! Knock it off, you two."

"Well, you're such a handsome man. We're not used to seeing you like this."

That's all I could stand. I'm not the vainest person in the world, but they made it sound like there's something wrong with me. I just couldn't sleep, nothing more than that. Because I had so much on my mind.

After a lengthy pause, we made our quick getaway.

"Paul, well, I'll just say it. I've started hearing rumors about you." Then, Lizzie looked nowhere else but straight up into the dark clouds above, as she captured my full attention. "Wait. You want me to tell you this?"

Although I was a bit startled, of course I wanted to know as much as possible. "You're talking to me or God? Yes, Lizzie, please tell me."

"OK, someone had mentioned to me th—"

"Wait a minute. Who's *someone*?"

"Oops…Paul, I really can't say."

Lizzie and I continued running, but I actually had to stop once I heard what came her glossy lips next, "I'm sure it's not true, but they told me you might be positive. From Justin, because of…what he does."

'Are you serious?' I thought. "Lizzie. Stop. Justin?"

"You know, don't you?"

"Know what?"

"That he's a hustler."

What Lizzie had divulged to me wasn't all that unbelievable, but I immediately had to correct her. "Justin? A hooker? I wouldn't have a clue. I highly doubt it though. But, so you know, Justin and I have never had sex, not even close. Justin doesn't have AIDS." Why was I still talking?

"Oh, that's good to know. For you guys. I mean, what a relief. So, you're OK then?"

☠☠☠

Although it was way past my bedtime, Mommy, Daddy and Bobby had plenty left on my plate for me to do. They'd been planning something pretty big for a real long time, even practicing their parts over and over again so they get it just right. Now the time's finally come to do it for real.

Since I'm a small fry, I still don't know how to read books or nothing, but from their instructions, they're getting ready for something that's all about Satan and the Sea or something like that. It's Ritual Number #3, and they always get so worked up whenever they get close to finishing these things off their list one by one. Don't forget, Number #7's supposed to be the biggest deal of them all. I don't know what that one's all about, but I'm sure it's a real humdinger.

Daddy, Mommy and me all got into Daddy's cherried-out and

spit-polished royal blue Nash Rambler, with lots of Bekins boxes of junk crammed inside. They kept talking about all the thingamabobs Bobby was supposed to bring along. As usual, he had collected a bunch of animals from our neighborhood and the local dog pound. Based on what always happened before, it shouldn't be a surprise to nobody what's going to take place tonight.

In the rear end of our car, Mommy had filled up our trunk with her best and sharpest cutting knives from her kitchen silverware drawer at home. "I'd like to donate these to the cause," she had told Daddy right before we all left Oakland.

Since Mommy called it a donation, I at first figured that the knives would end up with The Good Samaritan people downtown. I was wrong though. I should have figured it out, like I said, based on before. I can be so naïve at times. Duh. Out of the mouths of babes, right?

As I minded my manners on Mommy's lap in the front seat, Mommy said, "I packed the flashlights and two canteens of butane. That should be enough. Don't you think?"

"Plenty. It'll still be twilight by the time we pull up. I only hope that numbskull won't get lost."

"He's the one who suggested Half Moon Bay. I'd imagine he'd be able to find it just fine."

"A full moon over San Gregorio beach. Perfect."

Come to think of it, the moon is extra shiny tonight. Daddy's right. Perfect is exactly what it is. In some real secret, hidden and tucked away place behind a grove of Christmas trees that hadn't been chopped down yet, Daddy parked his car on some gravely road with barely no one else around. And from inside the warmth of the car's bucket seats we just sat there for a little bit and waited for the people still left there to leave. A few minutes after none of the stragglers were in sight, Bobby out of the blue, pulled up directly beside us. It was all the dogs barking he'd brought with him that woke up the whole neighborhood, if there had been any neighborhood nearby.

"Bobby, shut them up! Right this minute!" Daddy yelled out.

"Okey doke," Bobby replied just before shooting three of the dogs he'd just let out of his car. The gun shots echoed in the waves you could hear from the Pacific Ocean directly in front of us.

"Bobby! You moron. They're supposed to be live. You idiot!"

"But…you told me to shut them up."

"No, no. Now we can't do it. I can't believe this." Daddy was furious, as mad as a hornet.

"Hey, same difference. Don't get so worked up."

"Oh, boys. Let's move along. Since we're here."

I vote the same as Mommy. Yeah, just do it and get it over with. I didn't care. I wanted it all to be done with so I can just go back home to the snuggly crib in my own bedroom.

Somewhere along the lines, Daddy agreed to just go ahead with it all. Mommy helped Daddy start up the campfire with bunches of pieces of driftwood and the gas that gets it all started. There we were, just us, and all the animals still cooped up in Bobby's car, except for the three dead dogs, all by ourselves right next to the huge, noisy ocean. It would have been a perfect place to have a weenie roast or barbecue or something. Oh, well, maybe for Mommy and Daddy, this was the next best thing.

Getting the show on the road because she's the hostess with the mostess, Mommy said, "What would you like me to offer first, Master?"

"You two, let that furry beast out. A delectable morsel for Our Almighty Satan."

That poor kitty was crying out so much right before it got stabbed in the belly. I hope it finds its way up to the pitch black sky from the beach campfire. The kitty didn't put up a fight too long in the fire pit though. The first few screeches were enough to wake the dead, but then it got real quiet again. Not a sound could be heard when Bobby next threw one of his squiggly snakes into the pit. It did tons of squirming at first, right after getting its head chopped off, and then it turned jet black like everything else in the fire. The flames grew bigger and bigger, just like when stuff gets offered into our fireplace back home.

As Daddy watched a crow still flapping its wings burn to a crisp, he yelled out, "You never loved me. I'm your son! Take that, Ol' lady!" Daddy got so excited about the whole thing. I guess he forgot all about the part when Bobby went out of order by shooting the dogs first instead of letting them die in the fire pit like they're supposed to. Then things got back to the same old, same old when Daddy began touching hisself down there again. Then Bobby started doing the same. Next it was Mommy's turn to do it too. I knew I'd be next. Right after the touching begins is when they come over my way and start doing me. That's what's proper. That's the way it all goes. Always.

Before you knew it, everything was burnt up. All the dogs, cats, birds, snakes and even a few lonely spiders that had been roaming around inside our house. Now, they're all up in the night's sky. Since all the animals were gone, all that was left was the four of us. The three of them kept doing what they're famous for. But, something happened by surprise. Right in the middle of Bobby poking me in my bottom hole, one of the pieces of wood split straight apart from the very hot fire, and a tiny spark landed right on top of me, resting on my tum-tum.

It wasn't on me too long, but I still cried while I twisted and turned. It hurt so bad. I couldn't stand it. The three of them didn't help me. Mommy really wanted to, but the other two wouldn't let her. Bobby liked watching too much. He seemed to like seeing me wiggle, cry and burn. With his hands, Bobby picked up the little spark of wood that had fallen into the sand and put it smack dab in the middle of my belly button. The sizzling was all my tummy could hear. Not to sound like a sissy, but that's when I fainted and never woke back up.

☠☠☠

"How about MacArthur Park? They've got a great smoked chicken salad," I told Jenna on our way to a mouth-watering lunch nearby.

"Sounds good. I'm starved."

"Oh, you know what? Let me grab my mail. I'll be right back," I said while leaving Jenna at the front entrance of my building. This gave Andy, the doorman, the chance to engage in some heavy duty one-on-one flirting with Jenna, something he loved doing whenever she happened to visit. Unfortunately, this made her a little uncomfortable. Actually, it made her ill at ease whenever *any* man flirted with her. "What'd you get, sweetie?" Jenna asked with a coy smile and a hand around my waist. Sometimes Jenna pretended that we're girlfriend-boyfriend whenever she becomes a little insecure around others.

No big deal. I could do worse. As I looked down to the two pieces of mail I'd just received, both from New York, I was relieved and disappointed at the same time. Tracy had, at long last, sent back my 1991 daily calendar, my irreplaceably precious diary of tasks, accomplishments, and long list of unmarried "to-doables." The other was something I didn't want to be reminded of. A cardboard-reinforced envelope from the New York City Roadrunners Club, the Marathon. "I'd forgotten about these, my finish line pictures."

"Oh, let me see."

"No, please. After lunch. So, tell me what's up in L.A.?"

"Well, my mom found an apartment in Malibu, only a few blocks away from me *and* she died her hair the same shade as mine."

"She's not a blond anymore. But, I thought they had more fun."

"A brand new life, she says. She'll be able to take care of my dogs more often, too."

"The sister you always wanted."

"Paul, come on. I want to…see those pictures."

After running into two to three of my high-octane neighbors at the bar, and the small talk that goes with that, Jenna and I were seated at a cozy table for two in MacArthur Park's ficus-filled atrium. Without further delay Jenna reached for the envelope containing the photographs that I'd intentionally placed on the floor. "Now? Before eating?"

"Of course. I want to check you out. You in your little white running outfit. Those legs."

"I wore the gray one. It's called a singlet."

"May I?"

"Yes, please. Put me out of my misery and open the damn thing."

As Jenna carefully ripped apart the top of the oversized blue and green envelope, I wanted to keep my eyes closed as she sifted through the snapshots. I just knew they'd be awful. Me looking identical to death in the worst race I had ever run.

Why didn't she just shoot me instead? I thought.

"There you are. Oh, Paul. It's cute."

"Please. You're still such an actress, you know."

"No, seriously. You look good. Not that tired at all." Then, like a line straight out of a daytime soap, Jenna said, "Who's the woman you're with?"

"What? What woman?"

After hearing my response, Jenna shoved the peculiar photo into my face to show me. It was entirely too weird. "My grandmother."

"What? In the race?"

"No, of course not. The resemblance. She died before I was born."

☠☠☠

"Mom, what was your mother like?"

"My goodness, Paul, she was wonderful. Everyone always had something positive to say about her," my mom said, nearly glowing as she reminisced about her mother.

"Like what specifically?"

"She was so generous. Always inviting the neighbors in. Making them spaghetti. Coffee. Anything."

"And, you said that Grandpa really loved her."

"Oh, definitely. No question about it. He had red roses placed on her grave every week, every week right up until he died. Daddy loved her so much."

"How strange that she and I were born on the same day."

"It is, isn't it? Well though, the truth is, you weren't supposed to be born then. You were a whole week late. Daddy kept telling me, wait, wait a little longer. And, that's exactly what happened. You were born on the same day Mama was born. That made him so happy."

A peaceful feeling came over me as soon as I heard my mother say the word, "Mama." Mom had said it in a loving way and inside, that felt so nice. "She and Shirley got along well?"

"Oh, yes. Shirley always got into more trouble than me. But, yes. She was so young when Mama passed away."

"She died when she was only forty-two, right? That's *sooo*

young."

"Oh, it was terrible. No one could believe it. Much too early," Mom said with a somber tone.

I could tell this was all beginning to make my mother rather sad, so I decided not to continue. But, then, to my surprise, Mom wanted to go on. She shocked me by saying, "She would have loved you so much. What a shame she never got to know you."

"I'm sure I would have loved her, too."

That's when Mom lost it. She began crying. Something else was going on. I had no idea what. Something made me want to ask a few more questions, waiting a few minutes though until after Mom had time to compose herself. So I did. It didn't seem to be inappropriate at all. "And, how did you feel when she died?"

No answer. I decided to stop right there.

Inside her 1978 blue and white four-door Buick, hidden behind that same Denny's, Mom and I just sat there together. In the quiet of the dimly-lit, nearly vacant parking lot, in such a peculiar location for our conversation, I let my mother relieve herself of the feelings she had probably kept inside for so long. Not my initial mission at all. I was looking for answers, but everything else is what needed to come out it seemed. When the time felt right though, I found that I was compelled to ask one more question. It wasn't necessarily relevant, but something inside myself made me ask, "What did your mom think of Dad? Did they ever get to meet each other?"

My mother glanced over at me at lightning speed. As if I was meant to ask such a thing, she at first had no answer, but then when she was ready, Mom said, "Yes. They met only once. A few months before Mama died. Right after your father and I graduated high school."

I continued. "How did that go? Did they like each other?"

Having to think first before answering, my Mom said, "Well,

I'm sure your father liked Mama. He never said. I don't know."

"And, what did your mother think of him?"

After swiveling her head to the left, then to the right, Mom answered in a murmur, "On her deathbed Mama told me, 'Whatever you do, don't ever marry that man'."

MILE FOURTEEN

"Some days I wake up and ask myself, 'Why'd I ever marry you, woman'?"

"Oh, Marty. You're such a fooler."

It was nice to see Mommy and Daddy acting lovey-dovey with each other for a change. They're a different kind of people when Bobby's not around. Not like strangers, just different. He really gets their dandruff up. One time, when she thought I couldn't hear, Auntie Shirley whispered to Mommy that Bobby's a bad seed. I think that means he's not all that hot. I don't really know what kind of seed I am.

Mommy and Daddy were getting ready for their anniversary, their fourth one altogether. September twenty-fifth is both a good and bad day for them in their history books, 'cause something else happened then, on their anniversary day. It was when my baby sister went up, up and away. She was my age now, right around two when she left. It's a crying shame I never got to meet her.

Her whole name was Maria Frances Jacobson. From what I hear tell, Bobby always pronounced it "Mary" though. Sometimes as a joke Bobby calls me "Little Mary Sunshine." But, duh, I'm not a girl. That doesn't even make sense. He's not really the brightest guy. All that electricity they put into his head didn't do him one bit of good. From what I can probably guess, he used to do the same things to Maria that he does to me. Maybe that's what makes him so confused these days. I'm a boy and that's just not the way it's supposed to go. Maybe somebody should tell him. Anyways.

The way Mommy and Daddy made up their day was just like regular people. None of the usual junk went on. During the morning, Daddy went out and bought Mommy roses, some really long red ones. Mommy was so surprised that she actually started to cry. Nobody got me nothing though, 'cause anniversaries are just for the married people, not for little squirts like me. That's OK. I just minded my own business, doing what I liked best anyway, playing with my collection of Tonka toys and Lincoln Logs. They're the funnest. A world of caution though, don't put the Lincoln Logs in your mouth for more than a few minutes or else it'll stay red all day long.

Mommy was in the kitchen, not washing dishes for a change, cooking up a great T-bone steak and mashed potatoes dinner for two. Oops, and broccoli too. P.U. For me, just Gerber's strained carrots. Daddy had the day off from his police work, killing colored people, so he just loafed around on the couch all afternoon, not touching hisself or nothing. There was such a different feeling inside our house. Even the singing coming from the Pointer's church didn't bother Daddy. He just sat there listening as they sang *In the Garden*, and just when he thought no one else was, I could even hear him humming along. We knew the words to all the songs from way before 'cause they sing the same ones over and over. I like that. You don't need to guess the way it goes.

Not once during their special anniversary day did Mommy call Daddy "Master." She just said "Marty" out loud when she needed to talk with him. So simple and easy.

The telephone would ring once in a while, with all different well-wishers calling up to say, "Happy Anniversary." I want to have this same special day with my wife whenever my anniversary day comes around. I hope I last longer than Maria did. Lord rest her soles. No big difference though. Getting to be three or four is the same as being ancient these days. With what's going on in Cuba, and that Cold War with those red people in Russia, maybe the whole world's gonna be over for us all anyways. Who knows?

The phone call that never came in though was the one from Bobby. Maybe he forgot the phone number. Well, that's Bobby for ya.

☠☠☠

In my comfy crib, under my blanket, it was oh so toasty. It was a magical feeling to have everything be so easy. Mommy and Daddy had been nice to each other all day and all night long. That meant that they were nice to me as well. It was all perfect. I loved it. Even Tillie was in a good mood. Not one single banana chunk hit the wall or ceiling. Everything all went down so smooth.

Since the beginning of time, or at least from the day I was born I mean, I had always just figured that all the stuff that happens in our house is like everyone else's, even though it's so different on television. But, I'm still not so sure.

Mommy and Daddy's anniversary was proof in the pudding that, no, it's not like that everywhere's else. Treating each other kind and nicely is the way it's probably supposed to be. Not to mention a whole lot better. But, somehow, somewhere, something went way off kilter. I wonder what made Daddy dive off the deep end like he did, and want to start up all this Satan jazz. The voice that lives behind my scarred-up belly button tells me that it was really Bobby's doing all along. He's a hard nut to crack sometimes. Don't get me wrong though, it takes two to tango. So, I guess it was Daddy and Bobby together that got things going the way they did, and maybe Mommy just came along for the ride.

Oops, speak of the devil. "Open up. I've got somethin' I need to talk about," Bobby said while nearly pounding out our porch screen.

"Oh, Marty. Please don't answer," Mommy whispered to Daddy.

"Barbie, he can see us," Daddy told Mommy as he waved to Bobby from our supper table.

In his grubbiest Navy blue dungarees, Bobby said, "I can tell you're in the middle of dessert and all. But…you got today's paper?"

"Bobby, this is our anniversary dinner."

"Oh, yeah. Congrats about that. The paper?"

"Bobby, can't this wait? I'll give it to you tomorrow. How's that, buddy?"

"No, I got to find out now. Lickity split. The groundhog. It's…Groundhog's Day."

Daddy and Mommy just looked at each other.

"Did he show his head or not? Number #4." Then he came right over and knocked on Daddy's head just like it was our front door. "Dumbbell, hello!!"

"Number Four. Yeah, what about it?" Daddy said while getting up from his dinner. As he headed into the living room he picked up the neatly-folded *Oakland Tribune* that was resting atop our davenport.

Almost tearing the pages in two as he let his fingers do the walking, Bobby squealed, "Where is it? Where is it?"

"Groundhog Day was six months ago."

"Bull crap."

"Bobby, it's always midway between the Satanic Solstice and Demonic Equinox. It *prepared* us for Number #4."

"Oh, yeah. That's right. *Think*, Bobby. *Think*. OK. I'm gonna get myself one anyway. Consider me gone," Bobby said while heading back towards the door.

"Bob, you want some rhubarb pie before you go?"

"No, Barbie. I have to run. It's gotta be fresh. Springtime fresh. Get it?" Bobby said while laughing like Soupy Sales right after the cream pie hits him square in the puss. Then, while running as fast as lightning past me, he said, "Hey there, squirt."

Bobby's such a kidder. I never saw him kill a groundhog before. This should be interesting. I've really only seen groundhogs on *Bugs Bunny*, never in person. I wonder if they really talk as lazy as they do in cartoons.

"A slice to go?"

"No, gotta run. I'll be back," Bobby shouted as he stumbled over our front steps.

That poor, old groundhog. He won't even know what hit him.

☠☠☠

"Have you ever thought of getting a pet, Paul? A dog? Or cat? Maybe even a hamster?" Jenna asked me as we walked along the dog trail next to the bay in Mill Valley.

"Jenna, you're so cute. I don't really think a pet's the answer."

"I wouldn't know what to do without my dogs. They're with me for life."

Jenna made me recall what it was like when I had a little black kitten, Misha, in my high-rise apartment, although it was for such a short time. Remembering what that was like was painful for me. The truth is I never felt like I deserved to have something, even a little thing like a kitten, love me. How absurd is that? Totally insane. My excuse for finding him another home was that I didn't like the mess he used to make, the chaos, disorder, uprooting all my potted plants. Ripping my satin comforter to shreds. Well, maybe that was part of the reason after all. Or, was it my intense fear of finding him strolling along my balcony railing hundreds of feet above the ground when he overheard my voice while I was at my next-door neighbor's apartment? Being so young and needy, he wanted so desperately to be with me, and this left me terrified. I also didn't want to be responsible for his death. Misha ended up with a nice family though. I'm glad about that.

"Jenna, do you feel that you deserve to be loved?"

"Um, yes. Well…of course. Why not?"

"You don't *ever* think about that?"

"No. Of course I deserve it. Who doesn't?"

"That psychic lady told me that I will have a relationship only after I realize I deserve to have one."

"You never told me this."

"It's that second time. When I called her. I wanted more proof…you know, to figure out if she's for real or not."

"And?"

"I had asked, 'Who's going to be my first relationship?' And, her answer, 'Someone you have seen twice before. *M.* Matthew. It will be like a marriage, but without the paper. It won't last long, but will open you up to other relationships. You will have many'."

"Seriously? She never said anything like that to me.

"That's because you've already had one, some. Wait. For me, she still repeated the same thing though. This will never happen, until you find out the cause of your unhappiness."

"Same old story. You going to do anything more with that?"

"I still think about what she'd said from time to time. Meanwhile, life goes on."

"I'm not going to give my two cents again. But, if you want to hear—"

"I know you'll tell me anyway. So, go for it."

"Paul, no offense. You're beginning to look like one of those worn-out hustlers on Polk Street. You know, someone who *used* to be cute. You're always tired, full of stress. What I'd like for you to do is either figure this out or not. But you need to get better."

"Jenna, you're right. I'm not being indecisive about whatever's next. It's just taken over my whole life. I can't help the way I look."

"You know, I don't care what you look like. It's not about that."

Again, I could tell that Jenna really cared. But was this whole thing some wild goose chase? My life has unraveled, all because of what this stranger told me in between phone calls to her local video store and more than likely Round Table Pizza after that. Or was there really more going on than I had even realized? Things in my life weren't getting any better. They were actually getting much, much worse. Parts of me wondered if I even wanted to go on anymore. "I still think about Justin a lot."

"Oh, Paul. I still think about Charlie too. For the moment, you've got to forget all about him and put yourself first. This is all about you now."

"You're scaring me. You're getting that serious look again."

"Stop it. I *am* serious. Actually, since we're on this, I had another dream about you."

"If Keanu Reeves isn't in it, I don't want to listen." Jenna just looked over at me and rolled her eyes. Her attitude told me that it's time to sincerely consider any ideas or suggestions being offered. Not to joke around so much. There isn't time for that. "OK. You've got my full attention. Go."

"Well, it had to do with this calendar scenario she talked about. This 'by the end of the year' thing."

"Yeah, the calendar."

"You're sure you want to hear this? No matter what?"

"Yes, of course. No matter what. Go, go, go."

"You were so depressed. By things not working out. You couldn't or didn't come up with the answers you were supposed to. You had reached your limit with everything."

"Yes, my limit with everything…"

"And, so. You decided you didn't want to go on." Then Jenna made a diving motion with her right hand flexed downward. "Paul, you jumped off your balcony. Onto Washington Street below..."

I looked down. Not to Washington Street, but to the ground we were standing on top of. "Oh my God," was all I could say.

"…with fireworks going off in the background, reflecting off the bay. It was a celebration of some sort."

☠☠☠

It had now become mid-December. Winter was days away, but in the San Francisco Bay Area they're barely noticeable. Not compared to the winters in the Sierra Nevada's or back east. Still, the wind blowing through the City from the Pacific carried with it something potent and powerful. Its force was intimidating.

On a morning when neither of us was in the mood, Lizzie, a little hung-over, and I, forever weary, hit the pavement with nothing but resistance. Not running into Miss Francine this time, Lizzie was the smart one, wearing her chartreuse Gortex outfit with a few deliberately-placed, nipple-high reflective sequins, shielding her size 44-E jewels from the almighty elements of nature. A winter storm watch was announced by the U.S. Weather Bureau, but that meant little to us. We had our miles to do, so out we went.

It was Sunday morning and the financial district was like a ghost town, completely empty of the normal chaos inhabiting our hometown Commuter-ville on weekdays. As we crossed a deserted

Embarcadero, we ran into someone unexpectedly that we both knew. It was a neighbor living in Lizzie's building. "Funny seeing you two on a day like this," he told us.

"Rain or shine. This is what we do weekend mornings. Do or die," Lizzie said.

"How very disciplined."

"Sometimes I wish we weren't," I said back.

"And, stranger. What are you up to? How'd things go in New York?"

"Not today. Let's talk about something else. Please."

Matthew, a handsome and friendly 40-ish dark-haired man I had had sex with a few times about a decade earlier knew not to delve further into my east coast disaster. "I just recently returned myself. Yes, it can be harrowing."

"Are you just heading out? Or coming back?" Lizzie asked.

"Actually, heading out. May I join you?"

"Well—"

"Of course," on-the-make Lizzie interrupted, knowing full well that Matthew travels both directions.

I usually preferred private time while running. Also, familiar paces are what suited me most. Order, control. But, flexible was something I needed to learn. Why not begin now, I thought. "Well, how was *your* trip, Matt?"

"Oh, you know how New York is. No matter how much you need to accomplish, there's still plenty of fun to be had."

"That's the truth. I try to see as many shows as possible whenever I'm there."

"New York rocks. Expensive though. Especially happy hour drinks."

"I only went to one. *Lost in Yonkers*. By Neil Simon," Matthew told us.

"Oh, I saw that when I was there, too. I loved it," I said in between breaths. "Not what I expected though."

"Paul, I had the same reaction. I was looking for something light and funny."

"And, it wasn't. It was serious. It makes you think."

"It certainly did. Made me think about my family. My mother."

Oh my God, that's exactly what it did for me as well, yet I never voiced this to Matthew. Even while running, I still tend to be more private than open. "My friend, Trish, saw it with Mercedes Ruehl when she was there. Loved everything about it. Recommended it above anything else," Lizzie told us.

"I went because this woman said I needed to see it. 'Many messages,' she kept telling me."

"And, were there?"

"Oh, most definitely. If you're open to that sort of thing. But, then again, I went to be entertained. I was just humoring her. Some tarot reader I visited while killing time right after a fantastic Greek lunch downtown."

You've got to be kidding me. "A psychic woman? Where was that?"

"Bleecker Street, I think. In the Village."

MILE FIFTEEN

Auntie Shirley came over and she had the greatest news to tell. At first I thought she'd say she was finally going to get that pageboy haircut she'd always wanted, but instead Auntie Shirley told Mommy and me, "I'm going to have a baby."

Daddy wasn't home, but I'm sure he'd be excited the minute he'd hear what's going on. Inside, I was jumping for joy 'cause pretty soon I was going to have someone to play with. In so many ways I wanted to tell Auntie Shirley how happy I was for her, but, mainly because that's all I knew how to do, I just stretched up my arms and reached out.

"Oh, no one's going to forget you, sweetie," she told me.

That's not really what I was going for, but still good to know. Just like Fluffy, I never want to be forgotten. I figure, nobody does. In my head, it's like the newest baby in the family would be the one that takes over for Maria, my sister that's already gone. Maybe Auntie Shirley would even have a girl, and she could name it something like Maria, the name everyone's already so used to. Marianne might do in a pinch.

"What did Lester say?"

"Oh, he's pleased as punch. He can't wait."

Out of nowhere, Mommy's turned into a pickle puss for a little bit. The words in my tummy told me the reason why, and then the proof of it came only a few minutes later, right when Daddy walked through the front door with his police motorcycle crash helmet still on.

"Hi, darling."

"Hello, Marty."

"Hmm," was all Daddy said back.

"May I tell?" Mommy asked Auntie Shirley in a hushed-up voice.

Without being cautious, Auntie Shirley said right away, "Of course, sis."

"Darling, Shirley's going to have a blessed event. A baby. Isn't that wonderful?"

Without really answering what Mommy had just said, Daddy's first made-up reaction was to say, "Just don't let any ideas like that come into your head." Daddy was fibbing.

Mommy became instantly frightened, and told him back, "Oh, of course not, Mas—, Darling."

Auntie Shirley, even though she sometimes gets scared of Daddy, was still never afraid to speak her own mind. She said, "Well, the rest of us are happy. That's all that matters."

"No, good. Good for you. I'm sure Lester's real proud of himself," was all Daddy said back to her. Next he walked into the bedroom to probably take a nap, and then slammed the door behind him. In between, he patted me on the head, but didn't call me "Short Stuff" like he usually does.

When Daddy had gotten far enough away, Mommy whispered to Auntie Shirley, "Yes, of course we're excited. Marty included. He truly is. It's difficult for him to express what he's feeling sometimes."

"Yeah," was all Auntie Shirley had to say back.

The two of them, now out of sight, stepped into the kitchen. I was left to my toys and Mr. Do-Bee from *Romper Room* on the television set. I was happy. In my playpen I already imagined that my new playmate was right in there with me, both of us having a gay old time.

☠☠☠

"Something's going on. I can tell."

"In relation to what, Paul?"

"I don't know. I keep waking up. Always in between three and four o'clock."

"That's interesting. I've known many people that say they wake up at that very same time."

"No kidding. I wonder what it means."

Matthew just shrugged his shoulders while doing his best to shrink my head. Letting me continue was the right thing to do. But, before being able to go on, I let my mind wander to my immediate surroundings. I thought about the Castro district, the area in which Matthew's office is located. "I never did ask, but do you live nearby? In the Castro?"

"Paul…what does this have to do with *you*?" Matthew asked as he crossed his arms forcefully in front of his body.

"Oh, right. You know, once I'd heard someone say that when you wakeup then, you're supposed to pay close attention to what exactly it was that woke you up in the first place. They say that's when God has something to tell you. Right around those hours of the morning."

"Oh, I'd never heard that."

"Well, in my case, waking up then is even more of a mystery.

Since I don't believe in God."

"You're not religious or spiritual at all?"

"I was raised Catholic, but that went out the door a long time ago. Anything having to do with God never seemed to interest me."

"That could change."

"Oh, I really doubt it. I'm pretty clear on that. And, you're...Jewish?"

"Why don't we get back to you. The reason why you keep waking up. If it's not God talking to you, then what is it?"

I smirked a little as I heard someone loudly yelling, "Die, Mother Fucker!" outside Matthew's Market Street office. Curiosity made both of us look towards the window. But inside myself, whatever compassion that happened to live there, made me realize that even the street people that inhabit downtown San Francisco are entitled to their own personal agendas. Maybe yelling is their self-prescribed brand of therapy.

Before the interruption, Matthew was being flippant but still asked a very intelligent and relevant question. I felt pressed to come up with some sort of answer, since, duh, that's sort of the whole point of my being there. "Like I'd said before, something's going on. With my life. More and more, it's like things are becoming more urgent. Time, you know what I mean." Just as I said that a dead leaf from Matthew's ficus tree gently fell down onto the floor silently.

"You're going back to that, um, seer, in New York. What she told you."

Matthew, and his own special way of referring to the psychic, had become so predictable. No pun intended. He always called her the, "um, fortune teller," the "um, psychic," or the "um, reader." Always, always, always. What does that say about his impression of her?

"Well, maybe. Yes, um, I am. But, again, it's not what she said. It's just what she initially made me think of. The jealous person. Meditating against me daily. How nothing good will happen in my life until I 'figure it all out'."

"But, I think you are."

"Perhaps. But, the clock's still ticking. And, I have no idea if I'm getting any closer to answers than I was in the beginning."

If Matthew was going to respond with another "hmm, interesting," I was ready to bolt out the door. After all, he's a smart guy, but, with only a few more minutes remaining in our session, I was looking for dialogue with a little more punch.

"What about that dream you started to mention? Now I don't recall if it was a nightmare or what exactly. But, you'd said that your father was wearing horns. Anything more with that?"

A good one. I had completely forgotten about that. I'd just brushed it off as being completely bizarre and hadn't really pursued it any further. "Well, I was going to—"

"Oh, Paul. I'm so sorry. I should have brought that up earlier. Our time's nearly up."

Much like Regis Philbin minus a sidekick, Matthew always knew exactly when it's time for his next guest. That's OK. His question was one I'd like to ponder more, later on in private. Maybe that wasn't a Halloween photo after all. I'll have to look into that, I thought.

☠☠☠

"So, you're sure there was never any picture taken like that? At some party? As some sort of joke?"

"Oh, no. Not to my knowledge."

"Maybe Halloween?"

"No, I don't think so." Mom appeared to be so genuine, like

she truly wanted to help. She looked as if she was as eager to get to the bottom of things as I was.

"Well, maybe I should just forget about it. It is kind of crazy anyway."

"Hon, I'm sure that's the best thing to do. This dream probably meant nothing."

"I'm not so sure though."

"To me, it's simple. That's how you see him."

"Dad?"

"Sure. I'm surprised this, um, psychiatrist you're seeing didn't tell you."

"Psychologist."

"Same difference."

"Go on."

"You're angry at your father for abandoning us. Leaving us with so many debts. Leaving me. You see him as mean, evil…a demon."

"I never thought of that. Maybe that's the way *you* see him."

"Oh, no. Marty. I never think about him much. It's you I'm most concerned with. I'm sure with that Justin out of your life things are going to be much better. To me, it sounds like he only thinks of himself."

"Well, all actors are like that. A little narcissistic."

My mother was making sense. Maybe having Justin out of my life would be the one single thing that would change it all around. Still, I felt like I needed to ask one more time, "But, you're not jealous of me? Right?"

"Oh, my, Paul. Never. I love you to bits."

"And, the acting thing. You're somehow OK you didn't end up pursuing it?"

"No. Never. It was modeling that interested me more. Posing in front of the camera, I thought, was always fun."

"You never told me much about that."

"Not much to tell. It didn't go very far. It was your father mostly. He's the one who kept pushing me."

"You know, again I've got to ask..."

"Yes, Paul," Mom responded cautiously.

"Since I don't know much about Dad, did you two ever disagree? Or, during the time you two divorced, was there something negative going on? That I witnessed?"

"Oh, you were too young. Maybe a little bickering here and there. Normal for anyone two people about divorce, I think."

"But, Dad really loved you? When you first got married?"

"Oh, yes. I guess so. Maybe."

"You don't sound so sure."

"Well, I don't think he could ever really love a woman."

☠☠☠

Wearing no tiara or diamonds this time, bauble-lacking Lowell responded to my begging and pleading by saying, "No. Definitely not that one."

"Lowell. But, Keanu Reeves."

"Oh, my God. If you say her name one more time, I'm going to scream."

"But, it's supposed to be really good. River Phoenix is in it, too."

"Who's she?"

"River Phoenix is a man."

"I know that, Miss Moviegoer. *My Own Private Idaho.* Are the B-52's in it?"

"No, I don't think so."

"Then why'd they name it that?"

"Lowell, do you want to go? Or not?"

"OK. Let me throw on my frock and let's fly."

☠☠☠

"So, you didn't get to see Miss Reeves naked, and you're not Gloria Gaynor. Will you survive?"

I heard Lowell ask me something, but I had no idea what. "Hmm?"

With an unusually and out-of-character sympathetic look on his face, Lowell asked me, "This movie made you think about him, didn't it?"

"Yeah."

"Because they have the same birthday. That's what did it."

"Oh, no. Not at all. That's just a coincidence. It was that scene at the campfire. When the River Phoenix character opens up about how he really feels."

"I knew it. But, Pauline. In the movie, in life, they're the same. Justin's straight and he's a hustler."

"Lowell, you don't know that."

"Well, we do know he's straight. And, if he's not a hustler, what is he?"

"He just feels that he needs to use people in order to get ahead, to make it."

"I don't even know what you just said. Whatever it was, is nonsense."

"No, whatever he is, I know he loves, loved, me. He said so."

"Witches honor?"

"Witches what?"

"Hello! Samantha. Endora. Ser—"

"Oh, yeah. Right. Well, he said it to me after I'd said it to him once."

"He was probably just being nice. I'm sure he only said it while trying to figure out what he can get out of you next."

☠☠☠

Hustler? Or not a hustler? Well, it was over. A done deal. I guess spending even one more second wondering about such a thing would be a complete waste of time. But, while remaining sleeplessly alone in my bed, all I could do was think. Even after having popped *French Lieutenant's Boys* into my VCR, my mind still focused on the one that got away.

"You know love. He doesn't. He knows about one-tenth what you do about it. You think you love him, but you don't. That's *not* love," that psychic woman had said to me immediately before being interrupted by the video store. How could I give so much credibility to someone who spends that much of her daily life rewinding?

Maybe all this was true though. I'd have to agree that a person, a person like Justin, would never be able to love anyone else, when all he knows is using them. Being able to genuinely feel love for a person you're only trying to manipulate is not love. It's not possible. It's something else altogether.

"None of it will happen. Nothing. He will change. He will come back into your life. Only if you discover, only if you remove this negativity. You must find out what made you so unhappy. You must do this now." These words were like a mantra to me. Playing like a record over and over inside my head. At times it became deafening. I couldn't stand it.

As the glow from the still-lit offices across from me illuminated my path, I traipsed my way into the kitchen. Finding something salty or sweet tucked away inside my refrigerator might soothe me, I thought. No cheese, no salami, not even Jell-O. Nope, I was wrong. But, there was something unexpected that caught my eye as soon as I stepped back towards my bedroom.

A flashing red light was flickering on my Caller ID box near my phone in the living room. On its screen was a number I was very familiar with, a number that routinely gave me so much pleasure upon seeing it. Justin had called me while I was at the movies. I hadn't noticed the light before. As I stepped over to my phone I pressed the button on the side of the box, clearing Justin's number from its memory. Now it read nothing. I never returned Justin's call.

MILE SIXTEEN

If it's not one thing it's the other. As per usual, whatever was supposed to go right didn't. It all had to do with Number #4, but that one was just going to have to happen some other day. Something had gone wrong again, or they weren't able to get some doohickey that needed to go with it. Whatever. Although I'm curious, I don't mind waiting to find out later. On Sunday morning television programs they tell you that patience is a virtue. I think that comes from the bible or *TV Guide*. I'm not really sure. I get the two of them mixed up sometimes. Watching television's fun, I do it all the time.

But don't get me started on all those ads they run for the Emergency Broadcast System. It really frosts me when they put those smack dab in the middle of my *Rocky & Bullwinkle* cartoons. And that sound they make that goes with it, it scares the daylights out of me.

"It's ruined. Completely."

"Oh, Marty. It just means the time's not right. That's all."

How come Mommy forgot to call Daddy, Master? "What did

you say?"

"I beg your pardon…Master." There we go. All's square.

"I need to forget that this day ever happened. All this time and effort…gone to pot."

"But, Master. It only sets us back a few weeks. A month or so tops."

"No. We'd have to start from scratch, from the very beginning, all over again. More than anything, it puts us out of order. It's not the way to do things. In their proper order *every* time."

"Oh, Mar—, Master, you're too hard on yourself sometimes. For you, it's always all or nothing. Life might be simpler if you someday find a middle ground."

☠☠☠

"It's the perfect present."

"Oh, Bobby. I don't know. I was thinking more along the lines of a nice surprise party. You know, with Pauly's birthday coming up and all."

"Nope. No, si—r—ee. Needs to be somethin' more."

"I don't know, Bobby. A movie?"

"Yeah. Just you and me. We'll make it Hollywood-style. Just for Marty. He'll love it. The perfect donation for Halloween."

"Marty doesn't do things that way though. You know how he gets. Everything has to be in order, done the right way."

"Mart needs to take a load off. Pop open a few more beers."

"Drinking's never the answer."

"I'm joshing, Barbie doll."

I vote for the movie, but no one's asking me. I couldn't wait to be a grownup so I can go to the movies myself once in a while. Watching Debbie Reynolds when she's Tammy on the movie screen is something I've never done. Maybe Mommy'll sing her song just like Debbie does. Mommy and Daddy were always proud that they could both carry a tune. Since I'm just a baby, I'm not too good at singing yet. But, I've gotten really good at lip-singing, especially when *American Bandstand's* on over at Auntie Shirley's house. Her all-time favorite's Chubby Checker, but she doesn't turn it off if they put Fats Domino on instead.

"Maybe I'll be sly, casually run it by him first. If he flips his lid, we'll go with Plan B."

"Sounds like a plan, Stan."

☠☠☠

The time I got to spend with Jenna was becoming less and less, mainly because of all her current projects at work. I couldn't wait to see her. First though, was something I dreaded, a meeting with my agent in Los Angeles. Walking into his office in Century City had always attempted to be a pleasant experience, so I was expecting more of the same at this pre-arranged reunion.

"Your name?"

"Paul Jacobson."

"And, you're with?"

"Him. You. This agency represents me."

"Oh, I had no idea. Sit down over there."

Being un-welcomed this way, in what was known around town as the 'has been' agency, was definitely not a good sign. Actually, for me, being in Los Angeles for any reason was never a good sign. I tried my best not to take the bad treatment by the new blond and bee-hived receptionist personally. This was Los Angeles, this is L.A. life. A place where respect for others is replaced with superficiality, disdain and indifference. A culture where cordiality is interchanged with impersonality. I was so used to it. But, I happened to be feeling more than vulnerable on this particular visit.

"Paul!" some other insensitive behind the opaque plastic partition yelled to me, lashing out in my direction. While I began to stand up to go inside, another assistant ushered me in by saying, "Come on now. Go right in. You're here for the Scientology casting? Gardner doesn't have much time for you, I'm afraid."

"But, he's the one who called me to meet with him."

"Sorry. That's the way this day's been going. Go."

With an already disgusted look on his face and way too much grease in his permed ponytail, Gardner never asked how I was, never even said hello. "You're too gay."

"What?"

"That's what the C.D.'s say." Insider shorthand for casting director.

"Who exactly said that?"

"Doesn't matter. Brandeee, where's my tea?" Gardner yelled out.

"Are we having lunch today?"

"Yeah, right. No time for that. One of those days. "

"Gardner, I came all the way down from San Francisco to see you."

"Now, Paul. That's the whole problem."

"That I drove down from the City?"

"That you live there. The other agents don't like it. Personally, I don't care. You've either got to be here, or New York, or…you're out."

"Out."

"Yes, out. Living in San Francisco doesn't cut it. It means you're not serious enough."

"That's how they see it? That I'm not serious? Even though I haven't missed one audition because I live there? Driving down has never been a problem, Gardner. You know that."

"Oops, no time for a dissertation. Either here or New York."

"But, you'd said that the agent I'd met in New York told you I didn't have enough stage credits."

"Right. So, that cuts out New York, doesn't it?"

"Gardner, maybe now's the time to tell you. I've been giving a lot of thought to quitting. Quitting all this."

"Paul…I hear the same thing daily from every actor that's ever stepped into this office. Tell me something I *don't* know."

Something inside me had become a combination of angry and thoroughly disgusted. I began realizing that I deserved something so much better, although I had no idea what that was. Gardner and I went at it a few more rounds, but by the end of our conversation, if you can call it that, I'd become quite clear about one thing. "Gardner, I'm glad I came here. I'd like to terminate our working agreement."

Without even one question being asked in response, Gardner instead raked the fine gravel in his miniature Zen garden sitting atop his Feng Shui-ed desk and said, "Fine. Sounds good to me. I'll have the papers faxed to you. You sign them, fax them back, and we're done."

"No. I'd like to do it now. Before I go back."

"Done," was the last word out of Gardner's mouth.

Walking through face-lift central, Century City, looking for my dignity and the forgotten locale of my parked car, was a lonely and sad experience. It was the end of everything. My so-called big-time acting career had come to a screeching halt. Not in search of a new and better agency, not considering different but somewhat related career options, I knew acting was over for me.

Spotting my car in the sprawling Century Square underground parking lot was like winning the lottery. As I walked over nearer to it though, I began to hear the sound of tires squealing on the slick, polished pavement. Some red car, speeding through the covered parking with no other pedestrians nearby, was aimed directly at me. It looked deliberate. It was like a scripted chase scene from some Hollywood movie or a routinely bad episode of *Dynasty*. This time though minus the underpaid stunt doubles. I had only one second to feel terrified. If I didn't jump out of the way, immediately, I'd be history. All I kept seeing was red, red was coming at me. Red is what would be gushing out of me if I didn't act with the same lightning speed as the Porsche convertible pointed directly at my soon-to-be ex-actor's body.

To my surprise, just like in an action adventure, I jumped onto the ground and rolled and spun my way to avert disaster. How did I know to do that? Maybe I was being a little overdramatic. Maybe not. But being bruised and cut up didn't matter compared to being auto-assassinated.

When I had seen that the car had passed, and when I had realized that no one would be firing multiple rounds of ammo in my direction, I just laid there still, with my heart thumping out of my chest. After it stopped pounding more than a million beats per minute, I thought of Jenna. Surprisingly, dinner with Jenna was all that was on my mind. Would I have a great story to tell her, I thought. If she tells me that this was one of those meant-to-be things though, I'd feel most obliged to pop her right in the mouth. Hearing anything like that was something I wasn't in the mood for.

☠☠☠

Wearing Roy Orbison sunglasses to cover up her black eye, Jenna replied on cue by telling me, "Oh, Paul. I'd never say that."

"I'm only kidding. It's just that you do mention that from time to time."

"Well, I do know for certain. This was *not* meant to be. It was completely random, and you've just got to put it out of your mind."

"Oh my God, Jenna. It was terrifying."

"Made you forget about your meeting with Gardner though. Didn't it?"

"Please, please, please don't tell me it was meant to be."

"Paul, I'm hurt. Don't you trust me? I promised you I wasn't going to say that."

"OK, OK. Where's our dinner? I'm hungry. Dodging speeding and out of control hit men really takes it out of a person."

Finally our seafood salads arrived. Protein-rich comfort food never looked so good. And it took on a whole new meaning this particular evening. Seeming to be way too in sync while munching down on our fresh-from-the-oven garlic croutons, I knew exactly what was going to come out of Jenna's mouth next. She just couldn't let the evening pass without repeating it for the record-breakingth time. Like I'd said, since I was already expecting it, it wasn't so much of a shock to actually hear the words. "Maybe this *was* a sign."

"Stop? Yield?"

"Paul…a sign. Going back to what the psychic had said."

"Oh, please. I think this softball accident of yours has gone to your brain. You mean, getting knocked off if I don't discover…the mystery of it all."

"I'd never put it like that. But, yes. How's that coming along, by the way?"

"It does enter my head, from time to time."

"It *is* nearly Christmas. December 25th. Only days left before New Year's."

"Yes, Mother."

As her eyes widened, Jenna said, "Please don't call me that."

"I'm only kidding."

"Hearing you say that gives me such a pain. Right here inside my stomach. Like a stab with a sharp knife."

"Sorry. Next time, I'll be more blunt. I'll use a spoon."

Rather than responding, Jenna just looked at me in the most matter of fact way possible. She was serious. Dead serious. "I know it's your life. But you need to look there. Your mother."

"I've already done that. We've had a thousand discussions about this by now. She swore on a stack of bibles that she's not jealous of me. She doesn't meditate against me. She says she never has."

☠☠☠

Well, I guess it was bound to happen sooner or later. There's this thing in me now called syphilis. At first they couldn't tell 'cause it's kind of tucked away, like in a junk drawer that's chocked full of extra hammers and crucifixes. But, it's down in there for sure. I wish they'd get it out. I heard them say though that it's inside there for good. You should have heard some of the stories Mommy was trying to make up about how I got it. Like, changing my diaper in a public restroom, my babysitter not washing her hands enough before she fixed my peanut butter and jelly sandwich on Wonder bread with the crusts cut off. None of them made a whole lot of sense. I guess lots of people just don't like to tell the truth these days, maybe since the truth's worth way more than a lie and needs to be locked up personally by Mr. J. Edgar Hoover.

If drinking more Hi-C or Welch's grape juice is the answer, then I say, "yes, ma'am." It's a done deal. Oops, I forgot, Bobby's got it too. As it turns out, we both got it at the same time. It's kind of like catching the flu bug. What goes around comes around.

On a morning where there really wasn't too much good news at all, Auntie Shirley came over to try and cheer us all up. "You, sit down on the sofa. Put your feet up. I'll do everything."

Auntie Shirley was being such a good helper. She washed and dried all the leftover breakfast dishes and even picked up all broken pieces from the plate Daddy had thrown down on the floor. As she grabbed onto a really sharp one, Auntie Shirley cut her pointer finger just a tad. This little cut actually made her keel over and faint, just like in the movies when they're called dizzy spells. I love Auntie Shirley to bits, don't get me wrong. But, fainting over a little drop of blood ain't nothing at all. She'd never last a minute in this household with all the commotion that goes on. I'm glad I'm man enough to handle it all.

Then, they switched positions. Auntie Shirley went over to our sofa. But, right before she took her seat, Mommy yelled at Auntie Shirley to sit on one of the cushiony chairs instead. It's because one of Daddy's top secret magazines was inside the crack right there. They're like the truth, supposed to be kept under wraps at all times. Just for spies, Nazis, or the Reds maybe.

Now, it was Auntie Shirley's turn to be nice. She told Mommy, "Barb, this'll pass. It's just not time. That's all there is to it."

"No. I'll never have another."

"They didn't say that though. Now did they?"

"Doctor Livermore didn't use those words. But, I could see it in his face."

"Count your blessings you have your little angel here." I second that.

"Oh, I certainly do. But, to have lost Maria and now this one. I know it's just going to make Marty want another one all the more."

"Barb, there's many families that have only one child."

"No, Marty doesn't think that way," Mommy answered, and then she whispered quieter, "Keep this just between us girls, but he thinks people will look at him funny."

"Funny? Funny how?"

Then, Mommy made her hand bend straight down in front of

Auntie Shirley. Not 'cause she has arthritis like Grammy J., but she was trying to say something with it. "He said they'll think he's a fairy. Not man enough to produce more children. Only having one isn't manly enough."

"Manly? I've never heard such nonsense."

"No. Like I said, don't tell anyone. But, Marty worries about his image sometimes. Wants people to see him as the burly, Superman-type."

"Well, he *is* a good wrestler, I'll at least give him that much. His secret's safe with me."

MILE SEVENTEEN

"And, you're sure it's not a symptom? Lowell, did you hear me?"

As I began to question the sincerity of his ears, he answered back coolly, "Oh, darlin'. You're fine."

"Maybe I just need more rest. That's all."

"All you need is a ho's night out." Lowell said as he tried subduing my overactive imagination. This time not dressed in a green-spangled evening gown, Lowell was in his hot pink pajamas with the bunny feet sewn in. Our Saturday evening ritual was about to begin in primetime, *The Golden Girls* promptly at eight.

"I heard the latest statistics. They're not good. And, tell me again, why haven't you ever been tested?"

Lowell didn't answer. Maybe he was as afraid as I was. "I'll find out when I'm supposed to."

"When you're supposed to find out what?"

"Oh, girl-een. Let me get you something. A Bloody Mary? Shirley Temple?"

"Lowell, you know I don't drink. A Shirley Temple?"

"I'm joking, you wench. Go fix your hair. You look like a train wreck waiting to happen. And, there's under-eye concealer in the cabinet. Pleeeze, help yourself."

The scary thing was, as soon as I caught a glimpse of myself in Lowell's bathroom, or should I say, his floor-to-ceiling reflective ego, I did look terrible. I actually considered using the available concealer. But, was it enough? "Spatula or putty knife?"

"Spatula. Don't forget to put a sheer layer of powder on top. It'll keep better that way."

As I started to apply the concealer to the canyons that lived underneath my eyes, I gazed longer into Lowell's mirror that was surrounded by beauty-tip clippings from *Ladies Home Journal.* I was in need of far more than a touchup though. What made me look this way? Instead of seeing what I needed to, I instead sought out distractions. "No, seriously, Lowell. This rash. It's not a normal one."

"Hon, if you go there one more time, I'm gonna slit my throat," Lowell said with his hands resting on his hips.

"It's just that it's been there longer than normal. Maybe it won't go away. Have you ever had something like this? It's spreading, you know." Now the size of a pinhead, and no longer flesh-tone, I feel I had every right to be concerned. Not even one sarcastic retort. Lowell must be getting tired, I thought. "Lowell, have you ever? Lowell?"

Not a sound could be heard. Maybe she, I mean, he did slit his throat. Well, it's about time. With my under-eyes now concealed as much as possible, I stepped out of Lowell's bathroom looking like a million.

"Pop. Pop, pop. Pop."

As I'd turned into the kitchen, all my eyes could see was a pistol pointed straight at them. Just like Lowell, it was fully cocked.

Standing there proudly, posing in between his favorite gold-framed photos of Madonna and disco diva du jour DeeeLite's

Miss Lady Kier, and laughing as hard as he could, Lowell took my life away from me, even if for a second or two. I was even more frightened than that attempted drive-by hit 'n run in the Century Square parking lot. Actually, even more frightened than I ever remembered having been. "Oh, Missie," Lowell started saying, still laughing hysterically at my violent fake murder. "If that don't put you out of your misery, nothin' will."

I was speechless. I was still speechless. I couldn't get out a single word after being sadistically accosted by Lowell's concealed six-shooter, the cap gun he uses whenever he dresses up as cowgirl Annie Oakley.

"What? Did I leave you brain dead? Oh, Missie. What a sight. I wish I had a picture of that face. Scared to death, while wearing a tad too much Maybelline underneath those tired, swollen eyes."

☠☠☠

Lowell and the solutions he had to offer just didn't seem to fix what needed fixing most. It would take many wellness weekends at Elizabeth Arden to cure the years of mess I had accumulated. I was becoming so lifeless, and the accusations Lowell was making about me turning into the Wicked Witch of the West were becoming valid.

Immediately between the St. Francis Hotel and Macy's, Christmas merriment was about to begin. Decorating the gigantic sugar pine tree at Union Square, under the most trying of conditions, was what I was watching. The wind made its trunk and branches sway in every possible direction, taking with it the hearty forested fragrance it had once possessed. With the thick fog coming in and the lights going up, illuminating the gray night sky was beginning to provide the perfect backdrop to the more than mysterious evening to come. Next I began my walk back towards the desolate financial district.

As I arrived home, never would I have imagined that helping Miss Francine carry her harp to the waiting pickup truck in the Golden Gateway Center parking lot basement could yield such amusement. She was readying to go to some elegant event at one of the most posh hotels atop Nob Hill. She didn't reveal which one. Somehow, that information needed to remain sequestered. All Miss Francine could tell me was that she was playing for a rather small group of her peers that meet in the exact same place, right around this same time every year. The middle Sunday that's always preceded by a full moon occurring in the same month of December. Perhaps without realizing it, I may have been enabling a cultish club of superstitious seniors.

"If it's too heavy, I can have one of the delivery men pick it up."

"No, Miss Francine. I'll be fine," I said as I tried lifting the wheels up over the sidewalk without breaking anything.

"Paul, my word. You're so strong and manly. I had no idea," Miss Francine said seriously not sarcastically without noticing my Maybelline Erase.

While feeling perfectly balanced at first, I somehow must have stepped back a little too quickly onto the brick-laden driveway leading to the underground parking. My right ankle turned sideways, I tripped, and I immediately found myself beginning to tumble backwards. The worst part about it was that the harp and its even more mammoth case were soon to follow. There was no escaping it. I had no choice.

I couldn't see Miss Francine's face, but I'm sure it appeared terror-filled. With next to no warning at all, I was attacked from both the front and rear. The fall to the pavement came first. Then, smack on my back, straight down. In less than a second later, came the harp and its metal-reinforced hearse-sized container. It was aiming directly for my chest, but because of the way my right arm had been hanging onto it, its intrusion missed the majority of my most vital vitals.

The pain I felt within the same instant was excruciating. It was as if a wall had collapsed inside me, and my body was the only place for the debris to spread. The impact took the breath right out of me. And although I was looking straight at her, I had no idea what Miss Francine was doing. My thoughts obsessed on my survival for as long as I stayed trapped. My eyes couldn't see. While still fighting to recapture my breath, and waiting for my vision to return, I began to panic. Battling for existence and experiencing hysteria-provoking situations were now in some strange way becoming standard for me.

I waited and waited. I waited more.

My hearing remained in tact. I could tell because my ears heard the words, "Paul, are you OK? Paul! Paul!" over and over again.

"I…can't see you," I yelled back only once.

"Lay still," I heard a man's voice tell me.

"Paul, Paul. Jesus, Mary and Joseph, Paul."

Immediately thereafter, I remembered nothing. I had passed out. It all became too much for me. I had no idea when I'd awaken next.

☠☠☠

The caskets were coming soon. I'm not so sure why there were two at first. Then I heard a voice come from over my left shoulder say, "Peace. Finally. It's all over."

Without turning around to see who it was, the voice inside me replied, "Yeah, finally."

"They've found theirs. Peace. It's what they've been waiting for. Isn't that wonderful?"

My head nodded yes.

"Now, it's our turn. We both deserve it. Don't you think?"

I figured out it must have been Jenna with some sort of chest congestion, maybe even bronchitis. But, when I turned around Jenna wasn't there. No one was. And, I didn't really even know exactly what she was talking about. "Jenna? Jenna?"

Nobody replied.

Being anywhere near cemeteries always used to be a little too spooky for me. Not this time though. Even after hearing voices coming from out of nowhere, I felt just like my imagination had told me, at peace as I found myself stepping closer and closer to the open graves I'd soon be standing in front of. But, there was something happening that baffled me even more. There were actually three holes in the ground, not just two. Maybe akin to an in-store promotion at Target. Buy two, get the third free, I thought. Right before my eyes.

There they were. Three holes in the ground. No one else had arrived yet. Just me. I was alone until I heard, "Don't you remember him? That was their friend. Dad's age."

Why was I hearing these things? Who's saying this? I didn't respond out loud, but from inside my head I said, "Please tell me who you are. Jenna?"

"I'm not Jenna. Today it's 'family only.' Just us two."

Since this speech-free method appeared to be working best, I continued. "Family. I'm sorry. I still don't get it. Who are you?"

"We've never got to meet. I always regretted that. I'm Maria."

"Maria?"

"From Berkeley? Maria Valles?"

"No, no, no. I know who you're talking about. I liked her a lot, by the way."

"We've never met, but you know who I am. And you seem to know my parents. You even know Maria Valles."

"*Our* parents, Paul."

Then, I remembered a story I'd heard about her. I had never seen any of the pictures that were taken of Maria, because they had been destroyed in some household fire, I was told. "You're my sister."

"Yeah, I know. I hope I didn't startle you. Like I said, I've been feeling guilty for the longest time. Leaving you all by yourself the way I did."

Then, inside my head, I couldn't figure out how this could be at all real. I continued anyway. "You died before I was born. You're *that* Maria?"

"I'm afraid so. I hope you're not disappointed."

"No. Of course not. But, why are you here? What's going on exactly? I'm a little shaken up right now." Then, while waiting for some sort of response as I imagined her resemblance to my mother and pictures I'd seen of my father, I noticed something that continued to confuse me. They were wheeling a third casket towards us and the open graves. This one didn't match the other two. It was different and unique. Darker. It completely stood out.

"Well, that's all of them. Three of them gone…at the exact same time. What are the odds, right?"

"Wait, I still don't know who that one is. But you do."

"You will when it's time, Paul. Not needing anyone. Being strong and independent. Finding things out on your own. That's what this is all about."

I could only stare in the direction of Maria's voice, the sister I had never known. Until now. What was going on? And, who was this person she was referring to?

"How did they die?"

"No one knows. It's a mystery, Paul. For you to solve as well. A lesson."

"Lesson. Like a riddle? Or some *religious* thing? That's what you're getting at, isn't it? But, Maria, I don't believe in any of that spiritual stuff, lessons. I never have."

Maria just laughed at me. Then, harder and harder. Like it was the biggest joke she had ever heard. What was so funny?

☠☠☠

"I had the strangest dream last night."

"Paul, that's perfectly natural. Considering your fall, what you've been through."

"Yikes. I keep forgetting. Ouch."

Then, it all hit me. Part of what I'd been feeling seemed so real though, not at all like some dreamt-up reaction I'd had just because I got clobbered. It all started coming back to me. Miss Francine, the harp, the fall. All of it.

"Paul, who's Maria?" Jenna asked me, as if she should know Maria as well.

"Maria? How do you know that name?"

"That's all you kept saying. Over and over. Your pal from Berkeley? The one in your theatre group you'd always told me about."

"You see, that's who I thought it was in the beginning, too."

"First things first. You sure you're up for a chat right now? Maybe you should be getting some rest."

"Well, remind me later. OK?"

"Oh, but before I take off, did you see the doctor who's taking care of you? Oh, my God."

"What…is he cute or something? A good-looking doctor? In this place? Highly unlikely."

"Oh, no. Seriously. And I think he likes me. He's kind of shy, and he told me he doesn't have any family to go home to for the holidays."

Just like in *General Hospital*, a delicate but deliberate knock came on the door as if scripted. Jenna and I both looked over at the same time. Now, with my eyes back to normal, I could see what she was talking about. As Dr. Stunningly Perfect began entering my semi-private room at St. Mary's on Stanyan, Jenna and I could only stare at each other in disbelief. In the most approving way I knew how, I told Jenna to 'go for it' with my much impressed eyeballs.

"Paul, you should be resting," the doctor told me. His eyes were as clear as holy water and his face looked like a young, tanned and shirtless Mel Gibson in *Gallipoli*, minus the Australian accent, of course. His voice, his distinctive tone, in the strangest déjà vu sort of way was somewhat known to me.

Without thinking much before speaking, I asked, "Did you ever do any acting prior to being a doctor?"

"You sound just like my mother when she was alive. She always wanted me to give that a shot. But, no. Only medicine for me."

In between face-to-face glances, I happened to look down at his name tag that stood out like a sore thumb, right there on his immaculately white-starched lab coat. Dr. Robert Schmidt. A German name.

In the most intrusive way possible, my best buddy said, "And, I'm Jenna. Jenna Holmqvist. Paul would have introduced us, but with his accident…"

"Sorry. My manners just sort of fly out the window every time I suffer a concussion," I said while trying my best to make them both laugh. Assuming as Jenna did that this modelesque-looking doctor with hair the color of a raven was straight, I did my best to get them talking about things more intimate than the weather, baseball and bodily injuries. "Jenna's in film production. In L.A."

Then Jenna gave me a scolding with her abrupt stare. "But I live here in the Bay Area as well. A condo in Tiburon." I could tell that she had, yet again, met someone she felt possessed the potential to be Mr. Right.

But, at the worst possible moment, a very cute blond girl stepped into my room. Methodically, or via divine intervention, she introduced herself to Jenna and me. She was so sweet. Her nametag read Barbie, just like Mattel's vintage toy doll. She appeared to know Dr. Schmidt very well. Quietly, she mentioned to him her plans involving someone else for the evening and asked when his shift would be over. The thing that caught my attention more than anything else though was when she asked, "Will you be joining us tonight, Bobby?" My mind couldn't stop thinking about that name long after the three of them had left my room.

MILE EIGHTEEN

"I'm gonna kill that Bobby the next time I see him. That stupid son of a bitch," Daddy screamed out as his face turned beet red like Heinz 57 sauce and his stuck-out veins stayed green.

"Marty, calm down."

These types of spats were getting to be so run of the mill lately, happening all across the map. Nothing new about it. Daddy was getting madder and madder at Bobby, while Bobby stayed being his same old self. A little hyper around the edges, but it's probably just the way he was raised. Maybe he drank too many Yoo-hoos as a youngster. That'll do it, for sure.

Whenever Daddy gets real fidgety lately, he starts doing something brand new, something he never did inside our house before. He begins cleaning his gun real good, a brand new ritual for him, from top to bottom just like the way Mommy does with her dishes in the sink, so his gun will look shiny and fresh every time. It's like he's getting it ready to be in one of those contests where you shoot the bull's eye, dead in its center.

"You didn't touch this, did you?"

"Oh, never, M…aster."

"You know what'll happen if you do," Daddy told Mommy with his mouth and his fist.

"I surely do, Master. I'd never touch it, never in a million."

Then, Daddy had a strange and wild look come out of his own eyes at the same time. After cleaning all the grimy goop out of his gun perfectly, he took it over to Mommy and started touching her with it. In her private parts even. Holy mackerel. That's gonna smart.

☠☠☠

"These are my new buddies. They've come to play," Bobby told Daddy and Mommy when he and his friends walked straight through our front door without knocking first.

"I'm Scotty."

"And I'm Manny."

I'd never seen extra people, strangers, come over before. Well, not for the kinds of stuff that Mommy, Daddy and Bobby like to do. It was movie night, and Daddy had the screen all put up in our living room. As Mommy began closing the curtains up real tight in all the front part of our house, one of the guys, the really extra short one that sounds like big-mouth Martha Raye if she was really a man, whispered to Bobby, "What's *she* doing here?"

"Hey, no problem, buddy. I'll handle her."

I don't think Mommy could tell that this guy was talking about her. But, she probably figured it out as soon as he started playing Little Richard on the hi-fi. The more normal-sized one with sharp eyebrows came over to me and made baby talk, which I happen to hate by the way. But, it's OK. He was just trying to mind his manners.

When the movie started up, it was one I hadn't seen yet, so I could barely wait to start watching. It's with real good-natured Army boys that were only wearing black colored clothes, sitting around in a circle, grabbing their peenies. And some of them were also doing things in it that just boys and girls do together before they make babies. I never knew that boys had the proper parts to do those things with other boys. But, it just goes to show, you learn something new every day. As long as you keep your eyes peeled.

"How about you, handsome?" the shorter one asked Daddy, while his fingers did a little dance on Daddy's leg.

Daddy looked kind of bashful at first. Maybe even big boys can turn into scaredy cats once in a while. The shorter guy sure acted friendly with Daddy a lot. But, instead of returning the favor, Daddy just kept doing one thing. While the shorter guy kept touching Daddy, Daddy only kept staring over at Bobby sorta nervous, like he wanted his mommy. He also looked hungry, as if he wanted to take a big, juicy bite out of a yummy fried egg sammich.

It sure was educational watching the all-boys movie. Without a doubt they make a whole lot more noise in theirs than the other kind. In the ones with womens, they're more quiet, more shy, and do whatever the man tells them. In the boy movie, they let their hairs down a little more.

As usual, it was Bobby and Mommy that were together. I wonder why they weren't the ones that got married in the first place. Funny thing, isn't it?

☠☠☠

Reaching for the phone to call that psychic woman, I knew, was the wrong thing to do. That's why my left hand only hovered. Right over the phone, a hand that didn't have enough courage to pick up the receiver. The other with no strength left to dial. What a sorry wimp, I thought. Or was I actually being brave without realizing? From my apartment living room, I stared out at downtown's Embarcadero Center Number #2 of five, a huge thirty-to-forty floor office building, directly across from me, and wondered.

Thinking about all the 9-5'ers inside them occupied my thoughts. How normal they must all be. Normal people living normal lives that take BART to Concord on the yellow line after they step out the door, buy a pair of *Phantom of the Opera* tickets whenever it comes to town, hold hands at the movies even during the previews, travel to Maui together for vacation and rub sunscreen on each other's backs, get paid what they deserve, aren't financially dependent on their mothers, make love instead of have sex, sleep next to someone without wondering which or how many diseases they've got. Experiences I longed for every time I happened to glance over. What an outsider, I thought. The majority of me realized that in my lifetime, I'd forever be living out a destiny that's lifetimes away from normal.

Even though it was never my quest or solution, I began listing in my head, numerically or course, all the things I felt obliged to have in my life before I died. Without having a clue as to when this would take place, the end of it all, I realized more than anything else that I absolutely had to have a relationship before I was finished with it all. It just wouldn't be fair otherwise. Living a full adult life, without ever having had an intimate relationship, was far more than abnormal to me, it's horrifically unjust. Maybe they were more like me than I imagined. Or was I truly the oddball outcast I always felt I was?

Every room still in unusual untidiness following my New York trip, I glanced over the top layer of the debris. Nothing about me was motivated enough to want to change any of it. Cleaning anything up just wasn't going to happen. It somehow displayed a clear representation of my life. The clutter, the chaos, the disorder. I was growing restless and I needed to get outside.

Whenever I got like this, feeling this overwhelming need for something, something enjoyable, I'd go out. Out for a walk. These strolls were exhilarating, always filled with anticipation, and I never told one living soul about them. They were necessary each and every time, the only way I knew to feel validated, worthwhile, and *not* alone. Whether it was the bookstores on Broadway or the adult movie theatres in Chinatown, I had to go. It never lasted long. Sometimes were better than others, but it was just something I *had* to do. When I was younger it was easier, trying to fool myself into imagining that one of the many anonymous guys I was about to have sex with would evolve into more. Fool.

After turning thirty and beyond, I'd abandoned that notion completely. I gave up on a lot of things completely. But, how could I change it all around? How could I stop doing what I felt was so natural? My only outlet? Maybe one of these guys would love me. But, then, I could never allow myself to love anyone I'd ever meet in one of these dirty, disgusting and disease-filled places. This pattern had been in place for years, and I had no idea how to break out of it.

Seeing the same gay videos several nights a week was like watching *The Tonight Show* on NBC at 11:30. Typical, usual, routine, and normal. This had become my regular nighttime ritual.

The guys I liked best were ones that were shorter than average, possessed a visible tan line, have brown hair, little body hair, brown eyes, darker skin, and are well-toned but not overly-muscular. Nothing out of the ordinary about this. Once Jenna had asked me, "How come you don't like taller, bigger guys? You always go for guys smaller than you." My answer, "Because I like to dominate them. I like to control, rather than be controlled." Just my own personal preference, I figured.

Tonight's guy ended up being a rookie, I could tell straight away. He was wearing a wedding band, a business suit, and acted incredibly nervous. Definitely a beginner. His eyeglasses made him look more like an intellectual, maybe even a computer nerd, but he was still real cute. I never asked his name. He never asked mine. That's the way it goes mostly. It's some unwritten rule. Small talk just ain't part of the plan.

Getting down to business was like breathing for me. But, for guys like this, it sometimes takes them a while to get started. They pretend. They pretend like touching a dick, someone else's, is a brand new experience, something they've never done before. I can't imagine something like this would actually make anyone nervous time after time. Even if you're married, and having sex with a guy is an occasional thing, it's something you'd get used to. Like riding a bike. At some point, the nervousness subsides, and you just do it.

It would be a little too unrealistic to think that there's anything unusually bountiful about me or what I have to offer, but the majority I've found, seemingly can't wait to go down on me, these "straight" guys. What's up with that? Rather than question it, I just accept. I like it. As long as it's not too confusing or uncomfortable.

This well-groomed guy in his smart-but-stylish-looking business suit was interesting and nice to look at, but he didn't manage to get the job done. I did what I could, but it's got to be 50-50. Onto the next. After patting this one on the shoulder, I whispered "thanks," and waved goodbye as I was the first to zip up and step outside the door of the video booth at one of the sleazy arcades on Kearny Street.

Never did I feel ashamed about doing what I did. I always felt that the guilt, the shame, the self-loathing would somehow materialize later, but it never did. The night was still young, and I had to feel satisfied. I had to reach my goal or meet my quota.

Whichever it was.

My next visit was to one of the sex shops on Broadway. I had assumed this place was like all the rest, full of horny juiced-up straight guys having come from nearby straight strip clubs, desperate to get blown. But, on this night, it was a little different, fewer 'first-timers.' Inside, there looked to be mostly people like me, gay men, seeking to do what we're used to, what's expected of us. To my surprise, a young, gorgeous blond guy came right up to me. Didn't say a word, because like I'd said, that goes against protocol. Not necessary.

He walked into his video cabin, looked me over aggressively, and began closing the door, but not all the way. I had to go for it. I'd be an idiot not to. He was just too cute, too eager. Touching his young smooth skin felt so good. For an instant, I felt as if I would want to know him better, longer, maybe because of his innocent appearance. But, been there, done that *many* times, I thought. He was more tender than the rest. More knowledgeable than the straight guys. Looking at this blond twenty-something, at his youth, I kept thinking about him as I asked myself, "Why are you doing this? When you could probably have anyone you want?" Maybe his answer would be the same as mine if I were asked. Who knows?

When we had finished, he and I did something that few others do. We smiled at each other when it was time to part. That normally doesn't happen, and often times confuses your one-time partner once you've clocked out.

I left with my needs fully met. While walking home down Jackson Street, passing by Clown Alley burgers I became hungry, even when I wasn't. This happened a lot. It's because of the delicious grilled bacon burger aroma coming from inside the kitchen. After washing my hands in the always-crowded washroom there, I sat down in my hard purple plastic seat to eat my double cheeseburger with fries. It was awesome. A perfectly satisfying evening that took me miles away from reality.

Gnoshing away, for me, was always like a religious ceremony. Surprisingly though, I flinched as I felt a barely-noticeable gentle tap coming from behind my left shoulder. I had no idea. Turning my head to find out who the tapper was made me smile. It was a neighbor from my apartment complex, Gilman. He's always jovial, never goes by his first name, is cool for a conservative Republican, loves tennis as much as me although I've only been able to beat him once, and always makes me feel good inside. "Hey, Paul. Midnight munchies?"

"Gilman. Yeah. I've got to keep my energy up," I said, while rubbing my stomach. "I haven't seen you in a while. How have you been?"

He answered, "Good enough," before abruptly changing the subject. "So…what's up?" Gilman asked, while looking at me with a snide grin.

"Oh, just trying to figure out what's coming up next in life, I guess. The New Year and all. What's up with you?"

"No, I meant tonight. What're you up to?"

"Um, just getting something to eat. These things are great, aren't they?" I said as remnants of rarely-cooked burger juice dribbled from my lips.

Something about the way he asked made me suspicious inside. He knew more than usual. I somehow felt this for sure. Gilman was always a perceptive guy, but many times gave the impression of being guarded like me.

Gilman nodded with confidence. He knew something. "Meet anybody interesting tonight?"

I began to get nervous. "What? No."

In my imagination, I assume, I'd always felt like what I did late-night was my own little well-kept secret. But, walking in and out of places like adult movie theatres on well-traveled thoroughfares certainly does become public knowledge to any passer by.

Gilman just continued smiling at me. Not necessarily in a disapproving way, but acknowledging that he knew something I didn't think he knew. Interesting.

Never did I feel obligated to chastise myself because of my late-night activities, it's just what I did. Pretty normal, to me. After the moment of embarrassment wore off, my goal was always to just get on with it. Looking over at Gilman, joined by his girlfriend of the evening, his midnight snack, was also something normal. Nothing new there. Sometimes I felt relieved that I never had to go through all the formalities of what 'straight' dating is all about, not having to wait 'til the end to get what I'd wanted from the beginning. It even seems a bit more honest this way. No hiding behind a fake smile whilst having to get through a multi-course meal together at some fancy restaurant, all the while hungering for something off the menu.

Never was I critical of Gilman though. We were both different, one straight, one gay, going after the exact same thing.

"Every time I see Francine, she still looks so guilty. You look OK though."

He forgot to say *Miss* first. "Seriously? I just got the wind knocked out of me, that's all. There's no need for her to feel guilty." Without needing to tell me more, Gilman's mere mention of it was enough for me to want to take action. "I'll talk to her. I'll call Miss Francine."

☠☠☠

"Miss Francine? Miss Francine, are you there?" I figured that calling close to ten in the morning was OK, not too early. It was a dreary weekend morning when I dialed her, and Miss Francine, when she finally spoke, sounded so pleasant.

Getting past the "how are you's" was the easy part. Never in a million years would I have been able to guess what would be coming next though.

"I needed to catch my breath. Oh, my."

"Miss Francine, are you OK?"

"One moment, Paul. My heavens."

"Well…Miss Francine, do you need help?"

A minute passed, then another. "I'm fine now. Something startled me. A vision."

I didn't respond right away, because I couldn't understand exactly what she was referring to, so I had to ask, "Your vision? Do you want me to come over and help you find your glasses?"

"No, thank you. *A* vision. Maybe I was daydreaming, Paul. I'll tell you. My son was killed…"

I didn't know if I should interrupt the silence, so I just waited. But, still nothing more. So, I said, "Your son? Near Seattle?"

Not sounding startled at my apparent knowledge of her son's whereabouts, she continued telling me, "In an accident similar. Machinery fell on him."

"Oh, Miss Francine. I'm so sorry."

"Similar to what I made happen…to you."

I was shocked. What made her think that? "You didn't *make* anything happen. It was an accident. I lost my footing. That's what happened."

"You remind me so much of him, my Nicolas."

"Oh…really?"

"He loves people. Like you."

"Well. That's nice to hear, Miss Francine. Thanks."

"But, he gives too much. Always giving, always there for everyone else."

"That's an admirable quality though. You must be so proud of him."

"Yes, of course. In my vision, daydream, I tried telling him to be more careful. That's why I'm telling you this now. Use caution, Paul."

I didn't really know what she was getting at, but I said, "I will. I'll be careful."

"You don't want your diversions to be your demise."

MILE NINETEEN

Ritual #5's going to be a real doozie, I could just tell. An all-out bash. Even the church down the street could probably guess something special's about to happen. They were singing real proud and extra clappy with their windows wide open for everyone to hear all day and night. Reverend Pointer sure did a good job of getting everyone wound up. The times when I watch church on TV the people inside mostly look sorta glum, like they're just waiting to go potty or something.

Mommy got herself up at the crack of dawn so she could fix her face up real glamorous like Ava Gardner while sitting the way the Queen of England does at her very own vanity table, real lady-like. Mommy even put on her big black hair for this special day. Only in private though. The drapes were shut real tight in our house, kind of the opposite from the church down the street. Before fastening the extra bubbly hair onto her head, Mommy made our house look like no one was at home. So that meant if anyone knocked on our front door like the Salvation Army, the Jehovah's Witnesses or the Avon Lady, they'd think we were absent. Something real, real special was about to happen. I could hardly wait to see what it was.

Daddy was totally excited too. He wasn't so grumpy for a change. He was being so much nicer 'cause it was going to be his really important day to remember, one he had been looking forward to for a very long time. "Elvira, did you commence mixing the venomous brew?"

Who's Elvira? And, what's a venomess brew? Oh well, I guess I'll find out sooner or later.

"Our sacred elixir. Most certainly, darling. First thing this morning."

It took me a while, but then I got it. Mommy and Daddy were playacting again. Like getting ready for a show they were going to put on. Not like the kind Mickey Rooney and Judy Garland do out of a barn though, Daddy and Mommy's version was the more grownup kind. Just like when Daddy turns on his movies from the projector, Mommy started putting out all her extra long pink rubber sticks that they use for their love time. They're bendy like Gumby.

It was all going to be so extra special. After this one's done, only two rituals are left. I wonder what comes after that. How come they'll stop at seven? Maybe seven's the magic number. It's always been my luckiest.

"Don't forget what to call me in front of Bobby tonight."

"Of course not, Mas—, I mean, Lucifer."

"I love it when you call me that. It really gets my blood boiling."

"That reminds me. Can you please ask Bobby, in the kindest way possible, to try not getting it on the carpet?" Mommy said, knowing how much neatness counts.

"The blood? That Bobby's a tough one to control sometimes. Once you get him going there's no stopping him."

"Well, dar—, I mean, Lucifer, I'm beginning to run out of excuses why our folks can't come over anymore," Mommy said. Then she whispered, "You know, the stains, the smells, the carcasses."

"We'll just say that squirt over there made them. Kids make all sorts of messes. It's natural."

"Hey, don't make *me* the heavy," I said from my insides 'cause I still can't talk out loud yet.

I could tell that this shindig was going to be a real whopper. By the time Bobby came over, I thought that things were going to get more and more upbeat and peppy, but Bobby was in more of a quiet mood. "My black shirt's still at the laundry," he moaned out slowly.

"So, you'll just have to be someone other than Elvis tonight," Mommy said.

"The King? Is that who you are when you wear that?" Daddy asked.

Bobby just looked sad. Somehow his feelings must have got hurt. Bobby's the kind of guy that always seems to do the best he can, but it's still never quite good enough. He tries extra hard at everything he does. "We'll find you something else. Marty, what've you got for Bobby?"

"Don't coddle him, Barb."

"Oh, Marty. Help find him something to wear. You must have an outfit that's just right."

"No, no, no. Then it's out of order again. Only *I* can wear my sacred beastly garb. Once he gets his grubby mitts on them, we'll have to torch 'em. Just like the rest."

Poor Bobby looked so blue. Why did Daddy have to be so mean to him? The more Bobby hung around our house, the more I got to learn about hisself. As it turned out, he didn't have no family at all. I don't really know what happened to his own mommy and daddy, but after all, every person needs to have one. You know what I mean? I guess Mommy and Daddy sort of became his extra family, 'cause his real-life one probably forgot how to find him.

Since Daddy ended up being no help whatsoever, Mommy did the next best thing. "Come, Bob. I'll find the perfect outfit for you."

The sight I saw next should have shocked me completely. But, not in my wildest dreams. Like there could ever be anything that comes along that would surprise me. After about fifteen minutes or so, Bobby stepped into our living room, where Daddy and I had been waiting. And guess what? Bobby walked out wearing some fancy-pants gown with pearls and sparkles sewn in, and if that weren't enough, new long red hair on top of his head. Like I said, I'm a tad more open-mindful than Daddy, but I laughed a little bit on my insides anyway.

"Well…what the—"

"What?"

"Now, who on earth are you supposed to be?"

"I dunno. Barbie, which one did you say I am?"

From beside her bedroom vanity table, Mommy yelled out, "Rhonda Fleming."

"Who?" I said, again just to myself.

Bobby started getting a little miffed by Daddy's put downs. Since Daddy had no other costumes to give, I think Mommy's answer was a real bright one. Daddy changed though, he began seeing Bobby differently. For the very first time, Daddy did something almost like an experiment it seemed. He touched Bobby, his new hair, and all his other parts just like the way he touches Mommy. But, Daddy was doing all this gently. With Mommy, Daddy was never gentle about nothing. Without even flinching first, Bobby let Daddy feel him this way.

"May I be of service to you now, Master?" Bobby said to

Daddy.

"Let me get the Instamatic. Wait a sec," Mommy said in a hurry.

Both Daddy and Bobby ignored Mommy and her photography idea. The look Daddy and Bobby had was like they had been wanting to do something like this for a coon's age. "Stay in there, Barb," Bobby yelled out.

Daddy started smooching with Bobby. Right there on his kisser. Why were they doing this to each other? Then I remembered those two stranger guys that came over to our house. I wonder if they had done the same thing. I'd never know, because they told my folks they didn't want me watching. "Gives me the heebie-jeebies," the pint-sized one said. Daddy, Mommy and Bobby never had a care about that. It must have been easier on everyone for me just to watch the three of them alone, I figured. My attitude has always been, the more the merrier. A whole lot more interesting than when Milton Berle dresses up like a dame, for sure.

It seems like Ritual #5 took a whole different turn than what they were planning though. Mommy finally came out of her room to play her part. But, Daddy made her read the words that Bobby was supposed to say at first. And Bobby read the words that were supposed to be Mommy's. Parts of it were the best playacting I'd ever seen, even better than when Orson Welles does it. And, it's a good thing the fire department wasn't around because there were burning flames all over the place in our house. Way more than just Tiki torches from the South Pacific, Daddy wanted our home to look like the for-real hell. You know, the place where Satan actually hangs his hat.

They made it sound like they were inviting him in. Satan, not Orson Welles. But, I think it's quite a long drive to come all the way up from hell just to go to Oakland. The night sure was a long one. It was a first-time happening for me to be poked in the bottom by Bobby dressed up the way he, I mean, she was. But, my purpose was never to question how or why. It's all just part of growing up.

The newest part scared me some. When Bobby started playing with the knives Mommy uses to chop up her chickens to make soup. At the same time Bobby was doing me rough, he pressed me lightly with the knife, kind of playing a game. Even with my private parts down there. One time he was real soft the way he did it, but he still made a teeny cut on the tip of my peenie that made me bleed a little. None of it got on the carpet though. That's the all-important thing. I didn't want to get blamed for some new mess being there. No, sir-ee.

Another thing cropped up that hadn't really happened since we were all at the beach campfire together. I went faint again, or whatever you call it, for quite a spell. There was a time when I actually fell asleep, right there, smack dab in the middle of everything. I couldn't think if it was going to make anyone mad or not, because I wouldn't have even known.

☠☠☠

There was a brand new girl I'd never seen before. She was like my mommy, a fresh new one, but she was so young. Maybe only a few years older than me. I could tell she was older 'cause she didn't have diapers on like me. "My name's Maria," she said gently.

Under wraps, I asked, "Yeah? But, who are you?"

"Your sister. I take care of you when you're sleeping. Actually, all the time. Maybe you never noticed."

"You understand me. When I say words inside, you get what they mean. That's brand new. Mommy, Daddy, Bobby and the rest of them never know what I'm talking about."

"They're too young."

"No, they—"

"Pauly, I understand perfectly. They're younger than you. They don't know any better."

"Don't you know how to tell time yet? They're *lots* older than me. Doy."

"You're a part of their—, you're their teacher."

"What? I'm not so sure I know what you're saying now. It's OK though, you sorta make me feel good just the same. So, that's OK."

"You do know that none of this is normal, don't you?"

"Really? I maybe figured that. Mainly 'cause I never seen Ward or June re-crucify Jesus on *Leave It to Beaver*."

"This is all they know. Someday you'll be able to—"

"Ward and June? Or Mommy and Daddy? Oh, never mind. So, it really isn't all it's cracked up to be. Is it?"

"Like I said, it's all they know."

"Am I ever gonna get to be a grownup?"

"Good question. It all depends on how much you want to be one."

"Right now, I want to be a grownup most of all, so I don't have to be a kid anymore. But, I still want Mommy and Daddy to visit me. I wouldn't know what to do if they couldn't be there to love me."

"Pauly, sweetie. I'm sorry to be the one to tell you, this isn't love. You're going to need to learn that someday."

"You sure? I should have known. That's OK. I'm pretty sure babies like me aren't the best play-actors to be doing the grownup stuff they like doing."

"You won't remember this though. None of it."

"For real? That's a relief. I'd kind of like to keep it to myself. You know, hush-hush. It's sort of personal. You catch my drift?"

"Oh, honey. You're supposed to experience this though, every bit of it."

"What's spearience? *Hello!*"

☠☠☠

Sometimes I never knew how to react. Well, not completely honestly, I mean.

While over at my friend and actress-turned-mommy Alice's house, I couldn't help feel the joy coming from her face as she began showing off her new baby boy, Daniel, to me. "He likes you, Paul."

"The feeling's mutual. He's so cute."

"No, really. He usually acts so differently around men, but with you he's so loving."

"Yes, what's your secret?" Alice's hunky but nerdy husband, Sam the cameraman, asked me.

"You got me. It's so easy though. Daniel's so agreeable. He hasn't cried once."

"No reason to. He's got it made…made in the shade."

I couldn't stop thinking about *Happy Days* after Sam had said that. What followed out of his mouth next was about a million and one 50's expressions you'd only be able to find on old *Dobie Gillis* reruns.

"Paul, are you OK? Watch Daniel's head. Hold it up."

"Oh my God. Alice, I'm sorry." For a split-second my mind must have wandered. I had nearly forgotten that I was holding a tiny baby in my arms. After realizing what might have just happened by accident, I caught my breath and Daniel was fine. Still never whimpering, never crying.

"Hey, don't worry. I've dropped him on his head dozens of times," Sam said jokingly. "Yeah, what's a conk or two on the ol' noggin'," he added.

What's up with the antique 50's lingo? I wondered. Holding David made me think so much about what I might have been like as an infant. I had no idea at what age people, babies, begin to have a memory. I didn't have any. That's normal. I think my earliest memories were of Kennedy being shot. Everyone my age can somehow recall what they were doing exactly when that took place. I don't remember Marilyn Monroe being found dead though.

I did, however, always seem to remember the most bizarre thing growing up. I knew that I began gaining weight at around five or so, maybe even younger. I'm not really certain. But, never having understood anything about human anatomy, as a kid I thought it'd just be simple and easy enough to cut off the fat around my stomach with a sharp knife. All by myself. As I'd spend time at my babysitter's house on Partridge Avenue in Oakland, I recalled asking her about that. She must have thought I was completely nuts. Then, she'd always go back to *Queen for a Day*, as we'd both try to figure out who was going to be chosen as the afternoon's winner. I guessed more correctly than Mrs. Pusey most of the time.

Looking into Daniel's baby blues, holding him, squeezing his chubby little thighs was like taking a glimpse into a time I was so curious about. My past. Again, it made me think of my mother. But, before I could contemplate more, Alice asked, "What are you doing for the holidays, Paul?" while she placed a paperback into the bookcase as delicately and as she embraces David.

"What? The holidays?"

"Yeah, you going back to your family?"

"Hon, Paul's from here. The East Bay. San Ramon? Your mother lives there, doesn't she?"

"Yes…she does. In the East Bay. May I put Daniel down? He's getting to be a bit heavy for me now."

"Paul, you don't look well. Are you OK?"

My brain couldn't come up with a knowledgeable response. Instead, I excused myself from Alice and Sam's living room, rushed into their bathroom, and began throwing up without warning. Nonstop for the next five to ten minutes. A surprise attack. I never saw it coming.

MILE TWENTY

"You can be honest with me, hon. Always. You're sure you're not doing drugs?" Giving back my most angry and snide look was all I could do. I was most upset because I still wasn't being taken seriously. "They're the work of the devil, Paul."

Not getting through, again, was starting to get on my nerves. "No, I have *never* done drugs."

"Maybe you should try sleeping on your spine. That might do the trick."

Again, all I could do was stare back at the absurdity of the superficial solutions, these improbable distractions, my mother was offering. Having let all this time pass was now making me furious. Not coming up with the answers was making me tenser, more fatigued, and took a major toll on my being. If this was a test of patience, I was failing miserably. The clock kept ticking and I couldn't stop it.

"Sleeping's not the problem. If I don't come up with answers…I don't know what to think."

"Paul, stop talking like that. That woman's a con artist."

"I wasn't even thinking about her. Even if she and I'd never met, I'd inevitably need to know why my life is like this, why all my effort is so worthless and gets me nowhere."

"I think you're doing much better than you think. It's just a stroke of bad luck. That's what it is. The tide will turn."

"I'm beginning to believe that tides don't turn. If our lives need to change, it all has to do with our desire, our determination to change them."

"It's that therapist person of yours, isn't it?"

Soon after hearing that, our conversation for the evening ended with intent. I changed the tide. The realization that I had gotten all I was going to get out of my mother came rather late. The rest was up to me. I knew this for sure. More and more, the major part of me began looking back to my childhood. For the past two months I'd been focusing on my life-at-present and everything that surrounds it. But, looking way, way back was the only thing I could do next. My past became a fixation and began to consume me.

☠☠☠

"Hey, man. It's so good to see you."

Although I'd been seeking him out all night long, when the moment finally arrived, I couldn't speak. Instead I cried. I missed him so much. I wanted our hug to last forever.

"Great party. Isn't it?"

"Did you get my letter?"

"Oh, hey, man. Thanks for that, by the way."

"How…how have you been?"

"All's cool with me, man. You? You get any good parts lately?"

"No. I don't think so." My held-back tears prevented me from constructing more than five-word responses. My emotions, during that moment, took over my entire being.

"Hey. Remember this? *Merry Christmas...Mary* who? *What's up with that?* That gets me every time." As he laughed alone, a trendy, twentied and tanned, bottle-blonded boy-girl couple yanked Justin away from me. "Gotta go. I need to network. You taught me that."

"I guess I did."

☠☠☠

For nearly the past month Jenna could only speak of one coming attraction, a movie that was about to be released on Christmas Day, a movie called *The Prince of Tides.* Other than what that bizarrely intriguing hippie couple in Central Park was arguing over, I hadn't really known much about it, but it's a movie Jenna and I both wanted so much to see together. All I knew was that Barbra Streisand was in it, she directed it, and almost certainly produced it. Because of those three ingredients alone, I wanted to go as badly as Jenna.

Jenna was my absolute most trusted and dearest best friend, so much like the sister I never had, but she possessed one nasty habit I absolutely despised. "Paul, I'm so sorry. I won't be able to make it."

"What?"

"Yeah," she said, while taking a brief pause to cough several times into her phone's mouthpiece pitch perfectly. And after making some overtly audible choking sounds following that, she continued telling me, "I can't make it...into the City."

"Well, maybe it's playing in Corte Madera or San Rafael. I could drive up there to see it with you."

"No. No good." Then, more coughing, choking and sneezing.

I couldn't believe this was happening. Perhaps because it's Christmas. A matinee ritual I was looking forward to, a private holiday outing specifically with Jenna, just the two of us, together.

The importance of the movie came after that.

"Well, have a good Christmas."

"You too, Paul." More coughing, choking, and sneezing. At least there was no gagging. "Merry Christmas."

"Yes. Same to you."

"I love you, Paul."

"I love you, too, Jenna."

The forces directly above must have been in charge of my call-waiting, because without having time to hang up, another call had come in. "Hey, Lizzie. What's up?"

Lizzie was in a carefree, pre-partying mood, just like always. "I'm headed to Daly City in a few. A manicure and a movie. You wanna go?" Being Jewish, manicures and movies were more traditional Christmas-holiday entertainment for Lizzie than what I was used to. Being Lizzie, these activities only set the tone for the after-hours merriment to come, regardless of religious preference. Perpetually, she enjoys getting at least a week's head start on New Year's Eve and the rest of the year.

"That's funny. That's my plan exactly, a movie. I'll pass on the manicure though."

"City or peninsula?"

"Well, the City. But—"

"I'm going to *The Prince of Tides*, the new Barbra Streisand movie at Tanforan. Are you bare ass?"

I just laughed a little. Then, I said, "I'd love to. I'll meet you downstairs in a few minutes. How's that?"

It's so funny how things work out sometimes. Almost freaky.

☠☠☠

I had no idea what to expect. It wasn't a musical filled with tedious show tunes, that much was certain, but I'd heard it was some kind of story about a southern-type family. Maybe interesting. Alice kept saying that the book was a must-read, but since I never read books, seeing the movie was my only option. Before the movie however, we tested the limits of the all-you-can-eat policy at a nearby unsuspecting buffet-style restaurant.

Noontime in nondescript Daly City, actually the perpetual gloom of suburban San Bruno to be most precise, and all the rows of strip malls that go with it, was drizzly and rather depressing. But, it's always like that in this part of the peninsula. Nothing new in the forecast there. "You do want to see this, don't you?" Lizzie asked, while flashing her soon to be touched up pomegranate-painted fingertips.

After being a bit surprised, I responded sarcastically by saying, "No, the only reason I came is because *Mama's Family's* being preempted today."

"Oh, please."

"I think that Sizzler breakfast was a little too much for me though. I need to find the bathroom before we go in."

Without knowing what was coming, I got completely sick unexpectedly, all over again, just like at Alice's house. Turning my morning meal into an all-you-can-eat-and-beyond glut fest, I guess, was a colossal mistake in judgment. Normally, I *never* threw up though. This was so unlike me. I had no idea. I'd experienced nearly every strain of the flu many times in my life, but this was something different. It came from out of nowhere.

Not saying a word to Lizzie after my cinematic restroom upheaval was more than OK. I was ready to get on with it all. Every day of her life Lizzie always maintained a great combination of sensitivity and fun. What a great balance. I wished I could be more like her sometimes. As we walked through the doors to Cinema Number #1, the main event in the multiplex, we found that it was packed full of impatient moviegoers. A ravenous crowd.

Miraculously still, we stumbled upon the last two seats together in the whole place. "Whew. Barely made it. The last ones. Meant to be."

"What?"

"Meant to *be*."

I don't recall Lizzie ever having used that expression before. While thinking about the notion of things meant to be or not, something I didn't know too much about, the previews started. Both of us nearly bolted out of our seats from fright as the volume came on full blast. Adjusting it seemed to take a full few minutes, but when they got it just right, Lizzie and I relaxed into our reclining bucket seats, munching on our three-times-salted popcorn.

As the movie progressed, it was different from what I expected. A psychological profile of this southern family. As Johnny Carson would say, "I did not know that." But, I found it interesting nonetheless.

"You *are* liking this, aren't you?" Lizzie shouted out to me in a whisper with a mouthful of Milk Duds.

"Sure. Oh, yeah."

Remembering what one of my English teachers from high school had told me once as we were reading *To Kill a Mockingbird*, "when you watch a movie or read a book, you're seeing yourself," I don't know why, but I began to see myself in the scenes I was viewing. The father was violent, but I knew my own father could never have been anything like him. The mother was materialistic and more concerned with appearances than all else. My mother was nothing like that. But, the main character I happened to identify with perfectly. Nothing in his life was working. And, things were only getting worse. I was the most fascinated with the flashbacks.

The story continued, focusing on the many interactions of this troubled man with his family, but mostly with his therapist,

Barbra Streisand. She was good. She saw things in him he had never noticed before. How come my therapist wasn't like this? Maybe I needed to try a woman and experience her point of view the next time around. Maybe this is what the movie was secretly meant to tell me, if they do indeed speak to us individually.

The main character's fraternal twin sister had many problems, but it was only a matter of time before the Nick Nolte character realized that his problems were identical to hers.

But, even before one very revealing scene was shown, I had a gnawing reaction that must have emanated from someplace outside my body. My response to a particular scene was all I could feel until well after the movie had ended.

When the credits rolled, I was left speechless. "Wow," Lizzie said.

I could only shake my head. I was in shock.

She knew not to probe. Again, it's this sensitivity-and-fun thing combined. Yes, I like that about her a lot. But, as we began walking out of the theatre, I happened to look down at my clammy hands. At the same moment I noticed it, Lizzie did too. "Holy shit, Paul. What happened to you?"

Lizzie said it so loudly. Everyone around us outside the theatre now was staring at my hands. They were dripping blood. Not a lot, but they were still bleeding. Perhaps they bled from my fingers being so tightly clenched to the arms of the chair in which I was seated.

I was still in shock. So was Lizzie. So was everyone else. But, she was quick-witted enough to know to take action. "Come. Come on," Lizzie commanded while overreacting.

Without even flinching, Lizzie whisked me into the women's restroom. Creating even more unwelcome, unnecessary drama, she turned on the water in the nearest sink she'd found and immersed both my hands underneath. The sting startled me at first. I still hadn't known why or how they had become like that. How could this be? I had nothing sharp with me, nor was there any reason for them to be cut. The blood was coming from the knuckles of my fingers mostly. This was a first-time experience for them.

"Lizzie, I don't know why. It's no big deal. Don't worry."

"Just settle down, Paul. Everything's going to be OK," she said, taking full charge of my wellbeing by wrapping my hands like two gift boxes in paper towels.

As Lizzie and I exited the restroom, the theatre manager came over to us immediately. His behavior, all business. A little bit nervous at first, but then he asked, "Did you cut yourself on your seat?"

"No."

"You tripped on something?"

"No, he didn't do anything like that. It just happened," Lizzie said abruptly.

All I needed to utter was a single-sentence reply, and everything changed. "It's what I saw. That's what made it happen." At that precise moment my bleeding stopped.

Before leaving the theater, I was asked to sign some waiver or release form they had. But, with my hands in the condition they were, Lizzie insisted on doing everything for me, even forging my signature when the theatre manager's back was turned. She's so cool.

"So, what's up?"

As her pace quickened en route to her racy red Toyota Camry complete with spoiler, I stopped mid-stride. "Lizzie. Wait. First, thanks. This was so unexpected. Thanks for helping."

"Yeah, yeah. No problem. But, what made this happen? What's going on with you?"

"I don't know. I'm not sure. It was that one scene. I remember my hands digging into the seat, the arms of my seat."

"*That* did it? What scene?"

Finding the words to describe it didn't come so fast. I mumbled at first, and then I was able to say, "The one where he was being raped."

"Those guys from the prison?"

"Yeah. I don't know what it was exactly. Everything about it. The rape. The gunshots. The killings. The bodies. Lizzie, this happened to me."

☠☠☠

What was I thinking? When we got back home after skipping out on her ritualistic nail painting, Lizzie wanted to go for a run, but she had to talk me into joining her. Although I'd always thought of Jenna as being the selfless reliable one, all I could do was recognize Lizzie's loyalty to me. Flaking out, on anyone anytime, is something she'd never do. "It's just a movie, Paul."

"I know. I liked it. I'm too tired though."

"So you're just going to let that Sizzler grease sit inside you all day? That's gross."

"Oh, please. You're making me sick."

"I'll go on my own. No prob—"

"OK, OK. I'll go. Let me put my shoes on and I'll be right down."

Running into my bedroom was like hurdling through an obstacle course. Clothes, brochures, souvenirs, tons of New York memorabilia. Mixed in with all reminders of my marathon trip the New Year was coming soon, and as usual, I had the pages to my new 1992 day planner laid out and ready for use, while my current '91 version rested atop the stack. Unfortunately, due to the breeze I created by my impatient rush, they all got scattered over my bedroom floor after they'd fallen off my nightstand. Every single day of the week in disarray. I figured out that I'd need about an hour or so to put it all together the way it should be. Later.

While lacing up the running shoe on my right foot, the phone rang in my bedroom. I debated whether to answer. It was my mother. "How's your morning been, Paul? You enjoying your Christmas so far?"

"Well, yeah, Mom. You too?"

"Oh, I've had better."

"You know what though? I've got to meet Lizzie downstairs in just a few minutes."

"Oh, I don't want to keep you. You go on ahead. I just wanted to wish you a Merry Christmas. "

"Yeah, I'll see you for dinner tonight."

"Absolutely…Oh, what?" Mom said to someone on her end. "Sorry, Paul. Diane's here. We're just about to go see that new Barbra Streisand movie."

My mind immediately went back to my time in the movie theatre, to what had just taken place there. Again, it could think of only one thing. That scene. "Mom, you have to watch for one scene, one scene in particular."

"What scene is that?"

"You'll know. There's a scene that'll come up, kind of near the end. What happened in that scene happened to me," I said while trying to pull a wad of gum that was attached to the back of a playbill from my left foot.

"You say it like you already know. The movie only came out today."

"I just saw it. With Lizzie. It's very…potent. I got real sick right before it started."

"Are you all right? My heavens. Maybe I shouldn't see it then."

"No, it has nothing to do with…you. It was this scene, what happened in it."

"Well, what exactly—"

"No, I've got to go now. Just make sure you watch the movie all the way through. I have a feeling you'll know what I mean."

"Well, I'll surely be on the lookout."

"So, I'll see you here at Shirley's at around five tonight."

"That's perfect. We can talk about the scene from the movie then."

"Oh, no. Definitely not. We can talk about it some other time. Tonight, we'll just have a nice dinner and celebrate." After having scraped off all the gum, I turned the playbill over and my eyes became transfixed on the play's title, *The Secret Garden.* My stomach gurgled at the sight.

With uncertainty in her voice, my mother finished our conversation by repeating once again, even more concisely this time, "Merry Christmas."

MILE TWENTY-ONE

"*J*ust like she'd told me, J.P. and I would fight about money, and we did," a miracle-cured Jenna said to me about her mousy interim love interest. This time it was *her* turn to be indecisive. To call or not to call? Was J.P. her soulmate? Charlie? Or some new man altogether? Maybe some questions aren't supposed to be answered. I do a lousy Doris Day impression, but that's the advice I happened to have on hand. Que será, será.

"I'd forgotten all about that."

"And…I'd go the rest of the year without having seen Charlie. This has *all* happened."

"What can I say? Scary. Ain't it?"

"I think what's the most scary is your story about that movie. I'm glad I didn't go with you after all."

"It was no musical. That's for sure. I liked it though."

"That's another thing. This may have been what she meant over the phone. That there was some 'drama' we're supposed to experience together."

"What? You talked about me? *Again?*"

"A long time ago. Didn't I tell you?"

"Jenna, I had no idea how many times you'd spoken with her."

"Oh, my God. You're all she wanted to talk about. I forgot about most of it, because it was just too ridiculous. Something about coming back to New York close to Easter, a time for celebration. But, seriously…in one ear and out the other."

"Easter's next year. I thought I wasn't even supposed to *have* a future.

"Of course you will. You've got to be here for my wedding."

Hearing that word somehow made me feel selfishly sad. "Absolutely."

"You're *not* thinking about all the stuff she told you. Are you?"

"Although she's a nutcase, that woman was a catalyst, Jenna. She got the ball rolling. I try to forget what she'd said, but it's true, *nothing* in my life has changed. She made me *want* to come up with answers. Maybe on my own."

Making sure she still felt needed, Jenna asked, "You're coming over later tonight? Like you'd promised?"

"Definitely. It going to be a long day, but I definitely want to see you."

"And my dogs."

Reluctantly I said, "Yeah…and your dogs." Once again, I'm more of a cat person.

☠☠☠

On the drive over to the East Bay, I noticed that during the course of my journey that the weather had begun to change, quickly. So much was going on in and around me. The grayness of it all was overwhelming. Almost like some sort of omen. The closer I got to San Ramon, the darker it turned out being, the worse the perpetual pressure inside my head became. Also, the other drivers and what they were doing was also turning chaotic. Changing lanes for no apparent reason, riding my ass, passing on both sides. Without rational explanation, one driver to my left flipped me off when I had violated no one. Why he singled me out I'll never know. I didn't deserve it.

To presume that most of the people driving in the area around me were white trash might be a little too judgmental, so in its place, I'll instead diagnose it as holiday stress and strain. But, while thinking about the drivers surrounding me, I had done the most absentminded thing possible. I had somehow allowed myself to turn off miles before the exit I was supposed to have taken to go to San Ramon. Now, completely lost, I was going to be late for sure. How stupid. The darkness above turned into rain, and the rain became stronger and stronger. Almost sadistic in patches.

☠☠☠

Shirley couldn't have been warmer when I arrived. She looked so happy, full of hope. It was great to see her this way, as if her cancer was gone and she was living pain-free. I was ecstatic for her, but Shirley somehow appeared to be most happy for me though, for whatever reason. I had no idea why. Nothing in my life was getting any better. What did Shirley know that I didn't? "You really impress me, Paul. You really do," Shirley said while having had a head start at the holiday eggnog.

"Well, thank you. But why?"

"I don't know. Just everything. Respect. Yes, that's the word I was looking for. Respect. I respect you, Paul."

It must have been the whiskey from the 'nog talking, because I still had no idea what she meant. "Thanks again. I like that. Respect. Then, I'd have to say the same for you. I respect you too, Shirley."

My mother had absolutely no clue as to what Shirley and I'd been talking about. But, she joined in anyway for fear of being an outcast. "I want to get in on this. I respect the both of you." All I could do, when seeing my mother, was wonder if she had actually gone to the movie as planned.

Shirley just looked over at me, gave me the most obvious camouflaged wink ever, and slightly slurred out, "She doesn't really get it."

My quizzical wink to her was less veiled.

Shirley then whispered to me, "She doesn't get what you've b—, *you*. Does she?"

"Oh, I do so. We'll talk about this later."

I thought for sure Mom was talking about the movie, but the rest of the innuendos landed completely over my head. Sometimes communication between my mother and me ends up being misunderstood and difficult to interpret, as if spoken in a different, foreign language sometimes.

Rather than discussing the respectful admiration we have for one another, and other diplomatic relations, Shirley went back to what she does absolutely best, her incomparable cooking. There's no question that having Christmas dinner at Shirley's house was the highlight experience of the entire holiday season, even better than Thanksgiving.

☠☠☠

It was Auntie Shirley's turn to take care of me, and she never suspected a thing. She didn't know I was filled up to the brim with my relaxation medicine. I don't know what you call it exactly. It's not like St. Joseph's aspirin, because it's yellow not orange. This was all Bobby's idea. Whenever they all talked out loud, they said I needed to be kept a whole lot more quiet. The word he used was "silenced." Mommy told Daddy that too many of the neighbors had been poking their heads around where they didn't belong.

"You sure are a quiet one today, cutie," Auntie Shirley said as she put my blanket over me to keep me cozy.

I didn't tell too much with my eyes, because they were just too tired to talk. I was getting to be sleepy all the time. Maybe there's such a thing as being *too* relaxed. Either way, Auntie Shirley loved me no matter if I could speak back too much or not. Right after Auntie Shirley tucked me in, I somehow started to feel really, really scared. I didn't know how come.

As my eyes began to close up for my normal one o'clock naptime, my big ears stayed wide open. I made them stay that way for as long as I could. I was afraid that I'd stop hearing her. I definitely didn't want that to happen. Auntie Shirley was watching her most favorite show of all time, *The Guiding Light.* Finding out what happens next is the thing she likes best. This program gets her more worked up than the way Bobby gets at nighttime.

The last words I heard were, "And now a word from our sponsors." I was gone.

☠☠☠

"She got that from me, you know."

"Her suntan?"

"Maybe that too, Pauly. Actually, her endless devotion to *The Guiding Light.* We would listen to it on the radio together."

"Grandma, duh. It's on television, *not* the radio."

"It used to be."

"I hope that keeps her coming back here. Watching our TV, I mean."

"Auntie Shirley comes back to be with *you.* You know that, don't you?"

"I always thought so. But it scares me too much to think about right now."

"What? What scares you so much, Pauly?"

"That Auntie Shirley'll be gone forever. I'm afraid that she'll go away and never come back."

"Your auntie's here to be with you always. You'll know this later."

"So, I'm going to stay alive then?"

"The only answer I can give you is…never worry about such a thing."

"How do you know how to tell me these things, by the way?"

"Just like your Auntie Shirley, I'll be with you always, Pauly."

My grandma sure does say the smartest things sometimes. I'm so glad she turned into an angel. I never knew the time she went away exactly, but it was a few years before I was born. Angels are the best ones to talk to anyway. Sometimes when I talk to regular people, they don't understand too good what I'm trying to say with just my eyes and from crying. And baby talk only goes so far, you know what I mean? With angels, I don't need to talk at all. They just seem to know everything ahead of time.

"I hope Daddy doesn't hurt her."

"Again, not to worry. Not now, never. You'll always be taken care of."

☠☠☠

I wonder how that happens. Isn't it funny that the only time I ever get to talk to my grandma is when I'm fast asleep? Oops, I meant to say, Grandma-Angel. Or maybe she was already an angel when she was here on earth. Who knows? I sure hope I turn into one after it's my turn to go.

Grandma sure is special. She looks kind of like Rita Hayworth, even though her boobies are a whole lot more normal-sized. No offense. Grandma never raises her voice to me, and the best thing she does more than anything else, is make me unafraid. And, in my book, that's the most hardest thing to do of all…specially when you never know what's just around the corner.

☠☠☠

With tears forming in both eyes, Mom said, "Your dressing's just like Mama's."

Shirley just smiled back, probably not wanting to evoke the same sad memories that came up at Thanksgiving. Their look to each other made me realize what it must be like to miss someone who's not around anymore. I thought about my mother specifically, how sad it will be for her to lose her sister, too. It felt to me like Shirley and my mom wanted to include the spirit of their mother who'd died so young at forty-two, but perhaps it was just too painful. Somehow I felt as if I was eavesdropping on a much-too-personal moment between them both, but what I'd witnessed made me feel so much compassion. Losing a mother while being so young, must be terrifying to a child. No one to comfort them. No one to take their fears away.

The rest of the evening was pleasant, but mysterious at the same time. My mother and I had much to discuss, I just knew it. There was also something about Shirley that made me realize how much physical torture she was in, not having the strength to lift heavy bowls and that chronic gut-wrenching cough. I had never known that much about lung cancer. I just knew it's one of the most vicious forms. In a truly heartfelt way, Shirley handed me a heaping plate of Saran-wrapped leftovers. I gladly took them from her, realizing I'd be enjoying the memory her cooking, the memory of her, for a long time to come.

After leading me out her front door, Shirley walked me to my car, something she had never done before. "You make sure to get some sleep tonight," she told me.

"I'll try. It's just…I have so much on my mind these days."

"You'll find out soon."

"What?"

"Stop thinking. I do too much of that myself at night. You'll figure it out."

Christmas evening continued to be puzzling. I had no idea what Shirley meant. One more time, I had to ask, "I'll figure what out?"

"Whatever you need to. The thing that's keeping you up at night. Figure it out *during the day* and you'll sleep like a baby."

Shirley's stirring premonition stayed with me my entire drive back home to San Francisco. Once again, I almost missed the freeway exit, this time to my own apartment. Inside my head, I was still so busy trying to figure it all out. Less than six days remained in the year. Emergency. It's as if my life depended on finding crucial answers in order to continue just as much as Shirley depended on chemo and radiation for her own survival.

"Merry Christmas, Paul," an unfamiliar voice said to me. I didn't know where it was coming from. Then, I received a tap on my back as I got out of my parked car, and I heard the same once more, "Merry Christmas, Paul." I turned around, but I found no one there.

All I could do was shake my head a little as I realized I was beginning to hallucinate. Getting sleep, any kind, any amount at all, was exactly what I needed. Not taking time to deadbolt the door behind me after closing it was fine. Checking my messages was all I wanted to do, then go straight to bed.

The first message was from my friend Alice, wishing me a Merry Christmas.

A nice nonobligatory gesture, considering she's Jewish. The next message that began, sounding tense and rushed, was from my mother. "Please call me as soon as you get this, hon." I figured there was just something she forgot to tell me, maybe our plans to get together the following week, or she wanted to talk about *The Prince of Tides.*

Before I could even pick up the receiver to return the call, my phone rang. The unexpected noise made my body actually jerk back. It was my mother. "Wasn't that a wonderful dinner? I'm absolutely stuffed."

"Hi, Mom. You called before?"

"Oh, I just wanted to wish you a Merry Christmas again. Nothing important."

"On the message, it sounded like there was something urgent you wanted to tell me. Is there?"

"No. Not anything I can think of. Well…"

"Yeah, what's going on?"

"Wasn't that nice of your Aunt Shirley to give you all that food to take home. Is that what you two talked about when she went to your car with you?"

"We didn't really talk about anything special."

"Oh. I figured she must have told you something rather important. She doesn't really walk all the way to the driveway these days, ever since she got so sick."

"Shirley told me that I need to get to the bottom of what's on my mind…so I can get some sleep."

No response.

"And I'm sure this is making you think about that psychic woman again. What she'd said to you. Or that movie even."

This time, I was the one who couldn't respond immediately. I was just too worn out. "No. That never occurred to me."

"Oh. Well, Aunt Shirley's only concerned for your health. Have you tried drinking warm milk with a splash of vanilla in it before going to bed? Don't microwave it though. I don't care what they say, those things still aren't safe."

"No. Maybe I will."

My mother, as usual, was being cryptic. There was something specific she was getting at, but I can only speculate as to what she meant exactly.

I never did drink warm milk. After turning off all the lights, I hit the sheets, but that's all I ended up doing. Again, it was Shirley's message that stayed on my mind. I wondered why my mother was so concerned about my conversation with Shirley. Everything inside my head, all added together, became a full-blown burden. All that thinking at night. Somehow I began feeling like Shirley knew something I didn't.

So much information was collecting in my brain. But, what was I supposed to do with it? Maybe it was seeing that movie that affected me so much. Why did that scene haunt me still?

A new memory was what I needed. As I reached for my VHS copies of *Power Tool, Plunge* and *Sausage Safari* from the locked suitcase in my bedroom closet, I began to feel pacified. My nonstop porn-movie marathon filled up the night and early morning hours until I was able to doze off.

☠☠☠

Waking up screaming terrified me. My vocal reaction must have been eardrum-piercing to every one of my neighbors, I'd felt the noise coming from me could have easily drowned out the sound of any foghorn nearby. My skin, along with my sheets and blanket, were drenched in sweat as I was forced to awaken. My body felt like it had been assaulted and I was powerless, not being able to defend myself.

MILE TWENTY-TWO

*D*addy came home singing like a lark, then he must have changed his tune 'cause out of nowhere he turned plenty mad again. Ranting and raving. Mommy said it's 'cause he didn't catch enough z'sss. That can turn a person into a real sour puss, you know. And, Daddy's only human. But, as it got into the night, Daddy wasn't just cranky and mad, he got extra mean, too.

"Shit," he yelled out when he realized we were out of toilet paper.

"What can I do to serve you, Master?"

"Get the hell out of my way. That's what. Where's my Armored Veil of Darkness?"

"I'll retrieve it for you, my Master."

"And crawl to me on your knees when you bring it. Then, spit on it."

"As you wish."

It was going to be one of those nights, I could just tell. Which one of us was going to get it the worst?

"Has that bird been squawking all day?"

Then, without waiting for Mommy to get Daddy's horny mask, Daddy walked over to Tillie's cage and opened her front door. Tillie was being shy and wouldn't come out, so Daddy took the whole top of her roof off. I didn't really know what was going on, but before I knew it, Tillie was flying all around our living room. And, while he still had his police costume on with his badge shining bright, Daddy took his gun out of its holster and shot Tillie dead. Splat! Her pretty black and yellow feathers flew everywhere and the rest of her landed right on top of Mommy's new Frankie Avalon album that was playing *Venus* on our phonograph.

☠☠☠

My one-bedroom financial district apartment still substituted for a virtual inventory warehouse. Now impossible to even guess what's underneath all the mess. Piles and piles of the same old shit, marathon memorabilia, playbills from the shows I had seen on Broadway, and tons of laundry, some of it at this point months old.

It was close to three in the morning and all the offices next door to me in the financial district, still lit up inside, were staring into one sole dwelling, mine, my paranoid mind imagined. There were no noises outside. Everything was dead silent. None of the talkative homeless people were yelling at street-level below me. But, when looking out my front window to the left, my eyes stayed focused on one thing, the Bay Bridge. Traffic back and forth. Day and night. The bridge was always active. In my mind I kept picturing all the different types of people headed to the East Bay on its lower platform. Oakland. My birthplace. Just on the opposite side of the bridge I'd been staring at for the past twelve years.

Reaching into my refrigerator for an ice-cold Tab was something I always did no matter what time of day to quench my thirst. To me, the purpose it served was the same as brewing a soothing cup of Chamomile tea. Of course the extra caffeine kept me up longer than I'd wanted, but I was used to that. With a comforting glass of less-than-one-calorie cola in hand, I walked back into my bedroom, tried to motivate myself, and decided to sift through piles of cum-filled laundry that my mother hadn't washed yet. "Have it sorted before I get there," she'd always say. Dirty underwear, t-shirts, socks, sweat pants, and all else were scattered all over my bedroom floor. Twice-used clothing that's first worn, then becomes a towel substitute after my countless self-pleasuring sessions.

On the absolute bottom of one pile in particular was my dingy gray singlet with my race number still attached to it. A glaringly evident symbol of my failure. The safety pins now rusted shut permanently, having been surrounded by all that sweat for so long a time. *Lost in Yonkers,* a dramedy about a mother's control over her daughter, *Six Degrees of Separation, The Secret Garden.* The New York City Marathon, the subway, Central Park, and yes, the psychic woman and what she'd told me. Memorabilia with some sort of purpose, I guess.

My newest memories. Based on what I learned, what I would imagine I'd be able to understand about sexual abuse, I felt so certain that I was taken advantage of at some point when I was younger. Physically abused. *This* is what made me so unhappy. My mission was accomplished. I figured out what I was supposed to figure out. What more did I have to do? Nothing, I thought.

Uncertainty still plagued me by the minute though. When something should have felt so finished, I knew I wasn't. All I could do was continue to doubt. But doubt what exactly? If only I could be patient enough to hang in there until the next morning, I thought. I'd just have to forgive myself for chickening out by dialing her up one more time. Just to make sure.

With only fifteen minutes of sleep, I awoke to the adult

contemporary sounds of Bette Midler singing *From a Distance* on my clock radio. It was six in the morning locally and I felt that making my call at nine o'clock Eastern Time was the right, most appropriate, way to handle things. Feeling like a nervous fool, I asked, "Debbie's not in, is she?"

"Who's calling?" the suspicious voice responded rapidly.

"Um. I had spoken with her about—"

"Who is this?"

"My name's Paul. I'm calling from San Francisco."

"You didn't send me the money."

"Oh…you're Debbie? No, I couldn't. I couldn't afford—"

"You will never have to worry about money. I told you this. None of it will come. You still have negativity surrounding you. Nothing good will happen. Only little things."

"But, I figured out what happened to me when I was younger. I figured out where my negativity came from."

"No. I do not see this."

"Seriously. I spent a lot of time looking back. I really did figure it out. Something happened to me when I was a child. I don't know who did it, but that shouldn't matter, should it?"

"No. No. It is difficult process. You are living under a dark cloud. It will bring you only pain. Nothing good."

Proud and feeling in charge of my life, I said, "Like I told you before, I'm going to therapy, too. I'll get better."

"I must meditate. I will stay up all hours to find answer for you. There is someone, someone close to you, continue still to meditating daily against you. Someone extremely jealous of you."

"Yeah. You said that already. When I saw you."

"This has not changed."

"No. It was my mother. She's the one who was jealous of me. We talked about this. She told me she's not."

Before Debbie could respond, I heard a click. This startled me before I realized it must have been Blockbuster trying to get through.

"I be right back," she said.

For the first second, I tried being as patient as I could. I didn't receive anywhere near the kind of validation I was seeking. I was more confused than I was in the beginning. It was more of the same old, same old. I'm positive I did everything I was supposed to. Click again. I hung up.

The very next second, my bewilderment transformed into panic. My freshly-cleared Caller ID display read, 'Unidentified Caller.' How did Debbie get my new number? There's no way I was going to answer. Finally, the ringing stopped. But then, about thirty seconds later, it began again.

With a more defiant, almost angry voice gathering force inside me, I took the call.

After a more-than-lengthy pause though, I heard, "Paul?"

"Jenna?"

"I was thinking about you so much last night. Even this morning."

"Whew. For a moment there I thought you were that woman."

"Really? I was also thinking about her, the psychic, just this second. You didn't send her any money, did you?"

"No. I told her I'm positive I discovered what, or what I think made me so unhappy in life."

"Paul, I told her the very same thing. I called her last night when I couldn't sleep. I was up all night because Wilma and Pepsi were so sick. I'd found this weird yellow powder in their food dishes. Anyway, she told me I'm still living under a dark cloud."

"I hope they get better soon. In the meantime, take a deep breath…dark cloud, negative block. Next, she'll probably be calling it an evil curse."

"Either way, I never sent her a dime. And I promised myself

I'd never call her again."

"Maybe I should do the same," I told Jenna. We talked a little bit more. I was able to extinguish the need to call Debbie back, but something inside me still felt like she was right, like I was still not finished. Something inside was nagging at me, that there was more to do, and I knew this.

Jenna always appeared to be so much more secure and stable than I ever was. Instead of wishing I could be as strong as her, I'm just glad that Jenna hadn't given up on me when it seemed no one else would have understood what was going on. Something must have happened in my life, something I didn't know about that made me feel so weak and out of control.

☠☠☠

"I ain't no fortune teller."

"Bobby, all I wanted to know about is the precise time of the full moon coming up. Look in the almanac," Daddy told him back.

"What's an all-min-eck?"

"It tells you when to plant seeds. That's what we're doing. We're planting the seeds for our future."

"I'll go to the library tomorrow. I'll find out for certain," my mommy said to them both as she puffed fresh pink powder on her rosy red cheeks.

"It has to be right on the money. For Satan's sake, get it right. Will ya."

"Number Six. The big one. The gig that'll save our spot in Hades," Bobby, and the bad seeds that were planted inside him, yelled out.

"You mean, Number Seven," Daddy said, correcting Bobby like a grade-school teacher.

Why do they keep calling it a full moon? They should really call it an empty one, 'cause I'm pretty sure no one lives on it. Just like before, I didn't know what they were talking about.

I've never been to the moon, so I'd never know how many Martians live there exactly. Maybe I'll get to go someday. Maybe it's on the way to where the Maker is anyways.

Bobby, Daddy and Mommy didn't look as excited as usual when they get ready for some of the big-time stuff they do. But, the moon seemed to be so extra important this time. Probably so they'd have better lighting. Or, maybe they're going to dress up like Dracula or Vincent Price. Those guys for sure need to have the full moon around for it to be scary enough. All I hope is that nobody ends up biting me on the neck. I hate when that happens. It always leaves a mark.

"Oh, Darkest Lord in Heaven, I rebuke you," Daddy said out loud as Mommy was feeding me my Beach Nut Peas n' Carrots. Yummy.

It was business as usual in my home by the time the next morning came, but some major changes were in store. That's for sure. Everything started turning really white at our house. All the drapes were still closed up real tight, but on the inside, it was like a bright, sunshiny day. Mommy decorated things up real good. She put a real fancy, while-laced table cloth on the supper table. And, there were about twenty or so fluffy white paper bells made out of Kleenex hanging from the ceiling in every room. It was like a big party you'd only see on *The Price Is Right*, right after Bill Cullen tells the people what prizes they've won.

"Marty, dear. Please bring the linen napkins down from the attic, when you get a chance. Will you, please?"

"Of course, sweetie."

Who? I never heard Daddy call that to Mommy before.

"I'll retrieve them for you, Master," Bobby said to Daddy.

What's going on? Did they trade their playacting parts again?

It's like our whole household had gone daffy. And everything had stayed this way all day long. Taking naps and playing with my Raggedy Andy made me so relaxed and cozy. I always liked talking to him best. He's my buddy. "How are you doing today, my friend?" I'd ask him. It's always proper to do that, you know. Maybe Raggedy Andy doesn't know manners too good, because he never answered me back. "Do you miss Tillie?" I asked. Again, nothing. That's OK. He must be more of a listener than a talker anyway. Some people are just built that way.

I learned a lot from my pal Andy. He taught me that it's OK to love made-up people.

"You're being such a good little mister today," Daddy told me as I was napping. Maybe I knew he was going to say this to me, something so nice, so that's why I pretended to doze off when I really wasn't anywhere's near being asleep. I'm pretty good at faking it. Either way, it felt nice to know that Daddy loved me. And when he said it, I knew he wasn't telling a fib. It's like he was telling me this from smack dab in the middle of church, a place where you're only allowed to tell the truth, instead of fudging it. If you didn't, you'd get kicked right out on your bee-hind. As Daddy pulled up the blanket to cover me up real toasty, he said, "No matter what happens you'll always be my little boy." Then he began to sniffle. Probably because Mommy pledged the wood furniture too much in my room.

When I opened up one of my eyes, Daddy turned away from me. And, there, standing in the doorway to my room was Bobby, looking a tad spookier than normal, like he might have that worked-up feeling going on in his insides. Not excited, not happy, not even like hisself. It's like he looked a little jealous, kind of the way Joe DiMaggio's face looks whenever he catches some strange man staring at Marilyn Monroe's chests. Before Daddy could see him, Bobby left the doorway. Daddy looked over at me one more time before stepping out of my room. It's the most calmed down I'd ever seen him. I'm happy for Daddy that he was able to make hisself turn into that kind of feeling.

When I fell asleep for real, I didn't even force myself to dream. I didn't need to. I felt so good inside. Daddy made everything so peaceful. For the first time in a real, real long time, I knew everything was going to turn out just dandy. I was positive that whatever happens from now on is going to be just like a carbon copy of Ozzie & Harriet Nelson's house. I always wanted to grow up to be like Ricky anyway. I finally get my chance to do that. Whoopee!

Hearing the pop of the balloon woke myself up from head to toe. Even though the sound was coming from the living room, it scared me tons. And although I knew it was going to get me into loads of trouble, I started to cry. I just had to. Mommy came in to get me as fast as lightning and picked me right up. Instead of telling me to keep quiet, Mommy said, "No need to cry, my angel. All's going to be fine. Just fine."

Mommy held me in her arms and I could tell she really loved me. I stopped crying because I didn't need to anymore. Everything was starting to change in a really, really good way. It's like when that Prince Charming-fella came back to find Cinderella's other shoe. I could tell that my happy ending was coming up just like hers. Mommy carried me into the living room and it looked just like the Magic Kingdom castle on *The Wonderful World of Disney*. There were white streamers and ribbons everywhere, so it was a mixture of a party and something quite grand.

"Put him down. We need to get on with this," Bobby told Mommy. Then he handed her a big stack of papers. After putting me in my playpen, Mommy joined Daddy and Bobby back at the dining room table. It sure looked real official over there. "You sign here, Barb," Bobby said.

"Now, which one is this exactly?"

"That's your marriage to me. You sign yours, too, Marty."

"I'm missing one."

"No, that comes later. Sign the one in front of you next. The marriage that joins you and I."

Daddy stared at that page an extra long time then he signed it. I was so confused. I thought Mommy and Daddy were already married. And how can an already-married man and wife marry an extra person? After Daddy and Mommy signed their important papers Bobby'd told them to sign, all three of them signed the next one all at the very same time.

"Perfect. We're done. Soon we three'll be legally wed to Almighty Satan himself."

MILE TWENTY-THREE

The Prince of Tides was all I could think about. That scene. The rape accompanied by the brutal shootings after. For a second time in a flash, I began imagining that something like a rape had happened to me early on, but that's just too absurd to consider being real. Nothing but fantastical.

On a morning when I felt a guilty need to try it one more time, I decided to go out for a soothing, snail's-paced mental escape along the Embarcadero piers. Slipping on my unlaundered running shorts though somehow ended up feeling nothing more than an unnatural. It was more than just apprehension I was feeling after having been such a long time. While trying to go down unnoticed, I ran into Miss Francine in the elevator when I least wanted to. I wasn't feeling so chatty, but I decided to be polite by saying, "How was your Christmas, Miss Francine? A good one?"

"Well, it surely was. Christmas is a wonderful time. To celebrate. Birth, new life, new beginnings."

"That's true. Isn't it? Fresh starts."

"Are you starting out fresh, Paul? Is that what you're doing?"

Miss Francine asked with a sort of milky haze in her eyes.

I had no idea what Miss Francine meant by that, but I pretended I did. I shook my head affirmatively, again being polite. "Yeah, I guess by going for a run. That's my fresh start, a fresh start to my day ahead. I haven't really run much since returning from New York."

"That's not the fresh start I was picturing."

Rather than asking Miss Francine what she was referring to, I just went on my way. Although it probably wasn't her intention, Miss Francine congested my head even more with extraneous thought at a moment when I wanted nothing more than to be free. I was determined to enjoy myself anyway. Running, running away, had always been my most primal ritualistic survival mechanism. And I was relying on it once again to do the same.

Although the sky continued to shine brightly, darkness was arriving once more. Along with record high winds in downtown San Francisco, the waterfront, as I headed up to Pier 39, was swelling like a tsunami. I could hear thunder emanating from the epicenter of San Francisco Bay, but there was still no sign of rain anywhere.

Putting one size 11-E foot in front of the other that matched felt counterproductive every step of the way. Although I was running ahead, it felt so much like I was shifting into reverse. I remember having felt this same way at the marathon. It was a painful torture, never-ending and lifelong.

Rounding the tip of Pier 39, the mega-San Francisco tourist trap, on my very short 2.9-mile run, somehow was beginning to rejuvenate me because of the fresh and moist sea air hydrating my face. The smell of green apple cotton candy created a naughty junk-food craving in the pit of my gut. And, the dozens of uninvited sea lions that dwell on the fiberglass boat slips there were barking up a storm. They made me feel as if I wasn't alone on my turbulent journey. Looking over to them made me wonder what it would be like having to face the cruel elements of nature on a daily basis. What a colossal challenge, I thought. On the pier's peripheral pathway, normally filled with endless amounts of vacationers, it was only me, alongside dozens of vocal sea mammals in their artificial native habitat.

The same second the first few raindrops began pelting the skin on my closed eyelids, my right calf began to cramp. This hadn't happened to me often, but when it did, the pain became unbearable. I was praying that my impromptu strangulation wouldn't last long. My prayers went unanswered though. Halfway along Pier 39, with no one else in sight, as I was about to keel over, I was lucky enough to grab onto a metal railing. I had no other option than to deal with the pain to the best of my ability. Alone there on Pier 39, writhing. The cramp lasted nearly a few minutes, and that was the most I could stand.

As the cold rain began drenching me, I could only half-limp half-walk my way back to my apartment. Memories of New York came flooding back to me. Blood on my t-shirt, bruised raw nipples, a chafed groin, and an all-over ache that took what felt like forever to go away. Not to mention the reminded agony of having failed so miserably.

Almost without even being able to unlock my apartment front door, I stumbled inside. Rather than easing my way in, I found myself being forced to run to my answering machine. I recognized the voice coming from it immediately as I picked up the phone.

Still getting an occasional job locally, my San Francisco agent, Barry, knew nothing about my plans to move on. Much like Gardner in L.A., instead of offering a cordial "hello" first, Barry began our conversation by telling me from his well-lubed throat, "Paul, we've got a commercial for you. The shoot is tomorrow. Overtime. Más dinero. Golden Gate Bridge. Upscale casual. You haven't gained weight, have you?"

"Hi, Barry. I'm fine. And you?"

"And try to butch it up a little."

"Is it extra work? A one-day shoot?"

"Probably two."

"Oh, gosh. I don't know. I just hurt my leg somehow and—"

"Guapo, I'm sorry. I don't have time. Sí o no?"

"What?"

"Can you do it or not?"

"Sure, I'll do it. What's the product?"

"Great. The A.D. will call you in a few."

"Barry. Barry?"

Oh my God. Why did I say, "yes?" I definitely didn't want to do this. I couldn't. But, the money would come in so handy. Still soaked in winter's bathwater, and having again cramped twice since the pier, I just sat at my desk chair holding onto the ended call in my hand. Before I was even able to let it go, the phone rang once more. It was my mother.

"Oh, hi, Mom. I thought it was Barry again."

"Well...what in the world did he want?"

"He asked me about doing a commercial. I said 'yes,' but I don't feel like I really can."

"Oh, hon. Call him back. You shouldn't do anything you don't want to."

"I need the money though."

"I'll give it to you. I'll put some into your account."

"No. I mean, thanks. But, I need to work."

"I thought you were going to give up on that acting. Didn't you want to be doing something more stable?"

"Well, I still have a few more goals. I'm not really sure."

"Go with your Plan B. Always have a Plan B. That's what I've always told you. How about being a teacher?"

"But that's what *you* always wanted me to do. I never did."

"You'd be so good at it, hon. Always have a backup. You may even like *that* better. Who knows?"

"No. I don't think I should call Barry again. Agents don't like it when you cancel out on jobs."

"Oh, I'm sure he'd understand. He probably has hundreds of other people who can do the exact same thing you're supposed to do."

Having heard the wrong words come out of her mouth one too many times, I just had to let loose. Without further hesitation, I said, "You've never believed in me, have you?"

"Well, what on earth?"

"You never thought I'd succeed as an actor."

"Paul, I'm extremely proud of you. I just know you'll make it…someday. The tide will turn. Perhaps something else on the side would be worth your while."

"Don't you get it? By saying that, means you don't believe in what I'm doing now, acting."

"Hon, you've been doing it several years now. I admire your persistence, I do. But if you think about it, not all that much has panned out."

"But I don't remember you supporting anything I've ever done, not one of the choices I've ever made."

"Oh, Paul. That's just not true. That time you took those computer classes. A reliable backup is the way to go, trust me. Better safe, than sorry."

My conversation with my mother didn't last too much longer. I always knew which way it was going to end, so there was no bother going through this replay of a script one more time. She had always been like this, but I never before would have truly accepted that it was because she didn't *want* me to succeed. I always thought that she was just too fearful of me becoming involved in a career with so many inherent risks attached. The truth was my mother didn't want me to ever be more successful than her. She was extremely jealous of me for whatever reason, just as I had imagined back in November.

☠☠☠

My how time flies when you're having fun. It's nearly Christmas already. October twenty-eighth had come and gone a few weeks back and I turned two without so much as a fuss, but that's OK. I'd heard Daddy whisper to Mommy, "No party for Pauly. We don't want him to get his hopes up." A hope is kind of like a wish, and better late than never, Mommy finally made my wish come true. On a sparkling clear day when Daddy and Bobby went off to do their police killing work right after they did their morning calisthenics together, my mommy made me a secret seven-layer birthday cake with special grape frosting and purple sprinkles. Exactly the one I'd dreamt about. It put me smack dab in the middle of Cloud 9.

"You're my little angel and you always will be. I love you, my little boy. I'll love you 'til the end of time. You'll always be my pride and joy…no matter what." I'm pretty sure Mommy had more to say, but out of nowhere, she excused herself and ran into the little girl's room. Maybe that grape-flavored cake went down the wrong pipe. Just before she left, I looked up at my mommy and wondered out loud. I said, "Did your Mommy make you surprise birthday cakes, too? What were you like as a kid? Did you ever have to do the things I have to?" I guess I'll never know the answers to all that.

Even though she was still gone, my tummy also told her, "I love you too, Mommy. And I always will. You'll always be my very own special Mommy." I hope my message makes it all the way through the walls inside our house to the toilet so Mommy can hear. That'll make her feel better, and put her mind at ease, for sure.

☠☠☠

"Well, why do you need to do that before the ceremony?" Mommy asked.

"It gets my juices flowing."

"But, why Pauly? Why not me?"

"My willie. He really pops my clutch."

As per usual, it was time for Bobby to do his business in me, just like almost every night. But, this time he was starting to be a roughneck because Mommy was making him angry.

"Let Bobby do what he wants. Did you find my lucky Lucifer veil yet?" Daddy asked.

"Do you really need it, dear?"

"What did you call me?"

"Master. Master, I'll retrieve it for you."

"This minute."

"Yes, right this minute, Master."

They were still giving me my yellow relaxing medicine, so I was extra woozy. It made the hurt from my leg a little bit less, so that was maybe a good thing. But, then, when I'd wake up, I just knew it was going to smart real good. Bobby had grabbed onto my right calf leg too tight last time, and now the color on my skin is like the outside wrapper on my dark blue Crayola crayon. Not pink, like normal.

During the whole time I was crying, I stared at Bobby. I didn't really care too much for what I saw. Mommy made a fuss because there was green gooey stuff coming from the tip of Bobby's peenie, and she never wanted Bobby to shove it inside me when it looked that color.

"Here's your lucky mask, Master," Mommy told Daddy after handing it to him gently. Then he slapped her on her mouth. And then it started to bleed a little.

Mommy then spit on the mask. "Don't you ever ask to be with Bobby. Don't ever ask to be with anyone. It's never your right, understand? You're not worthy enough to ask."

"Yes, Master. I mean, no, Master. I'm not worthy," Mommy answered back sobbing.

Then, for the first time ever, Daddy went up to Bobby and me, and he said, "No. Not this way."

"Leave me alone. I know what I'm doing."

"Bob, he's my son. Enough," Daddy said as he put his left hand on Bobby's shoulder.

Bobby looked straight at me when Daddy did that. Then he turned back to Daddy behind him. Bobby stopped what he was doing to me. I still cried the whole time, before and after, but at least I knew the hurt was over.

"Use this instead," Daddy said. It's always Bobby's peenie that he pushed inside the hole in my bottom, but Daddy wanted him to try out a new style this time. "Put some petroleum jelly on it first. That'll work just fine."

When Daddy took off his horns to give to Bobby, I thought they were just going to exchange playacting parts, but I was wrong. Bobby put a little glob of Vaseline on one of the tips of Daddy's horns, and then he started pressing it into my bottom hole. He started out slowly, but then he began doing it faster and faster. It hurt so bad that I was forced to go away for a while. It's like I had vanished into thin air and all that's left was my baby body in front of me. It was like I was watching a widescreen motion picture projector-version of myself, one that hadn't been rewound yet. It was way different from just looking into the mirror.

I stopped being able to feel the ouch. I could only see it all happening in front of me. Dribbles of blood started coming out slowly. And, from the moment Bobby first saw this he got real excited, waving his hands and arms up and down just like Imogene Coca does on *Sid Caesar.*

"Not so fast, Bobby," Mommy told him.

"I haven't finished. My essence hasn't come out."

I was still gone away. "Bobby. Something's wrong with Pauly. I can tell."

"No, damnit! I've got to leave my mark…or else it won't count. Go away!!" Bobby shouted out as he shoved Mommy strong enough that she hit the looking glass in my room. I don't know what it was, the shove, the shout, the mirror, or maybe it was just time. But, I went back to being the real me, not just the sneak peeper-version of myself. I was back. And I hurt real bad. As usual, I had to go to the hospital. It's a good thing that Oakland has so many, because each time I got hurt so bad they kept having to take me to a new one, 'cause whenever they'd take me, all the doctors asked too many questions. They'd started to become so nosy, like Curious George. Daddy and Mommy were getting scared that people on the outside were going to start knowing what they were up to on the inside.

While I was in a place with other babies just like me, it happened again. I got to see myself in full Technicolor and Cinemascope. A lot of me wanted it to stay this way forever. Wherever I was, was just so much better than the movie-version. It's like the baby I was seeing wasn't really me. It looked a whole lot like me for sure, don't get me wrong. But, it's like the me I was watching is the one that didn't really matter. It was like some actor, some really good faker.

"You ready, sweetheart?" a lady's voice asked me.

It's Grandma.

"We keep missing each other, but I'm with you all the time."

"I know. You talked to me before. A while back. Why—"

"To see how you're doing. To ask you what you want."

"Really?" What an oddball time to ask, I thought. I'm kind of right in the middle of something here. "I'm not really sure what I want. I like food a lot. Something to eat maybe. Jell-O. Grape, if you've got it."

"That's not really what I meant. Do you want to go back? Or stay?"

"Jeepers creepers. Pardon my French, Grandma, but that's a toughie. I may need to sleep on that one. 'Cause I'm still a shrimp, you know."

"No you're not."

"Oh, I am. I only just turned two."

"I'm always with you, sweetie pie. But the choice is yours. That's all." Then, before you knew it, Grandma-Angel was gone. And I didn't even get to ask when I'd see her again. I had a whole lot more questions, too.

Gee, come to think of it, I sure could go for some Jell-O, maybe with some banana chunks floating around in it. Jell-O always makes me feel a whole lot better, every time. Specially grape or cherry, but not lemon. Yech! Then, I started thinking about other junk that makes me feel good. Another thing I always wanted real, real bad was to have one day when I didn't cry. This was the main present I always wanted in life, to have this one special day. Twenty-four hours where nothing hurts. I know it's like a dream come true, but there's no harm in asking. Maybe this is what I'll wish for. But, from what I can figure out, the only way to ever have something like this, is to actually be the me that's *in* the movie, not the one watching it.

Even more than grape Jell-O, I want this real bad. One easy day. A day when no one's allowed to touch me. A day when no one would make me bleed. No hospitals. No infections, diseases or green peenies. Just one happy day. Wouldn't that be nice? Things are going to get a whole lot better. The tides will turn. If I went back, I'm sure I'd be able to handle it all somehow.

Without even having to say it out loud, I told myself inside my noggin, "I think I'll stay. I don't want to go…not yet anyways."

MILE TWENTY-FOUR

There was no question in my mind that I'm anything but positive. I was dead certain about it. Considering all the things I had done over the years, there's no way the result could possibly be any different.

On a rare dog-free afternoon, Jenna and I were at liberty to ponder what we both wanted from our respective destinies. As we ogled one well-groomed yuppie after another while cruising up and down Fillmore Street, Jenna said, "J.P. wants me to have an HIV test."

"I don't get it. You're a straight woman, not a gay man, Jenna. Why?"

"Because he's been monogamous so long, he feels it's the responsible thing to do before we become intimate."

"You two haven't done anything yet? My God. There's probably no risk whatsoever. I wouldn't even worry about it if I were you."

"Oh, I'm not worried." Then, right there before my very eyes, Jenna whipped out the San Rafael City Clinic free-and-easy testing timetable she'd recently acquired. "Maybe we should do it together. You and I. When's the last time you were tested?"

I didn't answer Jenna right away. I was much too embarrassed to admit, "I've never been."

"You're telling me you've *never* been tested?"

"That's right. I'm very careful about what I do, don't get me wrong. But I've always just assumed I'm positive. You know, because everyone else is. Gay men here, I mean."

"I don't know about that, Paul. You don't know for certain."

"Well, either way, I appreciate the invite, Jenna. I think you should go ahead without me."

It wasn't really about fear. It only seemed natural that I'd wind up like all the rest. I resigned myself to this realization long before. There was nothing new to the idea that I was preparing to make my exit, whenever that may be.

☠☠☠

"Die, mother fucker!!" was all I kept hearing as I looked straight down to the sidewalk twenty-one flights below me. The same, extremely outspoken homeless man wandered the same block of Washington Street, in between Battery and Davis, over and over again. Back and forth at least five or six times. It was close to four o'clock in the morning, and I felt that I was perhaps the only one listening to him. I couldn't really make him out in the darkness from a distance, but his harsh voice was unmistakable. "Die, you sick fuck!"

Rather than going to bed, I thought about that man as I sat on the deck chair on my balcony above it all, invisible to everyone beneath me. Even after he stopped, I remained on my balcony in the chilly night air. Looking across to the office buildings was not as interesting as thinking about that homeless man. And, I shouldn't even assume he was homeless. Who knows? Either way, it would be obvious to anyone that he was, in some respect, troubled. What I thought about most was how sad it was that this man was crying out so loudly, with a probable need for psychiatric attention, while no one bothered to listen. Normally I would think someone like this was nothing more than a nuisance. But this time I paid close attention to him, the man, rather than to the noise he was making.

Where did he move onto? I just sat there alone and wondered. Across from my balcony in a diagonal direction, I looked over to the geometrically-devised Hyatt Regency with its multitude of unsubtle exterior right angles. I reflected on what I was imagining when I'd initially seen it, from one of the first times sitting on my balcony in the middle of the night, nearly thirteen years earlier. I was twenty-one then, and what I wanted more than anything else was a partner in life, somebody slightly older than myself, someone I could share my life with. I believed I was unstoppable back then. I thought that I'd meet some stable visiting business executive in the hotel's stylishly affable cocktail lounge next to the lit waterfall, he'd find me irresistible, and we'd become a couple and be together forever.

Looking out, it's hard to imagine how differently my life would actually turn out. Nothing even remotely close evolved the way I'd hoped or expected. Instead of going for quality, I opted for quantity. Lots and lots of quantity. Somehow I convinced my mind and body that horny brief encounters with a wide variety of strangers was all I was worthy of. They were always convenient, uncomplicated, inexpensive, quick and satisfying, for the most part.

Without wasting any time, I leaned over my balcony railing, looked down below me once more to Washington Street in the financial district, but now seeing and hearing no one. I didn't want to be alone anymore, not on this restless night. I needed to be with someone, anyone. After listening to the silence of it all one last time, I stepped back inside my apartment, closed the see-thru balcony door behind me, and put on my shoes and jacket. I picked up my wallet and grabbed for any quarters I could find in my bottom desk drawer.

Heading down the elevator a little after a quarter past four in the morning wasn't really that out of the ordinary for me on certain occasions when I needed it most. Thinking that I'd run into someone isn't something that I ever would have expected though.

"Mr. Paul, how are you doing?" my late-night doorman, William, said to me nervously.

"I'm fine," was all I replied at first. Not much else needed to be said after I repeated the same. I had seen that the elevator I'd stepped onto had come from the twenty-second floor. That's where Miss Francine lives. Many, many times I had seen her positioned strategically with semi-flirty smiling eyes at William's cherry wood desk in the downstairs lobby. I didn't ask, William didn't tell, and that's perfectly fine. No one wants to be alone, no matter what stage they're at in life.

William and I walked through the garage, and as we parted company at his parked black Dodge Plymouth, he told me with a grin, "Take care now, sir."

After I'd exited the garage on the ground floor, I found nearly no cars or busses on the street. The financial district was deserted, especially barren for a mid-week Tuesday night. It was never a surprise while walking the streets that there were occasional others like me, looking for the same thing I was. I was being indecisive though. Should I go to Kearny Street, the nearest? Broadway, the busiest? Or Polk Street, the gayest? There were many all-night places, but finding the closest was my priority. Kearny Street it was. They all looked the same, but the Kearny Street Adult Cinema appeared the most out of context. It's in Chinatown, immediately next door to a poultry market with ducks hanging expressionless from their stretched-out necks in the street-front display window.

Adult bookstores and trashy movie theatres had become so commonplace for me. The endless variety of patrons always kept me coming back. By no means did I go to gay bathhouses though. I'd have to get fully undressed there, in front of other people, showing my body for that.

Nearly every time out I secretly fantasized that I'd discover someone who would end up being a potential life partner for me. It's strange though that I loved Justin so much, someone I considered a most-certain future mate, yet someone with whom I'd never had sex. Nonetheless, I was forever searching.

"Two dollars in tokens, please," I told the clerk who never looked at me when he spoke.

"Quarters work too, you know," the multi-swastika clad, scar-faced employee told the floor as if it should know better.

"OK. That's good," I replied for the both of us, pretending his retort was newsworthy.

As I passed the throngs of straight and gay porno magazines lining the store's shelves all the way back to the movie arcade, I also made sure not to make eye contact with any of the leeches that may be hanging out in the darkened maze of walkways there. In each and every adult bookstore, I knew exactly where the unprofessionally carved-out gloryholes were positioned, in between which distinct video booths. Some of the holes were higher, some lower, some were crudely cut out, while others had smoothed off edges, preventing splinter irritation of any kind.

Not seeing anything special, I decided to step inside the nearest booth just so I wouldn't be tossed out. Hearing the dreaded, "Drop tokens!" while the bookstore attendant pounds his fist on the door is enough to send chills up anyone's spine. Accommodating freeloading horny cocksuckers and cruisers is not why adult cinemas are in business. I dropped my first few tokens right away, just so I could get the process in gear.

Watching a movie or two always put my joystick in its ready position immediately. For years, decades, they'd all looked the same, and I recognized each and every inch of every actor and the see-through characters they played, intimately. Length *and* width. My preferences had changed over the years, having gotten started a time before in the pre-AIDS late-seventies. Moustaches and muttonchops didn't interest me in the least anymore. Jeff Stryker's still a modern-day favorite of mine. Or, to be exact, Jeff Stryker's dick still stood out as being my absolute favorite. I always had a soft spot for it whenever I'd get hard. But uncut remained a perpetual no-no.

On the screen, one scene in particular caused me to unzip almost instantaneously before sitting down. I had picked a booth with only one gloryhole in it, cut into the wall on my left. The rest of the booth contained a small plastic trash can on the floor. Cum-filled tissues, condoms, lube packages and emptied vials of Rush were its contents. Since I could sense no one peeping into my booth from the other through the gloryhole, I decided to get up, stoop downward and initiate the first glance.

There, sitting in his chair, a stranger was doing the same as me. His pants were pulled all the way down to his shoes and socks. And, from what I could see, his legs looked nice. All three of them. He had a nice tan line remaining, which I perceived as being an oddity for wintertime. Maybe he just got back from Hawaii. Either he didn't notice me, or he just had more patience. I was ready to go for it and I didn't feel like waiting anymore.

As soon as I pulled my eye away from peeking inside, I sat back down into my chair, and one second later noticed an index finger wiggling through the other side of the hole. I obliged without hesitation. I stood right up and plunged my erect dick through the hole. His moist mouth felt so good on it. Not being able to see what was going on, on the other side, was never necessary.

His technique was different than what I was used to. It felt smooth. I could tell we were both enjoying it, not wanting it to end. It wasn't just me. Then, he stopped. While looking down to the hole after taking one step back, I could see a pair of lips whispering something to me. I leaned down to listen.

He repeated something twice I could barely hear. "You come here, inside," the mouth said. It sounded foreign.

"No, that's OK. I'll stay here."

"You come inside here. Is better."

"No, it's all right. I've got to go soon anyway." That wasn't exactly the truth. I just wanted my usual anonymous sex to stay that way. On this night at least. I didn't hear anything back, so I went back to doing what I'd started. The stranger reciprocated by continuing more of what he did best.

Again, his routine motions were quite familiar to me, but he began doing something noticeably different after a brief pause. It felt intoxicating. It kept feeling good until I began to realize that it was maybe not his mouth I was having fun with. I wasn't sure though. I was caught up in the moment. I was so close to cumming that I was reluctant to stop. Having unprotected anal sex is something I *never* did. A most definite high-risk. Just a few more minutes, I thought. That's all I needed.

I sensed I was close, and with less than a minute more, I finished. It felt fantastic. I was euphoric. As I caught my breath, my body pulled away from the hole so I could savor the feeling, clean up a little, zip up, whisper "thanks" to the stranger and move on. But when my eyes were able to focus clearly in the dim compartment, I was shocked to see my entire penis covered in blood and feces. I almost fainted. It was a thoroughly disgusting and alarming sight, one of the most dangerous sexual encounters

I've ever experienced.

Using a wad of toilet paper wouldn't be nearly enough of what I needed to clean up. I was still so completely startled. I almost didn't know what to do next. Something propelled me into survival mode as I next, with whatever remnants of toilet paper I could get my hands on, bandaged my dick like a wounded soldier. After that, I hoisted both my underwear and my pants up, all in one single jerk. Whether I was fully zipped up or not didn't matter. I needed to get out of this place, go back home, and disinfect myself thoroughly in my own bathroom as soon as I possibly could.

I was completely panic-stricken as I nearly flew out of the booth I was in. I ran out the bookstore entrance and headed for a nearby secluded and hidden alleyway because of the overwhelming shame of the mistake I'd just made. Closing my eyes for a moment, I wanted only to imagine that this experience had never happened. But it did.

I'd be home in a few minutes. Everything'd be OK, I thought. Just a few minutes more and I'd clean up and sterilize every piece of my entire body.

"Die, Mother Fucker!"

I gasped immediately after hearing these words, and then I lost my breath completely. Before I was able to choke though, the voice that just shouted at me repeated itself and became more personal, "Die, you mother fucker!"

Right there in front of my face was the man I had heard about an hour before, from twenty-one floors above street-level. Wearing khaki-looking army fatigues of some sort, the man grabbed onto me tightly below my waist, my legs. He threw me down and pinned me to the ground, thrusting my cranium onto the pavement. My head pounded, but I wasn't phased enough to become unconscious. The pain I allowed myself to feel for one second was even more insufferable than the harp incident.

As my voice shook, my instinct told the man quickly, "Take whatever you want."

"I want you to die," he told me back. His face lit up after saying it.

I couldn't reply. I was too afraid. When I was able, out of my mouth, I delivered a mystifying reaction that was utterly and inexplicably inconsequential. I simply said, "But—I *need* to stay. I'm—not—," as soon as I spotted a faded tattoo on his neck. A black skull and crossbones with red italicized text underneath reading, *The Seventh Ritual.*

As miraculous and uncomplicated as it may seem, this somehow stopped him. Maybe because what I'd said made absolutely no sense, the smudge-faced man with eyes clearer than mine just stared back at me.

"Veritas vos liberabit!" he screamed into the dark sky. With my hands bound by the stranger's grasp, I lie there on the pavement of some Chinatown alley I'd strolled down only a few times before. He still hadn't taken my wallet. It appeared that he didn't even care about money. I wasn't really sure what exactly he wanted. Then, like I should have understood perfectly, the man muttered, "Vincit qui se vincit," while still on top of me. These two phrases remained incomprehensible to me, like they were spoken in an extinct dialectic code.

As drops of his spit continued to fall from above into my opened mouth, I told the man, "There's—more to—I have—"

"Need? Or want?" he asked me with perfect clarity.

"I want to s-s-tay. Like you." In the split-second that followed, an amazing thing happened. The man voluntarily let go of me. He got up and motioned with both hands for me to leave, to walk away. With my eyes, I asked, "I can go?"

With his hands still waving onward, they confirmed, "yes."

I got up and walked, not ran, down the alley, with my heart

pounding like a ticking time bomb. Nothing about me was afraid though. I knew it was pointless to run. I don't know why I didn't, but I peacefully walked the five remaining blocks home, rather than sprint. Something so strange happened to me. Deep inside my gut, I didn't feel scared of anything anymore. Not even death.

With my apartment keys in my back left pants pocket I reached in, took them out, and opened the securely locked third-floor, terrace-level entrance to my building. I didn't even care if anyone saw me. Part of me stayed numb and still dazed. Luckily, from the feeling I got, I could tell my head wasn't injured that badly, but it was definitely bleeding. In the time it took me to walk home, much of the blood had hardened on my skin and stopped oozing out of me.

In my apartment living room, I was slowly able to peel off all my dirty clothes and drop them to the floor. I took off everything. As I turned on the lights leading to the bathroom, my eyes took a moment to adjust to the intensity. They were traumatized just as much as I was. Stepping before my mirror was an experience I'll never forget. With nothing between the reflective glass and me, I just gazed across at the horror of it all. From the blood and cuts on my face to the bits of dried brown and red feces on my penis, I nearly vomited from the chilling sight.

Not being able to look at myself any further, I turned off the bathroom light without even cleaning myself off yet. I couldn't do anything. I had become virtually paralyzed by this terrifying nightmare in real-time. I'd been completely violated. From the combination of events and the contemplation of its aftermath, I didn't even feel victimized because I felt as if I had brought on the entirety of it all myself. All I could do was cry. In the darkness of the bathroom, I let tears roll down my filthy face, and I just stood there naked.

MILE TWENTY-FIVE

It wasn't like the fancy-schmancy wedding Princess Margaret's parents are throwing her, but all the folks in it sure were happy. I guess getting to marry Mr. Satan, the actual for-real Satan, is almost like becoming royalty. None of the other family was there, like Auntie Shirley, maybe their invitations got lost in the mail. Just me, Bobby, Daddy and Mommy. And, since Satan couldn't be there hisself, they used horns, a blood-soaked crucifix and burning bones in the fireplace to play his part. The whole thing wasn't at all playacting or for-pretend though, it was totally legitamint.

The biggest shocker of them all was that they let me be for a spell right after I came back from the hospital. For a few days, I just got to sit there next to Raggedy Andy in my crib all by my lonesome. It was as if I was sent off to Disneyland. Without all the rides, of course. I even got to watch more television too. It's a memory I put on the inside of scrapbook, the very front page.

Life was changing at our home on Hillmount. I think the way they worked it, after the wedding and all, Bobby was going to live there full-time now. That meant in the end, he'd be doing even more personal things to me than before, since he'll be right there and not have to ride across town on his chopper. But, if they're all going to be more busier with this extra Satan person, maybe they just won't have enough time for me, I thought. What took me by surprise though was the honeymoon. They decided to do it right there inside our house in Oakland and not in Niagara Falls, the Hawaiian Islands or the back seat of a Pontiac like most regular folks. I had a gut feeling I was going to be a big part of that, and I was right.

Bobby must have gotten a smidge confused though. From being newly-married and all he kind of stopped thinking right, because all the time he was on top of me, he kept yelling out, "Pleasure me, Mommy." Talk about your mixed signals.

Daddy wasn't home yet, but when Mommy came into my room, she told Bobby, "Maybe that's enough for now, Bob."

"I'm not done yet. Oh, M-m-ah-m-m-ee."

Sometimes he yells out the loudest when his juices get ready to empty out into my bottom. Other times he's more shy like a wallflower when he wears his blue, sad face. It's always been the same for me. I know not to cry *too* much, not to overdo it, 'cause when I do Bobby turns wild. It seems that he doesn't like to be not in control too many times. That's why him and Daddy get into their fights. They never want to trade off being the top gun, like Mr. President Eisenhower. They don't like sharing Mommy and they don't like sharing me. Daddy never ever does his business to me though, he always just stays being the watcher-person, the ringleader.

"I'm making your favorite for supper, pot roast."

"In a min-nut. This squirt's bein' a stiff tonight."

"He's just two. He doesn't know how to make the right moves like you and me."

"I can't concentrate. Get lost, willya!"

Bobby sure was being the eager beaver. Everything was coming at me a whole lot more tougher and faster than what I'm used to. It was hard for me to keep up. I tried my best to hang in there. A little blood was coming out of my bottom, I could feel it. It got to a point where the more red that gushed out, the happier it made Bobby. He began hollering louder and louder. But, oops, by accident, I turned into a party-pooper before Bobby got to cross the finish line.

☠☠☠

"Merry Christmas, cutie."

Again the channel changed and I was seeing the movie-version of me. Did I turn into an angel or something when I wasn't paying attention? I forgot to ask Grandma-Angel that from before 'cause there was too much other stuff on my mind at the moment. I sure felt glad to see her again, that's for sure. What a pleasant surprise. What was even better though was that I didn't have to be in the real world anymore, in the movie-version of my life, or whatever you call it. "Same to you, Grandma."

"I'm here to help you, Pauly. You can stay as long as you like, you know."

"But, not too long, right? If I stayed gone too long…I don't get my turn to come back, 'cause I'll be away for good. Isn't that the way it all works?"

"I guess so, sweetie."

"I learnt this from you already, but I think I get it now even more. The things that'll make me stay."

"You do? Wonderful. What?"

"If I want to deep down or not. If this all ends up meaning something in the long haul, later on down the road. That's what'll make me want to… stay."

"You're so smart for a little one. Most people never figure this out. So, your mind's made up then."

"Nope. Not really yet. I'm still sleeping on it. Get it?"

"Yes. I do, angel."

"Oh, so then I am—"

"I mean, Pauly."

"One more thing. I don't really get why they do what they do. Wouldn't it be a whole lot better *not* to be married to Satan?"

"Nothing's ever better. Never worse. It's life."

"And that's the deal, ain't it? Learning a little something from this whole shebang?"

"*Isn't* it? Sure is, sweetie pie."

"Will I get a bonus reward if I get to be a grownup?"

"Life *is* the reward."

"No toys or prizes or nothing?"

"Perhaps."

I'm so glad I had Grandma-Angel to talk to, even though she's not too comical like Lucy or Ethyl. She made me feel tons better. But there's a question that's still planted on my mind like a sunflower seed, so I had to ask, "Where am I anyway? If I'm not there, where's here?"

"I guess you could say heaven."

"Oh. I heard about that one all right. Heaven, from the songs Reverend Pointer's daughters sing in church and from those yelling preachers on Sunday morning TV."

"It's certainly well-known. The world over."

"So, being in heaven is like being on television or in the movies."

"Maybe it could be. You sure are the clever one."

"Well, you know what I think? I think I need to get on with it. Enough dilly-dallying."

"Sounds good to me. I sure do love you, my little angel."

"Little Angel? Good one. Ditto, Grandma. I'll see you again, right?"

"Anytime you need me."

☠☠☠

"Are you sure he'll be well enough?" I heard Mommy ask.

"He's a resilient little guy. He should be ready by then." Daddy told her back.

"Well, this *is* the moment we've been waitin' for," Bobby said, like he recognized it on our wall.

"Yes. Lucky Number Seven."

"The number seven has always brought me bad luck. I hope everything goes well."

"You're such a fussbudget, Barbie."

"Only men can be fussbudgets, Bob. Not women."

"What? Who made up that rule?"

"I'm just concerned. It seems rather drastic, darling. Is it really necessary?"

"Naturally it's worth it. It'll ensure our re-birth in Hades. All of us, united together in the sacred netherworld for eternity."

"Personally, I can't wait. Let's do it sooner."

"Patience, my friend. Everything has to come together in the most precise way, in order for us to be delivered unto the hallowed den of cataclysm."

"Marty, I'm not so sure people are going to believe what I tell them…after," Mommy said nervously. "Are you positive?"

"Cot death is very, very common. It happens when the baby's asleep. Telling everyone it was cot death will be just fine."

"And, Pauly will join us…down there? In Hades?"

"No, Barb, no. It don't work that way. He's the one *keeping us* from there."

"In the afterlife he'll simply move on."

"This troublemaker here'll come back and be a burden to some other family."

I wonder how they got it all so wrong. One thing I found out for sure during my brief stint in heaven is that there is no Hades. That's a made-up place. What made them pretend there is such a town as that? What made them believe there's really an in-the-flesh person as Satan? After all, he's not Santa.

It's also a pity that they thought I was ever a burden. I felt that I was always as nice as could be.

"Not crib death. Let's say somebody stoled him. Then, we can bury him in the backyard."

"Stole. Not *stoled*," Daddy said back to Bobby.

Instead of answering Daddy back, Bobby just glared at Daddy like a real meanie. Bobby and Daddy's jealousy of each other was growing bigger by the mile. Their tempers sure do flare up every now and again.

"I just don't understand why Pauly needs to..."

"We need to kill him so we can be rewarded."

"Offer! We need to *offer* him, not kill him. We're offering him to Our Glorious Master, Satan."

"Offer. Kill. 86'ed. Same difference. Either way, he's on his way to God's country," Bobby said.

Mommy's skin began to shiver as Bobby said that out loud. I wasn't so scared myself, because I figured they were just fooling and weren't being serious. 'Cause I mean, who would actually kill their own little baby boy?

☠☠☠

Jenna had always been extremely supportive of everything I'd ever done, and vice versa, but I just didn't know if I could tell her the truth about what I was feeling. What would she think of me? But, being my very best friend, means being able to say anything and not being judged for it. Jenna's open-mindedness is what kept us close.

"I think there was a murder in my family."

"A murder? Paul, I thought you realized that you were, you know, sexually violated."

"Yeah. That too."

Looking like she was taking me seriously, Jenna stared at my face and said, not asked, "A murder," while instantly validating my claim.

"Yep. Somehow I feel sure about this. I don't know why. Or what that would have to do with me or my life, but yes."

"Who?"

"Some man. From the talks I've had with my mother I've been able to figure out it was one of their close friends."

"And *he* was murdered? Or he's the one who did it?"

"No. He was the one who was murdered. One of my father's friends. His partner on the police force."

"And you saw this? Seeing him murdered affected you. That's what you're saying?"

"I'm not sure about that part. I just know there was a murder. From the conversations I've had with my mother. The cover of that playbill staring me in the face all night, and those words in its title, *The Secret Garden.* And, even looking back to the calendar I had from months before, a calendar page mentioning your name."

"*My* name?"

"Yeah. It just feels like there have been way too many coincidences with things having to do with both our lives. Yours and mine. Like we're twins on the inside or something."

"There have been. That's true. That car chasing me on the PCH. J.P.'s piano almost falling on top of me. The truth about my black eye. Similar stories. Honestly though, Paul, I think it's because that whacko tells people updated-up versions of similar stories."

"No, no. Think about it. You and I were told the *very* same things. *Too* specific. Jealous mother. Meditating against us daily. Competing with us. Not wanting us to be seen. Narcissistic. Not letting go of the control. All those things. I just thought that somehow our lives are intertwined."

"I don't really know, Paul. Similar destinies perhaps? A soul connection?"

"Jenna, I was curious, that's all. I looked back in my calendar to see when you began working as a producer. I maybe figured somehow that's what I'd maybe do after acting, production work. Because our lives, for the moment anyway, are so closely linked somehow."

"Go on."

"I looked back, and I'd come to a sort of blurry page that read, *'dead ficus…Jenna's house…underneath'*."

Jenna just went blank. "Paul, no offense. *What?*"

"I saw your name, but I didn't know what it meant. I'd written it in pencil and it was smudged."

Jenna raised her eyebrows and didn't say a word.

"That's where I used to keep my spare key. Under that plant."

"A dead plant. Dead ficus."

"Yes."

"I just have to go with it though. It all means something. I just know it does. That scene in *The Prince of Tides*; that Neil Simon play in New York, the girl controlled by her mother in *Lost in Yonkers*; this in the calendar; the girl that was raped and controlled all her life in the movie *The Color Purple*; in October, on my birthday in between scenes when I talked to Whoopi Goldberg on the set of *Sister Act*, that's all I could think about. And, Desreta Jackson being there too, Young Celie. Most of all, I keep thinking about that horrible musical in New York, *The Secret Garden*, lots and lots of other clues."

"Paul, I'm not so sure what to tell you. All I've got left to say then is since you figured it out, you're in the clear. Isn't that fantastic?"

"You would think so. I guess. I assume this is what I was supposed to figure out all along."

"Well, good job then. Congratulations. You did it. You're finished. Happy New Year!"

Jenna was one of the most intelligent and perceptive people I'd ever met. I felt so lucky that she was my best friend. But, as the late-afternoon of December thirtieth turned dark, I still didn't feel right about something. I needed to do one more thing and I felt completely certain about this. Something deep inside me desperately needed to drive to Oakland, to the house where I imagined the murder happened.

As usual I tossed and turned the entire night through, not being motivated to watch the ending of *The Bigger the Better*, nor sleep at all. How absurd, I thought. I'd talked myself into realizing that what I'd been thinking was nothing more than an overactive imagination at work, looking for answers that never existed in the first place. If I had actually known about a murder, I would have remembered such a thing. Something like that never would have escaped my memory, no matter how old I was when it happened.

Like I was living certain moments of my life all over again, at some point in the very early morning I was forced to awaken. I bolted out of my bed immediately. I awoke to the sound of two gun shots very close by. My bedroom windows were open and hearing such a thing wasn't so completely out of the ordinary. I walked to my living room while still in darkness, not being able to see anything unusual through my window to the ground far below.

I even stepped onto my balcony, remaining starved for answers. Nothing. Nothing at all.

Once more panic-stricken, I didn't know what else to do but go back into my bedroom. I turned on the lights and realized that my back was soaking wet. As my hand reached behind me to feel the wetness, there were dry, brittle flakes mixed in with the wetness. I looked down at my bed sheets, encrusted in blood, and realized that the blood came from my back. Again, while completely awake, I again heard two extremely loud gun shots. I knew for sure they weren't coming from outside at all. They were coming from inside my own head. Somehow, somewhere, I'd been shot.

MILE TWENTY-SIX

Journeying through Oakland's much less-known, nearly buried and forgotten, southernmost district near the border of San Leandro, was something I never did. Not once before did I have a reason to go there. This time, it's as if my life depended on it.

As I exited the deserted MacArthur Freeway southbound onto Keller Avenue, my pure white '89 Daihatsu hatchback four-seater instinctively knew where to take me. Up one hill, down another, traversing and crisscrossing through neighborhoods I wasn't at all familiar with. At first I came up to a street I did happen to recognize though, with many identically-constructed homes, appearing like they'd been built in the thirties or forties. There I was at 6040 Winthorn Street, in front of the simple, white-picket fenced house where my father's orderly and proper parents of British ancestry had lived when they were alive, a house where I'd spent much time as a kid. Like everything else in life, it had aged. Now, moss growing on the wood-shingled roof, while the once meticulous garden of flowers, fruit and fresh rhubarb had disappeared. Nothing bad ever happened there. I remember them fondly. Somehow, I was certain of this much.

Up, up, up. My car continued to lead me on my way until I reached the intersection of Partridge and Hillmount. I didn't know the street address, but I thought I'd have a faint recollection of our old house upon seeing it. My car stopped long enough for me to scope out what was exactly in front of me. But what I was seeing was yet another home that appeared extremely decayed and in need of repair. The lawn in front was brown, and so were the few leaves lingering on top. I continued to drive, trying to see behind the homes, hoping to discover something especially particular in the backyards. My car parked at will and I got out. I enjoyed walking around in the affectionate sunshine. It felt warm on my face, comforting, but I began shaking as a pack of concealed dogs behind someone's tall two-story wooden fence began barking hysterically.

My moving body became still the further down the street I walked, away from the dogs, away from Partridge. Then, I recalled my babysitter from long ago down the block there. But, no. I knew nothing bad happened there either. Against my nature, patience took hold of me.

Somehow, inside my head's memory, resided the exact floor plan of the house I had lived in such a long time before. It's like it had been implanted there decades earlier, yet something I had never noticed before.

It was extremely calm outside. No wind. No fog. A pleasant winter day in the Oakland hills. One more time I'd stroll down the quiet street. My eyes kept turning to the east side of Hillmount, to the row of simple homes there and an unassuming church at the very end. All that time, the only person to be seen anywhere around was a woman sitting on her porch, a very small deck raised up twenty-or-so feet above street level. In the same worn-looking house my eyes had first seen. Once in a while the woman would peer down at me, in between reading the book she held in her hands. I wanted to both communicate with her *and* not disturb her, but I lost my ability to verbalize my modest offering.

The woman looked a bit startled and even a little frightened. "Yes?" was all she asked.

"I hope you don't mind. I don't want to bother you. But, I used to live in this neighborhood as a small child."

"Yes?"

"I'm almost certain that I used to live in that house," I said pointing to the brightly-painted beige home next door to hers. Or possibly even this one."

She looked even more afraid than before. The woman said nothing back this time. She put her hardcover book down on the wooden floor of her front deck, and then crossed her arms in front of her chest.

With my right hand, I motioned in a slow circle as I began describing precisely the blueprint inside me, "Do you happen to know if that house over there has a kitchen here, then a dining room, a living room, a bathroom, and a smaller bedroom and a larger one here?"

Her right cheek without blush began to twitch subtly as she said, "That's *our* home."

At that point, I felt confirmation that I had lived in this woman's house when I was a kid. But, from the extra clues I'd been given, I needed an answer to one very specific question. Instead of asking though, I was only able to continue gazing up at her. I couldn't believe I was actually going to voice to a stranger what I had been thinking. "May I ask you another question?"

By being courteous she allowed me to go on, but I could tell she was growing more and more uncomfortable.

"Do you happen to have a dead tree in your backyard?"

This time she'd become the one unable to speak. It even

looked as if she wanted to escape back into her safe home if I'd given her the chance, pretending she'd never met me. "Yes." Then, she rose to her feet. Her face, like there was an FBI interrogator shining a flashlight directly on it, was illuminated by only a strategically-placed ray of sun. "Why do you ask?"

Her question made my body begin to tremble both inside and out. Then, almost violently, I couldn't make it stop. I wanted to answer her question, but I was afraid for myself and I felt like I didn't want to intrude on her life any longer by imposing my imaginings onto her. Being as respectful as I could possibly be, I told the forty-ish woman with white wavy hair, "I hope you don't mind me telling you this. But, I feel that a murder took place here."

I didn't know what kind of response to expect at all, but to my complete surprise, she answered with absolute calm, "Oh, my husband and I'd already felt that a long time ago." The woman's whole demeanor was different than it had been from when I first appeared. Maybe because she was able to remain so composed and still, I became calm as well.

I let go a huge sigh of relief. "So, you don't mind me saying this?"

"No. Not at all."

"This must sound so crazy. But, being here is very important for me."

"Like I said, my husband and I felt this from a long time before, soon after we bought this house. We were able to get rid of the negative energy shortly after that. Not one problem since."

I almost couldn't believe I was talking to this woman about this, a total stranger. A notion sounding so absurd. If she had been anyone else, she probably would have called the cops.

The combination of what I had been feeling so strongly for the previous several weeks, along with all this new information, seemed like the freakish kind of validation I was looking for. I felt satiated.

It's like I had just put into place the last piece of a jigsaw puzzle that had been missing for the past four decades.

"I don't know what to say. Thank you very much...for being so open about all this."

"Not to worry," she said effortlessly. Seeing that her words helped me so phenomenally must have motivated her to offer even more by asking, "Would you like to come in?"

My feelings, along with my courage, shifted sides once more. Again, I became paralyzed. My feet couldn't move an inch. They were still deeply cemented into the sidewalk a good distance below where the woman continued to stand. You'd think nothing would scare me at this point, but it just wasn't possible. "No, thank you. I don't think I can. It's too soon."

The woman seemed to understand perfectly and our meeting was about to come to an end. She came down the steps to say goodbye. But, before she did, she wrote down her phone number on a ripped out page from *USA Today*, with a portion of an article about devil worship appearing on its backside, and handed it to me. The last thing she told me was, "Happy New Year." I had completely forgotten that it was New Year's Eve, with less than seven hours remaining in 1991.

Part of me couldn't really believe what had just happened, but another part somehow did. The time had come for me to leave the neighborhood that I had once lived in, the home where everything had taken place. Discovering the murder I believed to have happened was exactly what that psychic woman had talked about nearly a few months prior when I was in New York City. So many of the mysteries that had lived so long inside my head were finally solved.

Suddenly the day's sky that began so brilliantly clear and sunny was beginning to turn morbidly cloudy and dark with what felt like a brutal storm rolling in. There's something else I just had to do before leaving Oakland though. From the other end of town I found myself wanting to take one more excursion, this time to northern Oakland, to the once-ritzy, still segregated Piedmont area. Again, my car guided me to my destination. I don't know why, but something about me wanted for the very first time to visit where my grandmother, my mother's mother, was buried. I only knew she was in St. Mary's Cemetery, but I didn't know precisely where. Unfortunately, the cemetery office was closed for the holidays.

As I pulled beyond the main iron-gated entrance, and while noticing the immensity of it all, I realized I would have to return some other time, a different time. Less than fifteen minutes remained before the cemetery gates would close. Amongst the mature oak trees and serene, forever green rolling hills, there were way too many gravesites, thousands in every shape, size and age conceivable. There was no practical way I'd ever be able to locate my grandmother. It was a definite impossibility. I attempted to find her though, at least for a few minutes anyway. Up one street, down another. Down one row, then a few, I'd walked. About to give up, I headed back to my trusty and wise Daihatsu. Then, in near disbelief, immediately in front of where I had parked my car, there she was. What I had noticed instantly before seeing my grandmother's name was her birthday, my birthday, chiseled on her headstone. She'd died at a young age about four years before I was born, but I just had to see where she was buried.

I wonder if my grandmother was ever as determined as I was. I had heard many, many positive things about her, but seeing her dated photo superimposed onto her discolored granite headstone that read, 'Forever and always, our beloved angel,' enabled me to see her smile. It was a nice smile. A truthful smile. It's like she was right there with me. If I could speak to her, I wasn't so sure what I'd say for sure, but "thanks" had to be in there somewhere. I may never understand how exactly, but because of my grandmother, who would have believed in me all along I felt, I had summoned the power to solve the mystery of my life. I was free.

With only one ray of sun remaining in the sky, I touched the headstone, and said "goodbye" to the person I believed naturally helped me the most in my life, someone I'd never even met. The minute I closed the car door behind me as I got in, a clap of thunder echoed all around me. The black sky opened up and heavy rain began coming down from everywhere. Lightning followed, in an instant illuminating what had become complete and sudden darkness.

My drive back to San Francisco was filled with an odd variety of unexpected events. At first, on the Bay Bridge doing 60, a silver stretch limousine directly ahead of me to the right all of a sudden lost a tire, and it began bouncing right towards me at rapid speed. Luckily however, I swerved into no one on my left, averting my own misfortune. Power outages began happening all over the place. On the Bay Bridge Toll Plaza, then in downtown San Francisco, the financial district, even affecting the electric garage door leading into my apartment building. After one of the maintenance men opened it up, I entered, went upstairs calmly, feeling more relief than I had ever felt before. It was silent inside. No noises were coming from outside as the thunder and lightning ceased the minute I got home.

It was a little past five-fifteen in the afternoon and there I laid face-up on my waterbed, ready to take the nap of my entire existence. I was exhausted after having played the role of a persistently goal-oriented private detective over the past two months. My brain had become as spent and lifeless as my body. But, before I was able to pull the shroud up over me, uneasiness began to brew inside. The year was about to come to an end, yet the feeling of not being finished was growing bigger by the minute. A gnawing impression was inside my gut, telling me that there was more to do, something I absolutely *had* to do. I wasn't really sure what though. What was left?

Steadily, this feeling kept growing more intense and unavoidable. It was a sharp, strong, and painful reminder. A foreboding knife thrust into the center of my solar plexus, then downward, deeper than that, into the pit of my stomach. The harmonious feeling I had when I first walked into my bedroom that afternoon was vanishing. One sitcom after another was coming up on my bedroom Sony Trinitron, but I wasn't able to giggle even once. I was just killing time. A need was arising in me, a dire need. Eventually I discovered exactly what it was, what I needed to do, but there was nothing about me that wanted to do it.

My mind flashed back for a second to that late-night attack by the tattooed homeless man. At one point, close to seven in the evening, I got up from my undulating bed and reached for the phone about seven feet away from me. I picked up the receiver and even began dialing the numbers. I was only able to complete the first eight of ten. I couldn't do it. I somehow felt that I didn't need to. My work was done, I thought. I found out what caused me to be so unhappy in life. What else was there left to do? What difference would one more phone call make? Especially one I had no desire to make. It seemed so unnecessary.

After putting the receiver back down for only one second, my phone rang immediately. I looked at the display to find a number I didn't recognize. The area code shown, '510,' was the East Bay. Instinctively, I answered without hesitation.

"Signora Campera?" the voice asked before I could even say, "Hello."

I was shocked to hear this name. Not enough to ask, "Who?" though.

"Signora Campera. A casa? Con te?"

I told the foreign-speaking person on the other end that they had the wrong number and they believed me. The insane thing was that my grandmother's last name was Campera, my mother's mother. Maria Gemma Campera. Why did I get this call now? How could they possibly have known to ask for that name in particular? I couldn't understand this coincidence. Just when I felt I'd become the victor, my paranoia became real as I realized that the battle for my soul continued.

Initially I wanted to pretend that this call had never come. It kept haunting me though, mainly because I knew exactly what it meant. On my bed, the sharpness of the pain coming from my stomach had become intolerable. I felt as if my stomach was converting into an active, modern-day Mount Vesuvius ready to re-erupt at any moment. If my stomach could speak, it would have commanded, "Pick up the phone and *call* your mother." For the next thirty-or-so minutes more, I ignored this proclamation. What difference would it make? What did I need another validation for? Did I need to interrogate my mother further?

Now, with a sense of urgency minus the fear, I again got up out of bed. It was close to eight at night. New Year's Eve partiers were beginning to descend onto the streets of San Francisco below me. I knew my mother would be leaving to go home from her nighttime job in Walnut Creek. The moment had become now or never. I just knew I had to do it. Unlike my last attempt, I was able to successfully dial all ten digits. My heart was racing a mile a minute. For every one ring, my heart pounded out about one hundred beats.

I was secretly, cowardly praying my mother wouldn't answer by the moment the fifth ring arrived. My prayers went unanswered though. On the fourth my mother said, "Hello. TransPacific Title."

It wasn't nerves or fear this time. On my end, I was speechless. I couldn't get one word out. The apprehension inside me graduated into full-fledged rage, a lifetime of anger that had never before come to the surface. I wasn't even able to breathe.

"Hello. TransPacific Title. Is someone there?"

I felt as if I was going to implode, then after, all my vital parts spewing outside myself. I looked down at my right hand in front of me. It was beet red. All the skin covering my entire body turned red hot and it burned. Rage had enveloped my whole being. In the midst of this revolution, along with my speechlessness, my mother hung up. Immediately, I dialed again.

After the sixth ring this time, an agitated voice said, "Hello. TransPacific Title."

"Who the fuck is buried in the backyard of the house on Hillmount?" I screamed out, loud enough for all San Francisco to hear.

As if there was a five-second time delay in our phone connection, my mother nervously asked, "Paul?"

"Who the fuck is buried in the backyard of the house on Hillmount?"

"I don't know what you're talking about."

"You're in denial, you mother-fucking cocksucker."

"I'm going to have a heart attack, Paul. I don't know what you mean."

"The house on Hillmount, where the murder took place. Who was it, you cunt?"

"I have no idea what you're talking about."

"You're going to rot in hell if you don't tell me. It's my turn now, you bitch."

"I don't know. I'm going to have a heart attack."

"The sexual abuse. The murder. You knew all about it." My red-flamed anger grew into an out-of-control wildfire. Out of nowhere though, my rage led me to offer a conciliation of sorts as I said, "I'll forget all about this...if you promise to get help."

"But, I don't know anything about this, Paul. I don't, I swear."

My mother and I went back and forth for the next two to three minutes. My white-flagged appeasement became a demand. Finally, my mother said, "OK. I'll do that." I don't know exactly what that meant to me, but something changed inside my body. All the fiery rage burning throughout me was extinguished. This, somehow, was exactly what I needed to do.

It was now a little after nine o'clock. Less than three hours remained in the year.

THE FINISH LINE

The biggest party of the year was just about to start right at midnight, Ritual Number #7, the one all the hoopla's about. Just like the big-deal wedding that went off without a hitch, this was going to be a real lollapalooza. Every time Bobby looked over at me was like watching Whimpy's happy face, the one from Popeye, when he gets ready to take a bite out of another juicy hamburger. This is the moment they'd all been waiting for. Seven more hours and it'll all be over.

Daddy was fired up as usual because he got called into work that morning. It's December 31st, the day before all the spirits enter into the underworld, wherever that is 'cause we don't actually have a basement. Bobby had ants in his pants. Mommy was nervous. I just ate my grape Jell-O with my Bozo the Clown spoon like a good boy. Just another average day for me. Bobby hadn't done his business to me in a real long while, and I was so glad about that. It gave the hole inside my bottom a chance to rest up and get back to normal size. This is the first time there were no scabs or bruises in it. It was as fresh as a daisy.

"I can't wait no longer," Bobby told Mommy.

"You can't wait for what?"

"You know," Bobby told her as he winked real big with his whole face.

"I don't know what you're talking about."

"Let's do it. Let's do it now."

"Not without Marty. We couldn't."

"We don't need to wait for him. He's an old stick in the mud."

"It would be wrong, Bobby. No, we can't."

"Don't tell me 'no.' There's no time like the present."

Bobby must have been one of those people that was born way too late. For as long as anyone can remember, he's in a hurry to do everything. It's like he's always playing catch-up. Mommy looked more jittery than a Mexican jumping bean. Just like Bobby told, I mean, ordered her, she got all the stuff ready in the fireplace for burning. Parts of Tillie's feathers were still in it, burnt-up pieces that turned as black as the Ace of Spades. It's a shame they had to leave her there, instead of burying her in the backyard with all the rest of the animals they killed. Tillie's a good duck.

For the millionth time, Mommy lifted me out of my playpen. So I'd have some company she brought my Raggedy Andy with her, then she put us both on top of her bed. Mommy hugged me extra long then she kissed me on top of my head. Bobby's always the one who flipped me over so I'd be facedown on my tummy. This time he didn't even pretend to be gentle.

"Careful, Bobby," Mommy shouted out.

"What difference does it make? Soon..."

Bobby and Mommy, just like always, took off all their clothes and stood there in their birthday suits. My tummy was feeling a little queasy. I guess I ended up getting so used to stuff being shoved into my bottom that now it's hard for stuff to come out. I was wearing my birthday suit just like the two of them, even though it wasn't anywhere's near October.

Bobby and Mommy started touching and grabbing each other all over the place, and then it was Bobby's turn to do the same to me. Just like G.I. Joe rushing into combat, Bobby was ready for action. He, Bobby not G.I. Joe, always liked the finishing up part best, but somehow, on this special occasion, his weenie stayed extra floppy instead of standing at attention. He's a real trouper though. "Damn it! Why now?" he yelled out as he pulled the pink plastic love toy out of his bottom.

"Maybe we should wait after all. It's a sign, Bobby. Marty will be home soon enough."

"No, let's get this done right now. Let me concentrate, will ya!" Bobby continued trying to do his business. His peenie finally pointed straight up just after he got done shouting at it.

I can always tell when Bobby was close to finishing up, because he'd always say as fast as he could, "Set us free. Most Holy Satan, set us free."

"I can't do it, Bobby. I just can't."

"I'm gettin' close. It has to be when I cum. Damn it, woman. You've got to deliver it unto me right here and now."

Mommy just shook real hard on her outsides. She picked up the loaded gun on top of the dresser. Her hands were shaking so badly that she was likely to shoot the ceiling by mistake if she wasn't careful. Maybe she should have gone to target practice before. My life was about to come to an end. This is what I'd secretly been wishing for all along, but don't tell anyone. Finally my wish was about to come true. I guess something about me deep down didn't want to be in the real life after all, like me and my grandma talked about. I still knew my Raggedy Andy was right next to me though. Soon I'd get to see Grandma-Angel up close again. Hot diggity dog!

Mommy still couldn't hand over the gun. Bobby began

screaming at the top of his lungs. Blood curdling. His body was pressed up so hard on top of me that I nearly suffocated. I didn't know if I could take it much longer. The more I cried out, the louder Bobby screamed. All I could see was darkness because my face was smashed down so much into the sleeping pillow. Soon, it would all be over. Ritual Number #7, along with my real life, was about to be finished up for good, the very last thing to be checked off their list.

"N-n-n-ow, woman, n-n-n-ow!" jittery Bobby screamed out as I could feel his juices squirt inside me.

Then it happened. Two very loud popping gunshots, just like on *The Rifleman.* It was all over. Right there on the spot, I realized that heaven sure was a whole lot like earth, 'cause the first thing I saw when my eyes opened was the pillow again. There were chunks of bright red stuff everywhere though, all over the walls, the bedspread, in front of me, on top of me. None of it was so clean and fresh looking. The red pieces that were on top of my skin felt like fire.

I wasn't dead at all. But, Bobby was. He took his last breath while he was on top of me, doing his business right up 'til the very end. I couldn't hear any words, but I was able to turn my body over, so I was tummy-side up, to see Daddy standing there in the doorway, with a teeny trickle of smoke coming from the gun in his hand. Both Mommy and Daddy looked like their mouths just kept saying the same words over and over again, "Oh, my God. Oh, my God," like they didn't know any others. Daddy shot Bobby twice in his head. No one shot me. I wasn't offered to Satan after all.

The hands on the clock ticking above Mommy's nightstand read four seventeen.

Mommy and Daddy were beside themselves. Daddy must have been pretty unhappy that Bobby and Mommy had started this extra-special ritual-party so early and ahead of schedule. Or maybe he had second thoughts about making me the offering. Maybe he was protecting me. Only a split-second went by, then Mommy was like a crazy lady with her full bottle of Mr. Clean. She scrubbed and mopped that bedroom for hours and hours. I still cried. I was so confused about everything, and I couldn't understand why I was still alive. How come? Now I'd have to wait even longer to see my grandma up in heaven.

Daddy dragged Bobby's body to the inside of our back door and it made a trail of red all the way there. The red stayed there the whole night long.

In the very, very early morning, way before the light came up from the underworld and went into the sky, Daddy pulled Bobby's body out to the backyard to the same hole where they were going to put me, right next door to Fluffy. The neighbors probably thought nothing about it, because Daddy had been doing some manly-type gardening work out there planting petunias. After Bobby was in the ground, Daddy covered him up with dirt and rocks. And on top of that, Daddy planted a sapling, a teeny tiny baby maple tree, the type that would later grow up to be big and strong.

Even though Bobby was the one that died, part of me decided to go up to heaven that night too. I'll miss that time in my life when all I wanted was grape Jell-O.

☠☠☠

Fifteen minutes remained in the year. Part of me believed that my mother did end up having a heart attack and died from the conversation we'd had just a few hours before. I began feeling guilt and remorse. I didn't want my personal discovery to be the thing that killed her. Knowing that she'd be long finished with work that night, I decided to call her at home at Shirley and Uncle Lester's house where she lives in their spare bedroom. My aunt was the one who answered the phone.

Cheery, bright, entertaining and a little sauced, my aunt wished me a Happy New Year, and I wished her the same. Following our very brief chat though, and immediately after asking to speak with my mother, Shirley said something she'd never said to me verbally before, "I love you, Pauly."

How odd, I thought, as I wondered why, as far back as I can remember, I've never referred to my aunt as *Aunt* Shirley. Hearing her warm sentiments made me feel so right. It made me feel as if she was secretly saying, "good job," without knowing a thing. My mother sounded exceptionally nervous while coming onto the phone, little was said. It's as if I was testing the measures I'd initiated earlier.

"Are you OK?" I asked her.

"Yes, Paul. I'm doing fine. Are you all right?"

I could tell that my tipsy aunt and uncle may have been in the background, so it was maybe difficult for my mother to talk. Little more of consequence was said. It was a test. My mother once again said "yes" when I reminded her of the promise she'd made to me earlier. Although it was an odd demand that I still questioned, its acceptance is exactly what I needed to hear.

After hanging up the phone in my bedroom for the last time, I walked into the living room, then onto my balcony twenty-one flights above the ground. Rather close by was the Ferry Building along San Francisco's waterfront. As always the clock tower was fully-illuminated. Only two minutes were left in 1991. The typical sounds made by New Year's revelers seemed to be surreal. It's like I was in a fog on a perfectly clear night. I was at peace with myself. I felt as if whatever it was that I had just accomplished was the feat of my existence.

I knew for certain that I'd indeed figured out the cause of my unhappiness. Looking straight down from my balcony made me think how effortless it would have been to end my life right then and there, a life that was headed nowhere. One step beyond the edge and my life would have been over. Just one step, inches away from my own mortality. Once again somehow, I felt that I'd escaped a bullet or two that were aimed straight at my head.

So many details were missing from the scenario I was building, but it didn't matter anymore. At the very same time I was consumed by two very different feelings, one overwhelming sense of freedom and one of fear. Immediately prior to the illuminated Ferry Building clock striking twelve, I ran to my front door and engaged its deadbolt. Reality was beginning to set in. I recognized that what I had imagined all along was indeed the truth, definitely not a movie. And conversely, all I'd ever known was a lie. I knew that from this point on, my life would never be the same.

☠☠☠

Pauly still lives inside me today. I'm turning fifty in a few months, but there's a big part of me inside that thinks and acts just like that little boy. Much has changed since 1959, but one thing's still the same, I suffer, everyone suffers. People suffer all the time, in a variety of ways, in different levels of severity. The trick to life is to accept any kind of suffering just as you'd accept pleasure. This is the secret to happiness.

I have more happier moments than I've had in years past, and I'm grateful for that.

Both my parents are still living and I feel lucky I've been able to get to know them again without judgment. There's good in everyone, I feel this absolutely. I still don't know too much about Robert "Bobby" Smith. From what I gather, he had no family and was missed by almost no one. He was my father's partner on the

South Oakland Police force and had been my father's classmate in the Police Academy prior to that.

I never return to the house on Hillmount anymore, there's no need. Been there, done that. On my last visit there many years ago now, a few dear friends helped me by digging up the backyard. We discovered that Bobby's body had been removed, but we found a wide selection of animal skeletons still in tact underneath a dead, rotting tree. I still don't know what would motivate a person to participate in something like devil worship. I'll just assume it was merely a bizarre and gruesome trend of the times.

After a fifteen-year absence, I'm back in San Francisco again, perhaps to start over. I've been waiting for this opportunity all my life. Close to fifty and I've still never had an intimate relationship with anyone. And that's perfectly fine. It's hard to believe there was a time in my life where the only person I felt I was worthy of being with was Justin. God rest his soul.

I've never seen that New York psychic again. I wonder if she still remembers to rewind her videos. Maybe she's got a DVD player by now. In so many ways, it's difficult to think that what I'd experienced sixteen years ago ever happened at all. My discovery back then was the moment I grew up. Life's harder when you're an adult. There's more to reflect on, less to plan for. I still want so many things. I remember my mother telling me that all I used to ask for was grape Jell-O and tuna fish sandwiches when I was a kid. It's good to know what you want. It keeps you alive.

What I want most is to be a part of life more, to be less of a spectator. I feel I deserve so many things now, to live life fully, not to be left out of anything. I want to be in the driver's seat, rather than remain a passenger. It's my turn. Change is coming. Big change. I can feel it. More than moving to a new city but living the same life, everything's going to be different, I just know it.

As I move forward onto the life I feel I'm now worthy of, I'll continue to glance back once in a while to remind me where I came from. To remind myself that I've earned a good life. I've worked hard for it. I tried my best to learn from every lesson that's come my way. I'll continue to have compassion for others as I try to imagine what their lives are like, their suffering, but I'll stop feeling guilty for beginning sentences with *I*. Becoming more selfish, in my case, is not a negative character trait at all.

This weekend will be the first of my new life. And, it'll begin in a most unusual way. I'll be getting to visit someone who helped me tremendously, and I'll get the chance to finish something that began perhaps lifetimes ago. On Sunday, I'll be joining my mother in Oakland, to visit the grave of her mother, my grandmother.

"On her deathbed, Mama told me never to marry your father. She said this over and over," my mother had confided to me a couple of times throughout my life. My mother did marry my father. They eloped to Las Vegas and my grandmother never spoke to my mother again. My grandmother died before being able to forgive my mom. Forgiving is a hard thing to do sometimes, but I imagine its rewards are enormous, infinite, even life-changing. This is what I hope to do on Sunday.

On Sunday, before taking BART to the Rockridge station in Oakland, I'll take a few moments to look back at where I've been, where I've come from. The next few moments I'll spend looking at my life now. The fact that I'm still here is indeed a victory in itself. I'm grateful for what I've learned from my mother. I've learned that without obstacles there'd be nothing to learn, nothing to overcome. Without life, we'd have no instrument from which to operate. My mother and father gave me life. Rather than providing me with challenges, they've given me abundant opportunities to learn and discover. My life has been very full, full of possibilities, and I'm grateful. I may not have set the world on fire, but I sure learned a lot while I've been here. Lifetimes. I love my mom, my dad too.

Again, with my grandmother right there beside me, I hope to be able to forgive completely and unconditionally this time. I hope to feel grateful. I hope to know love. And when I experience all this, I hope to feel free to take my turn. Just like all the others, this is the next lesson I've been given to learn. I'm ready now. The time is right. My turn has come, because I've decided to take it. My hope is to live a happy life at some point down the road. But for the moment, being strong, independent, free, and at peace suits me just fine. Definitely OK by me.

other books by Clint Adams:

My Watch Doesn't Tell Time
Don't Be Afraid of Heaven
Fear Ain't All That
Just Say Mikey

for more information, please visit:
www.ClintAdams.com